Kelly Creighton is t[...]   [...]e
series; psychological   [...]
collections *Bank 1*   [...]
Happy, and poetry c[...]   [...]
Underneath the Tree.   [...]
literary journal, sh[...]   [...]
short story, and was the recipient of a 2017/18 ACES
Award from the Arts Council of Northern Ireland.
Kelly was born in Belfast and now lives with her family
in County Down.

kellycreighton.com

@KellyCreighto16

THE NATIONAL
LOTTERY

arts
council
of Northern Ireland

SOULS WAX FAIR

Kelly Creighton

ALSO BY KELLY CREIGHTON

STANDALONE FICTION
The Bones of It

DI SLOANE BOOKS
The Sleeping Season
Problems with Girls
The Town Red

STORY COLLECTIONS
Bank Holiday Hurricane
Everybody's Happy
(co-editor) Underneath the Tree

POETRY
Three Primes
(co-author) Fun Poems for Kids

SOULS WAX FAIR

Kelly Creighton

FRIDAY
PRESS

First published in 2022
by Friday Press
Belfast

ISBN: 9798675622627

www.fridaypressbooks.com
@friday_press

For Ryan

...and while we wait in silence for that final luxury of fearlessness, the weight of that silence will choke us.

Audre Lorde

Art and the Opossum

1988

It seems to take forever in Ake Ghost Bear's rust-freckled pickup, with its damaged hood, transistor almost dead, and both wipers lost on another ride, but the girls finally get to Mystic, where, in a bowl in the Hills, Celena kills the engine and MJ's stomach flips. Almost every journey at their age feels like a pilgrimage.

What have I let you talk me into? Celena says through her teeth.

You have questions of your own, says MJ.

I do? Questions for a New Age kook?

I'm sure you'll think of some.

Wind chimes titter and the cabin door opens and out comes Madame Barb. She is wearing blue-black hair and a velveteen kaftan in midnight blue, and while she does not look like her sparkly photo from the newspaper, she does look like a woman with direction and the ability to direct, of that, MJ is certain.

Madame Barb approaches the pickup, her eyes burning into the windows at them both, little Lakota Sioux girl and little 'all-American' blonde.

She tells the girls to leave their baggage in the vehicle. They vacate their seats and follow. MJ can hear her breath steepen, and she thinks that Madame Barb must hear it too, because she announces, as she stalks ahead toward the cabin: If any of you are nervous about this ... if you don't want to know what the future holds ... you'd best hit the road. Then Madame Barb stands by the screen door, her hand on the handle. Well, what's it gunna be?

Celena stays silent, so MJ insists on both their accounts that they aren't nervous, that all they want is truth, just this one thing.

For a moment the girls surrender to Madame Barb's analytical stares before she shrugs, then pushes open the door, letting them inside. Maybe this is part of the experience, thinks MJ. Surely a palm reader who is not sharp and mildly threatening is not worth her salt.

Indoors it smells like cinnamon buns and tobacco smoke and is decorated prettily in clover greens and salmon pinks. The drapes sit in swags and tails. There are dishes of potpourri and a small pair of roller skates by the door. Madame Barb continues her directions, telling her new, young clients to sit around the compass of a pine table. Then raking her fingers through her crimpy blue-black hair, and rolling the sleeves of her kaftan, she sits and wordlessly reaches her hand out for MJ's. Madame Barb examines the nimble porcelain of the girl's hand, moving it like one moves a dish under a water faucet. Next, she pulls the same movement across the table and Celena follows suit, putting her warm square hand dutifully into the cold cradle of the woman's rumpled palm.

4

They sit in hush like that for five minutes but possibly longer, with Madame Barb comparing and contrasting.

Well, she says, you girls are gunna have hard lives and there's no sugar-coating that.

MJ figures Barb could have guessed as much by looking at Celena's brother's pickup, or from their clothes: MJ's mother has her kitted out with Family Thrift Center donations. She is wearing a turtleneck the color of caramel – it always reminds her of diarrhea – and under the table her swishy bellbottoms make her feel like an unfashionable mermaid.

Naturally, Celena is equally outmoded, in her Rolling Stones tee and those camo pants she has rolled at the waistband to keep north of her hips. She has braids in her hair and bison horn earrings in her earlobes. And money aside, no one from South Dakota has ever heard of a native person who does not have a hard life.

Celena leans across the table on both elbows, propping her chin up with her free hand. Her long black braids falling over her shoulders.

What age are you, Brave Bird? Madame Barb asks her.

Eighteen, Celena replies.

MJ coughs to remind her not to give too much away and secondly, to wake her up. Celena is going; the propping up of her head is always the first sign. Next, she'll stop speaking. Celena can fall asleep on you whilst you are in the midst of delivering a sentence, and usually MJ does not mind, she doesn't even ask Celena why it keeps happening or what she is doing to pre-empt these sleeping attacks.

The Ghost Bears are drinkers and MJ knows this vista, she understands that everyone – American and Native alike – hurt and medicate.

5

They all use some kind of self-administered epidural to numb themselves from the throat down.

But now, today, MJ very much minds the sleeping, since her mother has had to sell the old Buick Skylark and Celena is her ride home and the ride is long. And MJ does not want to die on it. Not now and not tonight.

Your mother's ill, Madame Barb tells Celena. Had all you children and then a hysterectomy, full cervix removal. It wasn't even her choice. Am I right about that?

I think you mean my aunt Wanda, Celena says in her deep syrupy voice. Wanda had a lot of babies, but they didn't survive. We are the ones that made it, she tells us. Took us in because my mom couldn't raise us.

Same thing, says Barb. She's like a mother, see?

I see that. Celena yawns.

They'll have got the junior doctors to do the surgery. She'll have problems later.

Celena just blinks. The gust of light coming in from the window emphasizes the deep creases at the side of the woman's mouth, and MJ cannot help but think of Madame Barb as a dummy. She watches her speak to Celena for a while, not hearing much but imagining she is being steered by a ventriloquist.

And you, Marilyn? Barb eyeballs MJ, breaking her out of her daze.

Me? asks MJ, though this is not the first time someone has referred to her as Marilyn.

It is always people of a certain age who remember Ms. Monroe from the movies. It began with the teacher who suddenly turned cold toward MJ the semester she returned to class in her training bra, her eyebrows freshly plucked into delicate arches at her mother's hands, and by Marjorie's excited insistence.

6

It's a compliment, her mother told her.

Anyway, MJ loathes the association.

What about me? she asks Madame Barb in almost a whisper.

You the same age as your friend?

MJ nods.

Sorry sweets, but I'm not real heartened by your life line, says Barb.

Which line is that? asks MJ.

Madame Barb frowns at Celena who is now spark out, she carries that frown to MJ, Barb uses her finger to demonstrate the line on Celena's hand.

This is what you want a life line to look like, she says, it's a good one your friend has … good for a girl of the great Sioux nation, you understand me?

MJ looks at the line between Celena's thumb and index finger, and how it curves down toward her wrist, solid and deep, and she looks at her own, seeing only how much reduced it is.

Huh! MJ says like she has lost a dollar and found a nickel.

Okay, Marilyn. I see a man …

Yeah?

It's your father, says Barb.

You can see him?

He wonders about you every day. He misses you bad.

I'm sorry, ma'am, says MJ, but I didn't come to speak to dead people. My mom made me promise not to. She's kinda superstitious that way.

I don't communicate with dead people, says Madame Barb, but I know Brave Bird's old man is deceased and yours is still in the land of the living.

Celena starts to snore.

My father was killed in a farm accident, MJ whispers.

7

Oh sure! says Madame Barb. I'm not talking about the man who was *like* a father to you, like the aunt of your friend here. I know your mother tells you he was your old man but you know the truth. You've always known it.

Suddenly she does. Or does she? MJ's mind rolls away.

I see ... Tennessee, Barb says releasing MJ's hand and readjusting her sleeves. Yep, he's in Tennessee.

Uh-uh. My father died when I was two, MJ balks, bored now and irritated their time is up.

She has barely any memory of her father. Chad McCord's accident slipped him under a crack like a letter gets kicked under a sideboard and forgotten about. MJ has never thought about Chad and categorically she does not miss him. She'd been too young, anyway. And yes, she does want to hear about a man, one who will love her and stick around. A good man.

Marjorie has had men over the years but they are never good, nor are they solely interested in Marjorie, not once they've met her daughter.

MJ hasn't tried to make it this way. She tries to stay out of their way and give them space but it is useless, as history has amply shown.

Maybe you mean one of my mom's boyfriends, she asks Madame Barb, who is now openly irritated by her.

What is your name, child? Barb replies.

Mary Jane, she says in a soft ruminative tone.

Mary Jane, sweets, I don't tell people what they want to hear. I told you from the start: I call it like I see it.

But my father is dead.

Let's not poison the pudding, Mary Jane. There's really only one person with all the answers, I suggest you go home and make her speak.

*

For drinking in the local tavern, Marjorie wears a crocheted top, washed-out Levis, and a pair of copper heels, and when she arrives home, kicks the heels off in the doorway. She goes into the living room for a nightcap, puts on slippers, a sheepskin coat and pours herself a Jameson.

Marjorie tries to light a cigarette in the shuddering light of the TV, her hands shaking. She is cursing her daughter for leaving the TV running when MJ replies: I'm watching it.

God! You scared me, says Marjorie with a jump. She turns to see MJ wrapped in a blanket on the couch. What are you doing up?

I have something to ask you, Mary Jane says, looking at the flakes of blue eyeliner at the outermost corners of her mother's sherry-colored eyes.

Marjorie sits on the arm of the chair, cradling her glass, inhaling her cigarette. I'm listening, she says.

I went to that palm reader earlier, Mom.

I told you, you're gunna bring bad spirits into this house playing with fire like that. Marjorie clicks her tongue.

Madame Barb said I have a father, and Chad wasn't him.

Marjorie laughs then she sees that MJ is serious and she rubs her brow.

So suddenly this crank tells you this, and suddenly he's Chad. Suddenly he's not *Daddy*? Marjorie says from of the side of her mouth, following the words with a glyph of smoke that shoots out like an arrow.

Was he, my daddy?

Marjorie pushes her hair back from her face.

—

9

You really want to know? Hell, she says, you're old enough now, being that you're eighteen. She pauses then adds: No, MJ, Chad McCord was not your father.

Then who was he?

McCord was just some calloused-handed do-gooder who liked to call.

Call? What for? MJ asks.

What do you think what for? McCord was a horny old bastard.

You were just sleeping with him?

On occasion. But he liked you, thought you were sweet – didn't that set the tone! He would give me a few dollars now and again, take us out at the weekends. He wasn't real handsome, but, you know, McCord wasn't bad in the sack. Grateful, you see.

Mom! MJ shouts. Her mother always takes it too far.

Like you don't know all about it! Marjorie settles her eyebrows deliberately.

What would I know about it? MJ sighs.

More than you'd ever pretend, I'll bet.

Chad wanted to be my father?

Poor old McCord! He wanted the full package: a woman and a kid. He never lived here, with us, or nothing, just the next farm over. Many times he asked me to move in, but you know, I never promised exclusivity. Marjorie looks at Mary Jane's questioning face, she explains farther – I couldn't. There was another man I was seeing.

Who?

Your father, MJ.

MJ is perplexed. So why didn't you just be with him? she asks.

Well, his wife wouldna liked that now, would she?

My father was married to someone else?

Yeah. Try to keep up, Boo.

So … you had a kid with a married man?

Wasn't gunna abort ya, was I!

I can't believe you just said that! MJ says hating just how whiny she sounds.

Made sure you were provided for, says Marjorie.

Barely, thinks MJ. The thought is followed by guilt.

She could never say that thought aloud. Her mother, MJ is convinced, thinks she has done and is doing a great job. MJ has nothing else to compare Marjorie's parenting style against but she knows it's a little off, a lot hard, and practically over.

And if you don't like it, you know what you can do, Marjorie tells her daughter almost as if she can tell what MJ is thinking.

It is always the same threat: live by my rules or leave. And isn't her daughter a good girl? Never brings any trouble to the door and does what her mother asks of her.

Doesn't Marjorie fondly acknowledge this on sober days?

Probably best to change the subject.

So, my real father is out there?

Somewhere … over the rainbow.

Where somewhere?

Memphis.

That's where the palm reader said he was. Tennessee!

Well, bully for the palm reader. Marjorie knocks back her whiskey then drops her lipsticky cigarette butt into the glass. I suppose you'll want to meet him now?

I don't think so, says MJ.

Yes, you do. You want to go and stay with him and why the heck not?

You want me to?

Why not?

I don't know, says MJ, you spend all this time letting me think one thing and then suddenly it's okay, I can go and see my father. Everything is cool?

Everything is *cool*, as you like to call it.

Great. I think …

What's stopping you going? Marjorie laughs. Not that damn boy from Agri-Supplies?

MJ laughs back.

He stopping you?

Don't be ridiculous, Mom! Ephraim doesn't factor in anything.

The first time Mary Jane experienced anything like Ephraim Shea she had been twelve.

That first Ephraim Shea was called Heathcliffe Noteboom: a scrawny, buck-toothed, stuck-out-eared, seventeen-year-old son of a rancher who Marjorie used to have do jobs around the place.

MJ is here, she would say on the phone and he would come around and burn beet-red in the face, practically dancing about on the gravel like he needed the toilet badly, add to that a lot of head-scratching so he didn't have to see her fully. Though it was obvious Heath wanted to see MJ.

Heath was the first instance MJ could recall of this unnamable discomfort that occurred in boys that came into her presence.

Marjorie would tease him: I don't want to see those strong hands on my daughter, do you hear me, Heath, she'd say. 'Cos then I'd have to get you by the balls and you wouldn't like that. Or would you? And she'd poke out her tongue.

It was all a game, and there had even been a small window during which MJ quite enjoyed the comedic theater of it. She was around fifteen years old, as she recalls.

A few months later, that window firmly shut. Quickly she became irritated by those boys who would visit, delivering, helping, lingering beside her when she was working, assisting her mother on the farm.

They always seemed to be waiting for MJ, willing her to say something to them. But she never could tell what.

Mary Jane would see their faraway eyes, and feel compelled to dilute the intensity of them with the offer of a bottle of pop. That usually made the boys shove their hands into their pockets and decline.

And Marjorie was never far away, so she could hear everything, so she could then lean herself against the boy – Heath Noteboom or whomever – when he spun out and made to leave in a hormonal fluster.

The boys – who MJ thought of collectively but who always called one by one – had been waiting for her to pounce or press herself against them, too. MJ saw that later. They had been psyching themselves up to make the move when she did not.

Talk in her junior year was that events played out rather differently when MJ wasn't there, that boys would deliver repellent or seed or food only to find Marjorie McCord drunk, semi-clad, and ready to seduce them. Half the boys in school claimed they had lost their cherry to Marjorie but MJ didn't trust talk.

Ephraim Shea was something different. With his broad, boy-man hybrid body, and his long black hair, he was different from the rest of Marjorie's playthings.

The second time he came to the farm, Ephraim made a move on MJ in the kitchen just as she was getting him a beer from the fridge, since he had asked for one instead of the soda she had offered him, to demonstrate his manliness. Ephraim had come at her, attempting to kiss her.

13

MJ stepped back and turned her cheek. She had been a little afraid, and not of having her first kiss, and not because Ephraim had a physically overpowering presence, but because of the way he encompassed the space that was her space, the way he was so very assured and entitled, so confident in himself that to rebuff him would be embarrassing for all concerned, but it was too late, she had pulled away.

I have a boyfriend, she decided to say, to spare his feelings.

No, you don't, said Ephraim, his expression ropable but pleased.

No, no … I do. I'm so sorry. She handed him the beer and folded her arms across her chest.

You saying you don't like me? he asked as if no one had ever not liked him before and her rejection had come as a massive shock to him. Like there must be something *wrong* with her.

I do like you, she whispered, knowing her mother was in the other room, singing to herself. Marjorie could sing, Mary Jane would give her that. And Mary Jane wasn't lying when she said she liked Ephraim, she much preferred any male who was not immediately silly at the sight of her, this was true. And she also liked any boy who was not left humiliated by Marjorie. Though other than that, Mary Jane had no specific feelings for him.

I know you're lying about having a boyfriend, Ephraim said, cracking open the beer and catching a mouthful before it puddled over the top.

Not interrupting anything, am I? Her mother tumbled into the room.

Like what? asked Ephraim.

A laugh rolled through Marjorie. Oh, I don't know … you don't have a crush on my daughter, do you?

14

This is where most boys bumbled that they did not, leading to Marjorie quipping: Good, can we get this job done, then? before leading them away by the sleeve, or linking an arm through theirs.

But Ephraim stood firm, with a wide-eyed sneer on his face. Now MJ was glad she had not let him kiss her.

Yeah, I have a crush on MJ, he replied. Everybody does, and I'm human, aren't I?

She had never seen her mother's face take on that shape.

Ripe with secondhand embarrassment for Marjorie, MJ turned to open the refrigerator taking a bottle of pop for herself.

You are *very* human, Mr. Shea, Marjorie said, with a quick twitch of her head. Well ... MJ is busy trying to get into a decent college and she don't need no boy to drag her backward, so you can just be human elsewhere.

Marjorie leaned against the door jamb, a hand on her hip.

Fine by me, Mrs. McCord, Ephraim said, though Marjorie had only taken on Chad's surname after he died because it was better than that hideous maiden name of hers. Crapper. People just assumed the Mrs. part, even her daughter had.

I'm not interested in the Agri-Supplies boy, I have college, don't I? MJ asks Marjorie, nodding back to that day.

Her mother cannot afford college and this is why she'd snickered at Marjorie's quip to Ephraim. What did a girl with killer good looks and a sweet voice have to offer without a college education? Plenty, Marjorie had already decided.

MJ thinks she might take a night class in music, work days any old where.

In the evenings, she will sing in a bar until some hot shot music manager happens to walk in and be blown away. Like that can happen in Rapid City! A girl can dream. Though, till now, no one but Celena has ever heard her sing.

Marjorie says she was once a singer: a musical career which MJ suspects comprised of a couple of nights of drunken warbling at some karaoke bar, and so it makes sense to her that Marjorie will not let her go. Singers like to cage birds, after all.

This little bird, MJ decides for herself, will take the same route but take it better and more committedly.

She wants the stability of exclusivity in all areas of life that her mother has not, and MJ is sure she can do it. She has this self-belief and she doesn't know how. Maybe it comes from her father, in which case maybe her chin does too, that slight cleft that Marjorie does not have. Her face is oblong while MJ's is a clean heart.

The daughter's brows are arched and dark, giving her an eternally surprised expression while the mother's are straight, over-plucked, untrusting.

Maybe MJ's father has the blonde hair gene, all the Crappers – dead now, the lot of them – were so dark. Marjorie's father Ted had had the affectionate nickname TexMex. Some were convinced there had to be the suggestion of Mexican in his blood and MJ liked the idea.

But what of her own father? This is when he first feels real, when she thinks of him having a face and questions whether he deserves for her to walk in and ruin the family he already has. Has already chosen.

MJ is undecided whether she should revere him for having kept his normality, or whether she should be angry he abandoned her.

Yet he has given them money:

a barebones allowance that stopped on her eighteenth birthday, which just about coincided with her mother's announcement that MJ would have to get into the workforce while her peers applied to schools.

But there is Memphis, she has always wanted to go there. So, the next morning MJ goes into her mother's bedroom and sits on the edge of the bed where Marjorie is nursing the ghost of a hangover.

Go away! she winces.

You must have a number for my real father, MJ says, if he's been paying money all this time.

He put it in an account, MJ, I don't know. Talk about it later.

No, we'll talk about it now.

He's in the phone book.

I'll need a name.

Art Garfunkel, says Marjorie, that's a name.

Art G–

Art … Garber, I mean. Garber.

You sure now?

MJ, let me sleep.

*

After her next shift, she calls the operator and asks for the number of one Art Garber of Memphis, Tennessee. There is one, an Arthur Garber. MJ scrawls the number on a napkin and at home lets her mother know she has it.

Every night, just before Marjorie heads out to the bar, she asks – You called Art Garfunkel yet? and MJ says – Nope. And after a fortnight or so, Marjorie, it appears, has resigned herself that her daughter is not going to seek out her father, so she lets herself worry about Ephraim instead.

Agri-Supplies Boy is coming around, you might want to make sure you are out of here, Marjorie says.

I'll be in my room, don't gotta worry about me, MJ replies.

Her mother and Ephraim will be talking downstairs and MJ will sit staring at the name and the number, thankful their home phone has been cut off because maybe she might have called Art Garber twenty times over.

Then Ephraim Shea will be crunching outside, making his way back to his motorbike when he glances over his shoulder, up at MJ's bedroom window, and she'll give him a little smile, unsure if he can pick it up down in the yard. But he will give her a small side smirk back that she knows is between them, just the two of them, and she understands her mother's games, the ones she plays with men. At times it can be fun.

*

A month later, she finishes her shift at Sixth Street Deli and heads for the payphone on autopilot. Unprepared she dials the number she has had for ages.

Can I speak to Art? MJ asks the woman on the other end, almost choking on the words.

Sure, says the woman. Darlin', it's for you.

Hello, says Art.

Hi, hey, says MJ, look … this is gunna sound real weird, it sounds real weird to me too, believe me. But I went to see a medium, no, I mean a palm reader. I don't even know why I went because I only wanted to ask if I'd ever find a man to … never mind! I don't even know any dead people … what am I talking about, she didn't even do that, and there's my dad, he's gone, I suppose …

I'm sorry, I'm not interested, he says and the line dies.

Fudge! she says.

MJ tries to phone again but the tone is now engaged. Why did I say all that, she rebukes herself, why did I not just say, hey, I'm Mary Jane, the daughter you had with Marjorie?

Oh, baby girl, says Marjorie when she sees MJ's rosy eyes.

I tried phoning Art, she explains.

Yep, and?

He hung up on me.

What a pissant!

No, he didn't know who I was. I started to ramble. Went about it wrong.

Booboo!

Her mother hugs her, gathering MJ's hair into a bunch and hugging her in a way that is just great when she lets herself be like this, when Marjorie lets herself be that mother.

Don't you worry about him! Hey, how did work go at the deli? Good?

I suppose. I made a few mistakes.

Who the heck doesn't? Tomorrow will be better. Living's learning.

You're right.

Get any tips?

A few. MJ hesitates.

Keep 'em. Marjorie winks at her. Hey, I made meatloaf for you. Come, sit.

The day after that, MJ comes home from her shift and her mother says: Hey, guess who I called?

Who?

Who, dummy? Who do you think? Mr. Garfunkel.

Art?

Yeah, Art! Who else but Art!

What did he say?

He laughed, when he heard what you did, he ruptured his damn spleen. He said to tell you sorry, and that he wants to see you real real bad. I told him that you look just like me and he's kinda excited about that.

That sounds gross, Mom. Plus, I don't.

Well, he really did like how I looked.

But I'm his kid, it shouldn't matter what I look like.

It matters, MJ. Only ugly people say things like that. You, Boo, don't need to talk ugly.

Talk ugly? Jeez!

He's kinda hot, too.

You sound like you're setting me up on a date.

God, MJ, you have a warped sense of things, girl. I'm just saying, if he hasn't let himself go, you'll see why me and him couldn't keep our hands off of one another. Marjorie loses herself for a moment. Damn! she exclaims, shaking a memory from her head.

I think I've just been sick in my mouth, says MJ.

Don't be like that. You wouldn't be here now if I wasn't so hot and he wasn't.

What about his wife?

Oh, right! Marjorie waves her hand. Divorced. He's remarried.

Are you annoyed?

Annoyed?

That could have been you, says MJ, maybe.

And be stuck to one man all my life? I don't think so, Boo!

Whatever you say! So, he wants to see me?

Sure does.

Does he have kids?

Sure.

How many?

I know he has some with the first wife, I know that much.

How many?

Maybe you *don't* know anything about sex, Boo. Garber and I didn't talk about that kind of stuff. Too busy.

What do we do now?

I know what you need to do, you need to date, because teens who don't date have a life of disappointing sex ahead of them.

MJ makes a throw-up sound.

And on Garber's part, well, he's gunna wire me some money, we're getting you a single ticket and you are … Marjorie makes an airplane of her hand … on your sweet way to M town.

A one-way ticket? So I'm staying?

He's your father.

Aren't you generous with other people's hospitality! Didn't even know I had a father until a month ago.

Garber's sweet, and he can be generous. He bought me a car once … The old Skylark. It was brand new, then … Marjorie stops. You'll like him, she says. You just will. I must see if I can locate an old photo of him but I don't think so. We probably didn't take photos. Not any you'd want to see. She winks. Old Polaroids.

MJ thinks she might be sick, no pretending this time.

*

In May, MJ takes the straight flight: Rapid City to Memphis. Art arranges to meet her at the bus stop. The third or fourth one, he'd told Marjorie – Tell MJ to disembark beside the car garage.

21

The bus passes the car garage and MJ, panicking, stands up. The bus driver watches her in his mirror, and two minutes later stops to let her alight. She lifts her bag and wrestles it in front of her and down the aisle where she looks out of the window. She can see the side of someone, a man, his hood pulled up about his ears. She goes down the steps and stands outside. The man in the coat looks at MJ, he gives her a look that is so deep it makes her feel like crying and smiling simultaneously. It feels stronger than any look she has ever felt, and many males have looked at her many different ways in the last six or seven years.

But she recognizes this look instantly, even though she cannot remember having felt it before: it is an all-encircling x-ray of a look that blots out every noise around her.

She feels like a bride on her wedding day in a cheesy movie, a bride who does not hear the person who is blowing their nose into a tissue, a bride who does not feel that the temperature has dipped even lower than she thought it would when she was thinking about the weather and planning her attire for the date.

MJ has a warm protective layer all around her. She can no longer feel the cold of Art's absence.

The top of his face is all she sees. These deep-set, but loving, see-all eyes. She cannot tell if his chin is hers for his white shaggy beard covers it fully. But it surprises her how much Art looks like a grimy-faced farmer, or maybe more like old Saint Nick.

He wears a coat that is the most unusual fleshy pink-red, the color of an embryo in biology class when there is a light shone through, for televisual and sex off-putting reasons.

And with his hood pulled up, like an enlarged head, an embryo is all MJ can think about.

22

Aha! Because she is his child she sees a child, and for a second MJ thinks she is glad her mother did not abort her. She has always found it to be a stupid remark when her mother says, At least I kept ya.

If her mother had have terminated the pregnancy, MJ wouldn't have been around to have any opinion. That would have been fine also. Life is tough. That definitely would have been fine; pre-MJ nipped in the bud. Now Art looks at her like a father looks at a daughter. With love and depth and bliss. She is glad to be here, to be alive, excited.

Art, she says. My flight was delayed an hour, so thank you for waiting.

His face moves, and again she thinks of a baby and the smile babies make that could be happiness but could be gas. Art mumbles, turning his back to her. This is emotional for him, too.

He is having huge existential thoughts, just like her, she is sure. She has not expected this. Has not expected her father would have a bicycle instead of a car. She must widen her pace to catch him up as he pushes it, moving quickly through the thickets.

I only found out about you a few weeks ago, MJ says. You're not upset with Mom about that, are you? I've always wanted to come to Memphis, I don't know why. A few kids I know are applying to school here. I know one girl, Dixie, who is already here. She's older than me. I don't click much with girls my own age. Well, there is Celena but she doesn't go to my school. She won't go to college. Probably I won't either, but if I could, I'd like to come here, to Memphis.

MJ pauses, hoping he will not think that she has only wanted to meet him so she might now have a college plan. She can't stop talking and thinks it best to acknowledge.

That day I called you, she says, I am sorry I talked so much but I was nervous, see. It's a worrisome thing to do, to talk to you for the first time.

He looks back over his shoulder, his eyes pinning hers. Art seems to sigh. MJ giggles, hoping it will chase away the awkwardness.

They walk through a forest of tulip trees, eastern white pine and wisteria. They walk for what feels like two miles. Every time she goes to ask him something she stops herself.

If she says: Where is your car? will he be disappointed in her? Maybe he just likes the exercise. He does look very fit. Wiry, almost.

Besides, MJ has no right to ask Art anything, as he asks nothing of her, just pushes his bike through the fern until they come to a little log house. The garden is overgrown with weeds, far worse than at the ranch back home.

Your house is nice, MJ says as they walk into the honey-hued living room with black bear themed d'cor. The rug on the floor and the cushions have black bear motifs.

There is a still on the wall from an ice hockey match.

The place looks clean enough though there is a bad smell, maybe it's coming from Art's coat. Maybe he needs a new one, maybe it is the only thing he could find before he left to fetch her. She is not ungrateful, she really isn't.

Hungry? he asks.

Yes, she says.

MJ's relief is at its highest pitch, glad of a subject Art has broached himself. He turns on the TV and sits down to watch a documentary, every so often glimpsing her from the corner of his eye.

You like wildlife documentaries? she asks.

Yep, he says, standing to fetch a knife and sharpen it without looking.

Do you mind if I put my clothes in the closet?

Art grunts a positive response. MJ goes to walk into the bedroom but he comes over and holds the handle firmly, he looks at the couch. Okay, he decides and pushes the door open, the knife is hanging by his thigh.

There is a clean pile of bed linen that Art pulls off the wood-framed bed and sets on the couch then he stares at MJ again.

I'll just clean up before we eat, okay? MJ says and Art nods.

She closes the door and starts to strip the bed, then she stops and sits down, slightly confused. She cannot see Art and her mom together, but maybe he was handsome when he was younger, MJ is not thinking that he is not now. She is not rude like that.

Looks aren't everything and she supposes he is intense. There is something about him, but she only feels warmly toward him through knowing that she is his daughter.

MJ doesn't suppose many women would find him as 'hot' as her mother once did. But then again, her mother can find sex anywhere: eggplants, burger buns side by side. Marjorie McCord is a metal detector for innuendo.

MJ looks at the stains and the small curly hairs on Art's bedsheet and resigns herself that she will sleep in her clothes and change in the morning. She is tired from travel and lies down, closing her eyes for fifteen minutes or so before her father enters the room without warning, startling her, telling her supper is ready. Still wearing that smelly coat of his.

In the living room, MJ sits on the armchair, with him on the couch, his spare bedding over his knee.

He leans forward and hands her a plate of meat. Nothing else. Where is your wife? MJ asks as she pitches a piece of meat on her fork.

Where is my wife? That is the question, Art says with a smirk.

It is the first time she sees him smile a smile that is easy and uncomplicated. But moments pass and she realizes he is not willing to answer.

This is good, she says, chewing. Lying. It is far from good.

Art goes back to his documentary and MJ looks around the room, at the intricate flock wallpaper in natural tones, and the drawings of black bears that are framed and on the wall. I like those, she says.

They're mine.

Really? she says. You draw?

Draw? Yeah … used to, he says, getting up suddenly and pouring himself a drink, forgetting to ask if she would like one.

Huh! says MJ. Art's art!

Suppose you'd be right, he murmurs taking a sip of water.

You're real good, says MJ. My friend's aunt Wanda makes these vases, they are real nice. I'd love to be able to make art. She's Lakota Sioux, my friend. I mentioned her earlier. Celena …

Art looks at her intently, a small smile forming around the edge of his mouth, she can see through his white whiskers. He is back to inscrutable smiles, and this one makes her think of Ephraim, the Agri-Supplies boy.

MJ puts her head down and chews some more.

I want to be a singer, she says.

Sing some, says Art.

No.

26

Fine.

No, I will, she says. If you really want me to.

Art looks at her with controlled eyes. He laughs.

Yeah, well, my dreams aren't big or nothing, says MJ. I just want to ... sing. I suppose.

My dreams aren't big or nothing, he says in a you're-dumb voice that makes cold water flush through her spinal column and makes her arms break out in goosebumps, and makes the meat taste stronger than it did, stronger and weirder than anything she's ever eaten before. What did you say this is? she asks.

Opossum.

Opossum? MJ laughs. No. What is it really?

Opossum.

Is that even legal? she cries.

Is that even legal! Art mimics her, his voice is lighter now. He takes another drink and looks at her sideways. MJ's throat closes over. Where did you get this? she asks meekly.

Back yonder, says Art.

Where yonder?

At the bus stop, just waiting.

Roadkill?

It's good meat. Food grows all over the planet, don't need to pay for it. His face twitches.

She wheezes when he stares at her.

Where is your restroom, Art? she asks, slowly rising, feeling the two pieces she has just about managed to swallow down start to make their way back up.

MJ makes it to the restroom just in time and vomits until her head aches and the black bears on the shower curtain leap out toward her. Art does not ask her if she is alright.

MJ just wants to be home. She feels like crying for her mother.

Don't puke on the floor, Art said. Tina done mopped it this morn.

Slowly, MJ lifts herself and washes her face. The bathroom looks pretty clean, the taps shine, the mirror has not a speck of toothpaste, no little hairs in the shower, none in the sink. A woman's touch: Tina's touch. She will be glad to see Tina. MJ wonders what kind of woman Art can get these days. If Marjorie could only see what Art has become! What would she say? Must have had my whiskey glasses on back then, Boo.

MJ tells herself that she will be able to get through the stay much more easily with Tina around. She wonders if she will sleep on the couch and Art on the armchair. She never pictured his place being so small, feeling regretful that he has been sending money he has clearly needed for himself. He has been supporting her and other kids, his ex-wife too.

It's by no means easy back home, but she and Marjorie always have food on the table, every night, while Art Garber has made do with flattened fauna that he scrapes off the road.

When MJ comes out of the toilet she sees a bowl of skin and guts on the kitchen counter. If she has any doubts that he has been fooling around now she knows he is not. He must have had the animal tucked inside his coat, and why wear a nice coat if it is only rubbing up against a dead animal?

I'm sorry, she says. She asks him if he is tired too and he says he is not. I think I might go to bed, if that's okay.

MJ goes into the bedroom where something tells her to put the chair against the back of the door, hoping that if he needs to get in to retrieve something, her father will not be offended by this action, or reaction, of hers.

MJ is in a molten mood with Marjorie, as she brushes her teeth with a smear of Colgate on her finger and without water. She lies on the bed moving the grit about her mouth with her tongue.

The TV blares for another hour before she can hear Art make a stubborn bowel movement in the toilet and repetitively flush it gone.

MJ thinks about Tina giving them this space together, which is really kind, when MJ thinks about it, she resolves that Tina will be the one to pull the seams. Men are oftentimes quiet and sullen, and a bit weird when left to their own devices. Seems like Art has always had women to look out for him. Maybe he has gotten lazy, MJ wonders, and finally, unable to drift into it, a dark wave of sleep comes and pulls her inside.

By sunup, she sees her face, frozen and rough-hewn in the blackening mirrored closet. She doesn't even feel beautiful here, and, her father or not, men always comment on her physicality, sometimes by what they say, other times by what they do.

Women certainly always comment: I was once a lissome little thing like you, or – if MJ refused salt on her fries during lunch in the loft, a waitress would quip: See, that's why you've got such a neat little figure. Male wait staff would say: No sauce for you, it's fattening and makes you come out in spots.

All these older people trying to preserve MJ's beauty on her behalf. They could not let her go past them without remarking. Well, aren't you darned pretty! just in case she had not been told before.

If I were only twenty years younger!

I suppose I'd better lock up my sons.

Not on my account, please, MJ once replied.

She was trying not to sound what her mother would call *ugly*.

As she brushes her hair before Art's mirrored robes she thinks of Marjorie, who has become crazily boy-mad since she hit forty, and along the months either side, and in truth, for five or six years before hitting that landmark age.

Then MJ pushes her mother out of her mind and rises, hearing someone outside. It is Art, who must have been out already and is now returning to the house, wearing that coat, and pushing that bike.

She quickly goes into the living room and turns on the TV, installs herself on the chair where she tries to focus on the red rims on Sally Jessy Raphael's glasses, on her colossal sparkling earrings. MJ tries to look comfortable, then Art sets a dead, squished squirrel on the table and MJ squeals blue murder.

Crazy girl! He runs at her, shouting.

She sprints into the bedroom and pulls the stained plywood closet against the door, it almost falls on top of her. She catches the fear in her reflection then cowers, crouching down and covering her head with her arms so she cannot hear him just so loudly.

She has never been shouted at like this. Never heard a voice like his.

Art stops shouting and begins muttering: There's a crazy girl in my house. Hello, police? There's a crazy girl, she's in my house.

The change in his tone alarms MJ more than the shouting or the squirrel or the fact that she is trapped in a room with a stained bed and a man who knows how to sharpen knives without even looking at the blade.

She packs her bag as quietly as she can, then goes to the window, trying to open it but it is stuck good and tight.

A woman driving by stops her car and gets out, humming to herself as she comes up a bald tire-made path. She enters the house. Something stops MJ from crying out for help.

Feel good today? the woman says to Art.

There's a crazy girl in my bedroom and I'm gunna call the police, he says.

C'mon, you wish there was a crazy girl in your bedroom, maybe that's more like it.

Tina, he says, you run and call the police. I'll keep her in there. Think she's stealing from me.

What have you been watching on the TV? she sounds concerned. Did you stay up late?

MJ hears the water faucet start, and the kettle boil, almost instantaneously.

Watching some weird shit, were you? the woman asks Art. Wouldn't have taken you for a Sally fan, thought you were gunna stick to documentaries, eh? Nice, calming nature programs.

I'll see her in prison before this day is through, says Art.

Will you now?

Yes, I will, Tina!

Tina hums some more in the bathroom, MJ hears the swish of the mop over the floor.

Were you unwell in here? Tina asks.

MJ moves the closet as quietly as she can, she has knots. She opens the door with her breath held. The woman looks through her amber glasses at MJ standing there with her mouth open.

What is going on here? she asks. Who in the world is this? She looks at Art.

The crazy girl! he shouts. Don't go anywhere, crazy girl, the police are coming for you.

Now MJ sees it, her father is completely cuckoo.

He's my dad, she appeals to Tina.

Dad? He don't have no family. If he did he wouldn't need me, she says pleasantly, almost amused.

No, I'm MJ … Mary Jane?

Tina pantomimes her indifference, throwing her hands in the air.

I'm his daughter.

Tina's face falls. Hey, girl, he do anything to you?

MJ grabs her packsack, heavy with all her apparatus, and she runs for the door.

What has she got in that bag? says Art. She's stealing my soul, sucking it out of me with her eyes, I watched a program about it.

I think we'll just let her go, Tina says.

*

The thought does not enter MJ's head to lift that phone in the sticky-carpeted reception of the hairiest motel she can afford and call Marjorie, instead she walks the grounds of the University of Memphis until she eventually sees Dixie wearing a neon pink Tee and denim cutoffs. She is standing under a canopy of southern red oak trees, chatting to a boy who is carrying a huge but slim black folder.

Dixie cannot believe her eyes. Dixie is beyond ecstatic to see her, wrapping her arms so tightly around MJ that she is choked by Wild Musk. She excuses herself from the boy with the folder – no introductions – whisking MJ off to the cafeteria where tearfully she tells Dixie all about Art and the opossum, over a plastic cup of Dr Pepper. Dixie reaches her hand across, clutches MJ's hand and smiles.

You live on a ranch and you've never slaughtered a prairie dog?

The old foreman did odd jobs like those, MJ explains. Or Mom asked a boy …

Oh, you sweet thing, you, Dixie says.

She insists on MJ bedding down in her dorm, her roommate is living with her boyfriend anyway and only returns to collect stuff from time to time.

No, says MJ but Dixie won't hear a word against it.

*

After a month staying with Dixie, MJ learns that they are a little alike, they both share the same theory that everything in life goes well, or does not, depending on timing, therefore Dixie prefers to arrive at frat parties just before what she has learned is hook-up time. That way the house will be quieter. That is if it has not already been broken up by the cops.

Go to a party too early and the testosterone levels are ridiculous, she says.

But somehow, this time she gets the timing wrong, and someone wearing the royal blue jersey and the huge orange globe of a tiger mascot head opens the door and sprays beer all over MJ and Dixie.

But mostly Dixie.

Great! she mutters, making her way to the kitchen to wipe herself off with a cloth. The Beastie Boys play on the stereo. People are talking in the hallway. MJ takes a beer from the ice basin, replacing it with the warm one she has had sloshing about in her purse. Dixie mixes herself a vodka cranberry. The drink is an ice breaker. Mary Jane has seen it work, some guy asks: What is that you're drinking? like it is the most interesting thing, and Dixie will explain. She has a whole story that goes with the drink, then they will get to talking about other things, Dixie and the guy.

33

Tonight though, nothing. It is just another drink and Dixie, just another girl.

They go into the living room where small clutches of people are engaged in talk in the corners. A couple is making out on the couch, a curly-haired girl is dancing around her purse in the center of the room.

Every so often someone shouts: Go! Tigers! Go! and a chant erupts around the room.

By the window, Jordan Pinault and Eric Nwafo stand side by side. They are kind of hard to miss.

Jordan is 6' 2, a 222 lb quarterback, white and sandy-haired, Eric – who goes by Ricky – comes in at the same height but is about twenty pounds lighter, black-eyed and brown-skinned, a wide receiver with dreads that come down to his chin.

Usually girls are on them like ants on a banana, Dixie has told MJ. But not tonight.

Standing directly in front of them, Dixie starts a bitty conversation with MJ, she can tell that Dixie is not even listening to herself, her eyes so wide and self-aware. She seems much too intimidated to speak to the men, which surprises MJ. When they'd taken the bus to school together, Dixie had always seemed impossibly confident and worldly, especially having two years on MJ.

She has talked so much about the two young men that Mary Jane McCord is already bored. She doesn't care that they play college football, nor does she care if they too are from back home. She barely recalls them from school and now turns her back, because they should be Dixie's view.

MJ is there for support, as invisibly as possible, like she is gravity or something.

Cool as you care to be, the curly-haired girl stops dancing and needs to get past Dixie and MJ, almost going through them.

The girl approaches Jordan and Eric, taking a lipstick from her purse which she uses to draw red war-paint stripes on their cheeks and across their noses. They all laugh. They don't say a word to each other.

MJ turns to better see how submissive the boys are as they are being painted. This interests her, like Ephraim in her kitchen that time, putting his feelings for MJ on a plate.

Then the curly-haired girl touches up her makeup and puts her lipstick back in the purse and Jordan, Eric and the curly-haired girl start to talk what sounds like football talk. MJ hears Jordan boast, above the music, that if a cat wanders in and breaks a game, the Tigers make it into soup, making MJ picture that tire-squished little squirrel.

Any plans for tomorrow? Dixie asks abruptly, but MJ cannot concentrate so she asks Dixie to repeat herself. Any plans? says Dixie, her eyes searching MJ's face.

What plans would she have, apart from serving at the bar where she works? And Dixie is already aware of her schedule, that MJ is only ever working, or making herself scarce or of use to her roommate.

Still, it's better than being home with her mother, MJ thinks when a hand taps her on the shoulder.

Yo! I know you from SD, don't I? Jordan asks her.

I think so, MJ says, looking back at Dixie who scarcely jerks her head enough for MJ to know she means, let's get closer.

You went to the same school as us, says Eric. You didn't cheer though. You should have.

I cheered at my school, the curly-haired girl says in a coltish tone.

Me too, says Dixie.

I could tell you practice yells, says Eric to the girl.

35

That's life, Ricky, Jordan tells him.

Best to strike while the iron is hot, Eric replies, pinching his nose to keep down a laugh.

Dixie went to the same school, says MJ.

She points at her friend like she is part of a presentation, remembering Dixie's orders to introduce them if MJ gets talking to the boys first.

I remember you, Eric says to Dixie.

You do? Dixie blushes.

Sure do.

Anything goes, says Jordan.

Ah, I get it, says MJ, this game you're playing: you're listing clichés.

Jordan laughs.

At the end of the day, says Eric.

Jordan punches him dead on the arm.

God, you are two doofuses, says MJ.

He is! says Eric, returning a measured punch.

You ready to go? MJ asks Dixie, who is watching the curly-haired girl who is watching MJ. When Eric rubs his arm, the girl breaks interest, taking an opportunity to caress his bicep before sliding the maneuver into a hug, and wrapping her arms around his waist and resting her head against his chest. MJ notices that he is all new muscles, popping. Jordan, too.

What's your hurry? You have to be somewhere? Eric asks MJ while squeezing the curly-haired girl like a kid squeezes a younger cousin he only sees once in a year, and palming her back like you'd pat a dog on its head. Making it clear that is the way he sees her.

I'm staying with my dad, he's expecting me, MJ says.

MJ and Dixie have agreed to stick to this story in the event that she gets caught staying in the dorm room.

You have some time, MJ, says Dixie, but if you need to leave that's fine.

—

36

But wasn't your father killed in a farming accident? says Eric.

Yeah, says Jordan nodding his head. I heard that, too.

How would you know? MJ asks.

Everyone knows your mom, says Dixie.

MJ bites the insides of her cheeks.

Admittedly Dixie is doing her a solid by letting her stay but these side-notes on Marjorie go above and beyond, which is one thing, and how it has always been back home, but now they are being written about MJ and that is not okay.

This is not the first time in MJ's stay in Memphis that she questions how much Dixie really likes her being around. There are remarks she chooses not to hear. There have been other parties, other young men, and when they have shown an interest in MJ, someone has got in their ear.

In another frat house, MJ once got speaking with a guy called Christopher, a nice guy who had a funny answer to everything. That night had been going swimmingly until MJ left him to answer nature's call, and when she returned, Christopher linked his fingers through hers, which was nice, until she turned her hands over saying he was looking for her wedding ring.

And there had been a similar scenario at the bar. MJ had paired Dixie with one guy before she got speaking with his friend, Louis.

Never let a man buy you a drink, she'd been told that in school, so MJ told Louis that she would get the drinks, returning from the bar carrying two jugs of beer to be confronted with a barrage of questions about her child: what age was he or she? was the father still on the scene? does everything go back to normal ... you know what I mean?

37

MJ refuted the bullshit on both occasions, though she sensed she was not convincing Louis any more than she had convinced Christopher.

MJ had liked Christopher until he looked at her with suspicion and admiration, remarking that he didn't mind on either account, husband or not. Like Louis did not mind that she was a mother, it was a one-night thing he had in mind. Louis had declared that he would still love to take MJ to bed, regardless.

Boy, are you beautiful, they'd both said.

Though Dixie still denies putting such ideas into their heads, MJ knows there can be no one else to attribute the blame. She was pissed at the time, but maybe in the end Dixie has done her a favor, for MJ does not want a man who will so readily live a lie, not even if it is her lie or someone else's, not even if it is only for a night.

It feels like school all over, she thinks, feels like before she met Celena Ghost Bear and clicked. Celena is not like the rest and MJ misses her realness.

Yeah, she was kinda hot, your mom, says Eric.

Then a lull, in which it feels like the right thing to do is walk away. Jordan's face says it, the curly-haired girl's face says it. Only Dixie does not want to leave, not now the time is right and she is finally in the company of touchable gods.

Are you gunna come here next year? Eric continues.

No, says MJ. I'm a singer, so I think I'll do that.

She doesn't feel like such an imposter anymore since she has braved (if only shakily) three open mic nights in the bar where she works. Success, MJ thinks, is like sleeping, you pretend to do it until you are. So far she has had a couple of short naps.

MJ has taken a while to open her eyes while she sings, to see if the crowd is looking back at her.

But she finds she listens too much, which is something she will have to work harder to block out. The cashier rattling coins in the register, doors slamming shut, redneck assholes who like to heckle her to show them her tits.

When she relayed this minor footnote to Dixie, Dixie looked Mary Jane square in the breasts and said: But would it kill you to wear a sweater that doesn't restrict your breathing?

MJ won't let them get to her or let them blunt her best and bravest moments in the future.

Singing is not a career, says Jordan stretching out. He is all hands, arms and wet pits.

But tossing a ball is? asks MJ.

Mary Jane McCord! Dixie reprimands her. That's rude!

It is if it gets you a scholarship, says Eric.

You can't get one for singing! says Jordan. Though you do have a good pair of lungs.

Maybe you *should* go, says Dixie looking at MJ accusingly again.

What does Dixie want from her? MJ hardly makes up her face before they go out because she feels too made up, like she has an unfair advantage. Doesn't Dixie want MJ to lead her to the nice-looking guys, just like Marjorie had? Like a girl breadcrumb.

The college experience is primarily about how much you can get laid, according to Dixie, and since MJ tracked her down, she hasn't, not once. Not one party has Dixie woken up after, feeling a little less civilized, and isn't MJ trying to remedy that?

Besides, she is living sweater to sweater; any money she earns is for food, for smokes and beers, and Dixie's vodka cranberry, even though the girl comes from money.

But MJ is not bitter. It's only a load of privilege, luck and money that allows a young person to live so poorly for the sake of reupholstering their brain, she thinks.

I don't need a scholarship, she says.

If you say so, says Jordan.

Money means nothing to those who have it, she thinks, and talk has always been that Jordan Pinault comes from a mega-wealthy family. Whether true or not, MJ remembers it now she is looking at the gold chain around his neck. It isn't massive, which means it is real. She wonders about the taste of it, about biting each link warm from Jordan's damp salty skin.

My father – my real father – is pretty loaded and he lives here in Memphis, so now excuse me, says MJ as she leaves.

Excuse you, says Jordan.

You know, money can't buy you happiness, Eric calls after her.

All you need is love, shouts Jordan.

*

After half of the summer term, Dixie hands MJ an envelope. Look, she says, my pops gave me this. It's a little rainy-day money and it looks like it's raining buckets for you, so why don't you take it?

MJ begins to look through it.

Jeez, don't count it, Dixie says. Goddam. So rude.

No, I'm not. I'm just …

Just … go home, says Dixie. Apply to your own college. This one here is mine.

I know what I want to do and it's not college, says MJ, and Dixie should know that already.

Dixie's face slackens. But this is my life, she says, you've high-jacked my life, don't you fucking get that?

I haven't been any trouble, have I?

Not in a way you'd realize, says Dixie. She gives MJ a tight, aggressive hug that is almost sore. MJ reels from it. How it differs from the one she gave when she first tracked Dixie down under the trees, speaking with that guy she liked and has tried this whole time to keep away from MJ.

Dixie asks MJ to call her, but to leave it a year or so.

*

She flies in over the prairies then catches the shuttle from the airport that always reminds her of a church. She has rarely visited either. And she goes into Rapid and walks the streets searching for a place to work.

She could try Sixth Street Deli again, but she also needs a place to rest her head.

There is this one motel that catches MJ's eye now she is properly looking. It has a flower of fire in the hearth and a leak in the roof, but there are buckets for that, with a sign beside them that says: free water, help yourself.

This is her language, that warm and quirky South Dakota humor. Rarefied it becomes homely, condensed it becomes home.

And besides the leak, the place is clean, at least.

MJ is prepared to work for meals and board, she tells John Kloster, the owner who has been called to the desk to speak with her, but it is not how he does things, he says.

John has a policy to pay his staff and pay her he will. He offers some numbers and MJ accepts, although she has no other choice.

She is covering the bar one evening when her mother walks through the door hand-in-hand with a young guy wearing denim, his hair shaggy and dyed black.

MJ watches them choose a table to canoodle at for a few minutes. She watches Marjorie preen herself as the man advances to the bar, searching his butt-pocket for his wallet. Marjorie is half-heartedly playing with a menu when MJ dips her head, feeling a chowder of annoyance and relief.

When Marjorie sees her, she stands and makes a beeline.

MJ, she says from part-way across the bar. What in the heck are you doing here?

Working, she says then MJ waves a cloth and carries on polishing. What can I get for you? she asks of her mother's companion.

Where have you been, Mary Jane? I've been going out of my mind, says Marjorie putting her purse on the bar.

MJ throws a couple of coasters on the counter. What about you? Can I pour you a drink, ma'am?

This your daughter? the man asks, pointing at MJ with a finger festooned with a skull and crossbones ring. A drywall screw in each of his ear lobes.

Don't be silly, says Marjorie, this is little sis.

MJ rolls her eyes. No change with you, I see.

No change with me, just going out of my mind since you didn't show up at Garfunkel's house.

Are you seriously still calling him that!

What would you have me call him?

MJ puts her hands on the counter, leans on it, brings her face close to Marjorie's. The weirdo you let inseminate you, how about that? she says.

Marjorie looks away. He could be a little weird, she says, I'll give you that, but mostly you're wrong, MJ.

A *little* weird? He lives in a hut, eats roadkill and rides a *bicycle*. MJ emphasizes the bicycle most, like it takes the biscuit for weirdness.

Then she laughs, mainly at herself, and because she thinks that if she doesn't she will cry at the thought of her running through the woods, him behind her with his knife inside his coat. Seeing his eyes and hearing his voice, they still terrify her.

MJ laughs about Tina, and what might have happened if she had not shown up. She laughs the tears back down.

No, baby, says Marjorie, I don't know who you are talking about, Garber called me worried out of his tiny mind that you never showed up.

He's lying.

What's he got to lie about?

'Cos he's a freak.

Marjorie's man coughs, his Adam's apple journeying up and down his throat. Marjorie smiles at him but speaks to MJ: Well certainly, Art's a little bit of a freak. MJ, this is Jeff.

Howya doin'? Jeff asks her.

And that embryo coat? MJ says – she can smell the house again.

Embryo coat? asks Marjorie. Sorry about this, Jeff.

Don't worry about Jeff, cries MJ, worry about your daughter being attacked by some creepy weirdo.

Who did you wind up with? Wait … did he *tell* you he was Art?

Not exactly.

So, what … how did that happen?

You know … I got on the bus, I got off the bus. My plane was late. He was there, he looked at me, he walked ahead like, I don't know, follow me, or something …

MJ!

I'm lost, says Jeff lighting a cigarette.

So was she, says Marjorie, laughing.

It's really very funny indeed, says MJ. And on a one-way ticket, what a responsible mother you are.

Oh c'mon, you're eighteen years old. Nineteen now, I suppose. Happy belated, baby.

You have a nineteen-year-old daughter, Marj? Jeff asks.

Oh, shut up, Jeff! Marjorie says and Jeff steps backward, looking hurt. No, I didn't mean … she says. Marjorie pulls at his wrists, trying to make herself minuscule and feeble, she strokes his face. Just a minute, Hun, just a minute. Okay?

I'll be over here. Jeff putts to the table.

Thank you, baby.

Thank you, baby, MJ mimics her mother and is reminded again of Art and how he spoke to her.

Marjorie's face grows stern. This is real effed up, she says.

You're telling me.

I was so worried.

Looks like it.

Don't be like that, MJ. I don't have the luxury of putting my life on hold. I have to work and I'm still a woman, for crying out loud.

What do you want? asks MJ. A Jameson?

You're too young to be working a bar. Besides, I don't know if I feel like a drink now.

You can't sit there without one. Maybe you should go home.

Marjorie's face tempers. I miss you.

And I miss you, MJ can't help but say.

So, you'll come home too?

I'll think about it.

I didn't do nothing wrong.

Not this time.

Not many times.

Marjorie is looking behind MJ's head, looking at herself in the mirrored wall, MJ decides.

MJ, quit this and come home, Marjorie whispers, looking blankly past her daughter.

Everything okay, Mary Jane? asks John. She has not realized that he was there.

All good, she says.

John smiles. Just seeing if you need anything before I go home now.

Not a thing, thanks John.

He puts on his coat and walks to the door. Glances back at her.

He *likes* you, Boo, says Marjorie.

And I like him.

No, he likes you. Know what I'm saying?

How do you know that?

It's the way he looks at you. From my vantage, he was staring at you like you were the only person in here.

And that's fine, isn't it?

He's just real old, that's a concern.

That's probably what Jeff's mom tells him about you. She's real old, Jeff!

Ha-ha, MJ. Hardly true!

But MJ thinks about it, he is older but being around John is safe and comfortable. More than that, being around John Kloster feels like slipping warm shoes on to cold feet.

*

A week later she is in the office with John. The desk is leaking with papers, he is counting out wages.

45

Now that they have had some heart-to-heart conversations and he knows of her plans, John is telling MJ that he will give her a gig one Friday night singing in the bar. MJ agrees on a price for five songs, slipping the booking fee into her pocket when the office phone screeches.

John answers it. Hold one moment, he says, then covering the mouthpiece. Mary Jane, it's for you.

She takes the phone and utters a damp hello.

Is this MJ? a man says.

This is she, she replies.

I'm Art ... Garber, your ... father.

Is this Jeff? she says. Has my mom put you up to this?

No, it's Art. And in a way, I suppose Marjie has, she told me what happened, that you thought someone else was me or that I was someone else.

Something like that, mutters MJ feeling embarrassed.

I still want to meet you, if that's doable.

Erm. MJ looks at John, who is rubber banding the last of the wads of cash that are all laid out on the table, he consults his employee pay book once more, puts his hands up and walks out.

MJ runs her eyes over the greens, she visualizes lying on a bed made entirely of crisp just-printed notes cold on her back. She feels breathless.

How? When? she asks Art.

I know you won't want to up sticks again, but it's hard for me to come to you. I'm self-employed, see. If I wired you some money, would you come out and stay with us? The kids would sure love to meet you, and Tracey too. Everyone was so disappointed when you — when we thought that you — didn't show up.

I'll come, she says. I'll get my own ticket though. Just need to see when I can get time off work.

Great! Have you got a pen? I'll give you my phone number and my address. No mistakes this time.

No mistakes, alrighty!

After he explains that he will meet her, or send a family member to collect her from the airport, Art says: I'm sorry I haven't been there for you, kiddo. Did Marjie explain?

Eventually, yes, Marjie did.

And I believe I hung up on you before, and for that, I'm truly sorry. His voice sounds clear and warm with just the right amount of authoritativeness.

I appreciate that, MJ says gulping back a little tear.

I believe you're beautiful, says Art, and you sound beautiful. You sound like you can sing, if that makes any sense ... I hear that you sing better than your mom.

She told you that?

Sure did. Your mom told me a lot. She's hugely proud.

Hmm, maybe. MJ has never thought of it like that, it isn't how Marjorie frames it.

So, I'll see you soon, kiddo?

You will see me soon, Art.

Okay. He sounds disappointed but she can't call him Dad. It just doesn't feel right.

Take care of your good self, he says.

Her hands shake after she hangs up, she is halfway down a Marlboro when John comes back into the office. Do you need something or no? he asks.

Time off ... hopefully.

Going somewhere?

Memphis.

Hey, that's pretty cool.

It is.

You'll need a plane fare. What else?

Nothing else, and I'll earn it.

47

I know, I trust you.

And I trust you, too, she says.

Well then, we're the trusty … team, together. Right?
Right!

And you are such a sweet person, he says, anyone else would have robbed me blind.

How do you know I haven't? she says and they trade a laugh.

John lifts a wad of money and holds it out in front of MJ who looks at it and makes an involuntary reaction: a warm sensation, beginning in her hands, tingling its way up her arms and warming her to the core. She puts her hands out to receive it. Pieces of paper and discs of metal. All and any of it, she loves.

I owe you a full disclaimer, says John, I was gunna ask you out, Mary Jane, for a meal, or to see a show, go someplace you'd like. I'm not trying to buy you.

I know.

But now, I'm bowing out. Take this money. Just take this and go see this guy. Maybe he'll make you happy. John throws his hands up. God, what a mess I'm making of this.

I don't care if he makes me happy or not, MJ says. John, it's not what you think at all.

God knows I'm getting old, he says, and I don't know if anyone has ever told you, but you are really beautiful. I mean, really *incredibly* beautiful. I feel like a fool.

John, stop.

Well, have they told you?

Oh, once or twice.

How silly of me.

Yes, silly of him, she thinks. MJ has eyes. She can see for herself that she is usually the prettiest girl in the room.

48

That is just something a girl gets used to, like being the tallest, or the shortest. She doesn't care. Not anymore.

Believe me when I say I'm not trying to buy anybody's affection, John says. So, we're clear.

MJ shakes her head, she taps the cash against her chin, she breathes in. Nothing smells better. And she adores him, and the boyishness of his cheeks, his smooth skin, the gray hair at his locks.

She also adores John's generosity, his powder blue Cadillac de Ville and the twinkle in his eyes. She hates to see his eyes without it. And right now, he is losing it at the thought of her not returning some kindness.

You could bow back in, she says. Or I can take you to dinner sometime.

Really?

And truly. I have been wanting to ask you.

Are you sure, Mary Jane? You've got your whole life in front, he says looking around. Is someone about to come in and tell me this is a joke? Are you sure we're not on *Candid Camera*?

*

It is the end of July and her last journey to Memphis – though naturally, MJ doesn't know it – when Grace collects her from the airport.

Hey, she says, anybody lose a sister along the way?

Grace helps MJ get her case into the trunk then stands back to take a long look. Hey, let me look at you. God, you're gorgeous! A real movie star.

Stop! You're gorgeous, too.

MJ looks at her sister, lanky and broad-shouldered, Grace looks like she was born to swim, right down to her tea-colored tan and long damp hair.

Your mom must be gorgeous, Grace says, and that would figure, right, seeing father was fucking the two of them at the same time: your mom and mine.

What age are you? asks MJ.

One month younger than you, I do believe.

MJ covers her face with her hands.

I know! I mean, Dad, right? Oh, MJ, you'll love him, he's very suave and cynical but such a bore, and his wife, Tracey, she's cool, and our brother, Aaron, my twin. He's alright. I used to hate on him so bad but he grew out of that annoying-ass stage in the last year.

He sounds nice too. I'd like to meet him.

You will. Good grief, would you look at that! You and Aaron have the same … Grace taps her chin.

Really? MJ puts her finger to the dimple on her chin.

But anyway, getting back to Dad, ha! Three kids the same age, and two different women. What a player!

It's hysterical! says MJ. And your mom?

She's pretty. No, she is pretty.

I mean, isn't she going mad about me turning up? About my mom?

My folks have been split up for years. Aaron and I were only three. She caught him with his pants down.

No!

Uh-huh! The babysitter. He's nothing if not a horny cliché, is Arthur Garber Esquire.

What was he doing in South Dakota?

Besides wetting his weiner?

Besides that, says MJ.

How Marjorie would love Grace, she thinks.

So, M… Grace starts, as she drives off …there was this Cheyenne man in Taos who started up a taco stand in the mid-sixties. Mum, Dad, and a business partner they brought on board, bought the franchise rights to the venture.

Then, she continues, they started franchising restaurants based on the founder's concept, changing the name to Taco Stax. They started small, sure: Memphis, Rapid City, Scottsbluff, Nebraska, then Torrington, Wyoming.

I know that place. The one in Rapid, it's on Eighth Street.

I guess. Now they have eighty-three branches around the states. Montana, Nebraska, the Dakotas. The branch in South Dakota is owned by someone else now. Dad sold a few recently. Made a prewty dowar, Grace says in a faux Chinese accent. Don't get carried away though, we Garber kids have to pave our own way. Art Garber's big on self-preservation.

They drive a half-hour until they are at the bus stop where the man MJ had mistaken for her father sits smoking. The lights ahead change and traffic comes to a halt as Grace slows the car.

The man – not-Art – stares in through the window, the same embryo coat that is black now, the only thing that has changed about him since she first saw him, months ago.

He is like a big chargrilled baby, MJ thinks, and he is holding on to the seat of his bicycle.

Can I lock this door? MJ asks her new half-sister, whose face is stenciled by the shadow of trees along the roadside, the trees MJ walked into and ran out off, crying. Waiting for a bus with both her eyes on the gap in the trees. Listening for the whirring of his tires.

Sure, says Grace, buttoning down the doors. He's a stinkin' creep, isn't he? Crazy Tony.

Is that his name? asks MJ.

That's what Aaron calls him. Aaron says he was once some big shot ice hockey star – back in the sixties.

What do you think Tony's waiting there for?

—

51

Pfft! He never gets on board any bus, I know that, says Grace. It's somewhere to sit, maybe that's it. Sit and have a smoke. Good a place as any, I suppose.

Maybe he lives nearby.

There is no nearby.

Crazy Tony flicks his cigarette butt at the car window.

Take it easy, Crazy Tony! shouts Grace. Hey, M, look at his bicycle.

What about it? says MJ, trying desperately not to look at those eyes that sucked her in and spat her out, she just wants the stoplights to change to green.

He just pushes that bicycle along, doesn't ever get on it, says Grace. Look at the tires. You notice anything?

There's no air in them, says MJ. They are completely flat.

Exactamente! says Grace just as the lights change.

The Other Truth

2014 – 2015

It goes like this:

One minute you're eighteen years old and leaving for school in Illinois, the next – a flash – and twenty years are gone. Now you are thirty-eight, and leaving Minnesota, traveling west through the artery of Interstate 90, back to your mother's ranch where the old homestead sits like a monopoly piece on a board of land. Here, only grain bins and silos rise above the otherwise flat horizon. It's here my parents planted themselves in South Dakotan soil a year before they wed. When my mother Bess was pregnant, my father entered one of those bins for some ordinary reason only to be overcome in a tidal rush of grain that crushed and suffocated him. Leaving bits of corn embedded in his lungs.

Leaving my mother alone, apart from the threat of me stretching out in her belly. When I arrive home early she is already expecting me.

The day you're late will be the day the world stops, she says.

I tell her that I will stay for a week or so, until I decide what to do about Rochester, and what to do about Mitchell.

Well, Helena, she says, God has a path for you, if you'll only meet Him halfway.

Bess has a red leather-bound hardback edition of the Old Testament, it gathers dust the way cliffs build themselves around prehistoric bones. I can't say I've ever seen any truth on its pages, which is not to say that I have ever looked, though I like to lift the bible each time I run back here, away from some drama, and inhale its wise grassy hue.

The bible has felt like the snakeskins I used to find on the prairie, when dogs were whistling and the summer sun would swell the trees, and frizzy cottonwood seeds would float gracefully.

I would find myself looking out at the shivering corn, leaning my hands on that warm leather skin. It always felt like my own limb: an arm that was not attached to the rest of me.

Now the bible sits atop a stack of old art books that have been long disregarded by my mother. She gave up the job at the art college to hold down this farm and I have not seen her lift those books in yonks.

Feeling like I owe her mother something – and in a sudden inclination of God's will, like I'm cutting carbs or committing to a two-day cleanse – I say: Sure. I will try to meet Him halfway.

But I still believe that doubt is better than faith.

So, when Sunday comes, I drive Bess to the City of Change International Church where they just love themselves some Bess Russo. Mostly on account of her having been married six times – which makes her exotic – that and my mother's lake of silver hair.

The church smells of coffee and cologne. Senior Pastor Ricky Nwafo is greeting every one of his flock. There is a sea of familiar faces. A couple of exes of my mother's. A couple of lays of mine. I have to do a double-take, but even Jordan Pinault is here.

Maybe I shouldn't be surprised, he and Ricky were always inseparable, playing first for the South Dakota Coyotes before transferring to Memphis, before joining the NFL and making it huge as Cardinals, and everything that means and everything that followed.

They are the same age, must be mid-to-late-forties by now.

Some years ago, Jordan retired from football and became a congressman. A republican, to Bess's disdain, who I think is actually Obama-obsessed.

I have a little-remembered memory of Ricky and Jordan and I clench on it here, in church, at the fast, vivid flowering, and the reaction my skin, spine and groin have taken to it.

I ice the memory down to stand and join in with the opening song but my heart barks. I suppose we all end up back here, back where we started.

Now Pastor Nwafo asks us to be seated and a broad-chested, big-bellied man in his seventies delivers the scripture reading from 1 Samuel 15:34 through 16:13. Kenechukwu Nwafo – he is credited in the Order of Worship, or Papa Ken – is Ricky's father. Boy, Ken has gotten old and gray. He tells us a tale of a band of brothers from whom the Lord is choosing a king.

The Lord was sorry, Papa Ken reads, and I listen up, never having realized that this a possibility before, a sorry god. Ken talks about one son who looks like a king, and the other who does not.

In essence, it is a tale about appearances being no substitute for matters of the heart. Then Pastor Ricky thanks his father for delivering the scripture reading.

I'm a lucky one, he says. You know, there are thousands growing up without the visible presence of a father here in the United States. In the media, this is what fathers look like: a god or a doofus. There is the Homer Simpson idea, stupid, crass … then there is the Cliff Huxtable character: a black man, educated and a good father. Can't we see now how that was ahead of its time?

The congregation murmurs in agreement.

I loved the Huxtable family as much as anyone, but are we ignoring the news stories about Cosby now? I wonder.

Pastor Ricky goes on to talk about love and manliness, how men need to stop worrying about being seen as feminine. Men need to be not manlier, but Godlier, he states, and the congregation agrees, as it should.

Saul looked like a king, Ricky says, but there was David and he was ordinary, he was not the obvious choice but he was who God chose to work through.

Pastor Ricky holds up a dollar bill. We might feel like this, he says, crumpling it up and stamping on it. Full of self-loathing, he says, and bad memories and brooking regrets. He takes a fresh bill from his lectern.

But look at this dollar, says Ricky, doesn't it look good: new and fresh and not crumpled up? Is one worth more than the other?

The congregation murmurs again.

An Oglala Lakota man with a stick and scratched face stands up in a row a few ahead of mine and walks along the aisle, he heads as if to leave but goes into the kitchen instead.

Alf, my mother's third husband, turns to watch and does not stop watching, and I hear Ricky all the more for it.

After, when we say our goodbyes and wish everyone a happy holiday I drive my mother home.

Doesn't Papa Ken look great? Bess asks.

He's huge, I say.

A lovely big belly, she says, I couldn't picture him without.

Did you see Alf? I ask her.

No? I mean yes, but only in passing.

Did you speak with him?

No. Did he speak with you? Bess asks.

He said, Hello, young woman, glad to have you home.

That's kind of fun, to see Alf again, right?

I suppose, I say.

You told him it was only for Christmas, right?

Yes, Ma. He was watching that man with the stick, I add.

What man with the stick? asks Bess.

The Sioux man.

Oh, with his face all scratched, or Jimmy with the lovely tasseled coat?

Yeah, the man with the face, with the scratches.

I think that poor fellow had a fight with the ground.

He was looking a little worse for wear.

Alf was watching him? Maybe Alf was watching out for him.

No, I say, Alf was worried he was gunna do something.

Like what?

How can I tell? Like the Lakota man might steal something. Who knows.

You got a lot from one look.

He watched him for ten full minutes.

You watched Alf for the same amount? asks Bess.

It was hard not to, there was Ricky … and Ma, this is why I have a hard time with the church, I say. Pastor Nwafo talking about marginalized people and, you know, how God knows what is in someone's heart, and also, at the same time that …

Alf's a good guy.

Yes, he certainly thinks he is.

He served his country. So did Mitchell, Bess adds but I don't take the bait.

Maybe Alf was wanting an opportunity to be a hero again, I say.

He was good to you.

I was good to him too. I was his ranch hand.

Hmm … that's true. He wasn't cut out for it. Didn't have farming instincts.

Or the patience, I say as I turn the car on to the ranch.

He's more patient now, being that bit older.

Right, I say.

Aren't you coming in, Helena?

I'm gunna go for a drive.

Sounds good. I'm talking to Alf again, Bess says, you should know.

Good, I say. He was the favorite of all my fathers.

She looks surprised.

I'm sorry, I say, I should learn to bite my tongue. Maybe I'm projecting.

You've had a week, with Mitchell and all! I get that's no fun.

Bess watches me reverse before she goes indoors. Then I go for a head-clearing drive under that white chest of sky when it begins to snow the kind of snow that stings your eyes. Soon, somewhere near Nemo, I get stuck. A Jeep in front dims its lights, a figure leaves a car and approaches mine.

When this figure gets to my window, I lower it to see Jordan Pinault again, buffeted against the wind, against the crystalline whiteness. Not one real-life sighting of him in twenty years and now twice, and in one day.

Need some help, ma'am? he shouts. It's gunna be a whiteout. They're closing the interstate.

I insist I'm fine and I try to drive on while he waits, knowing. But my wheels spin, so he helps me get my wheels dislodged using the shovel he winches from the trunk of his car. Noticing his pronounced limp, I hop out of the car and try to do it myself only Jordan insists that I don't.

Just getting over surgery, he says when I ask if he is okay.

Really, I say, I've always worked in hospitals. Not the medical side, managerial.

He looks at me with a squint. Did we ever date? he asks.

Maybe, I say, just as reluctant.

Then he asks for my number and I give it, because of course I do, it's Jordan fucking Pinault after all: Republican Senator, patron saint of overgrown boy-gods, and the kind of man who pulls himself out into a blizzard – even though he's hurting – just to help out a virtual stranger.

—

59

Only we are definitely not strangers but he obviously cannot remember that, and why would I expect him to? I'm no one to the likes of him. Oh, the things you do for your eighteen-year-old self.

*

A new year, a new man. And a plan. We are eating pancakes for breakfast in Tally's Silver Spoon when I tell Jordan I need to get back to work.

He asks if I'd like to volunteer at the animal sanctuary on East Saint Patrick Street. And I would do it without payment? I ask.

It is a registered charity and they have not got the funds to pay people, he says. And the community, social and psychological values of volunteering on a person are worth way more than cash.

You sound awfully like a senator, I tell him, putting down my fork.

He gets the check and pays.

A man with his own money, how refreshing, and I can't say anything, not when I did not decline the Cadillac Jordan bought me for Christmas from the showroom in Spearfish, the car with a snow shovel in the trunk tied in a red ribbon.

When my mother saw that automobile, she said: But Helena, you've worked so hard to get where you are. Don't give up that independence now.

Of course I laughed.

After my father died, she chain-smoked husbands, good men all battling something, like her mother before her. All of my stepfathers, Bess thought she could iron the kinks out of, wasn't happy unless they were more or less helpless.

None of them took care of her – not even good old Alf – so I have decided, I'm going to be taken care of. I'm going to let Jordan, and I'll look after him in return when he gets the subsequent prosthetic hip.

I wouldn't want to go through that alone again, Jordan has told me.

But personally, I like the thought of taking a break from hospital management, and I have always loved animals. Being an only child means animals have always been my friends, and the way Jordan is with them melts my heart.

By the end of January, I am volunteering at the sanctuary and also living in Jordan's home in Nemo, with his ritzy contemporary tastes: noisy wall colors, dolphin-shaped cupboard knobs and minimal furniture.

At home he has two dogs, Tibetan mastiffs, massive. Monsters, really. Bigger than me standing up. A girl called Dohna and a boy called Dorjee.

Jordan brings them to the off-leash park and the rest of the day they are somnolent.

They wake to bark at sounds during the night but I'm getting used to that. It is almost reassuring.

*

By March the mastiffs' clean odorless coats are having their annual molt, so I attack the house with a large lint roller in each hand, after the maid has left. By now my life has become an intoxicating mix of daytime soap operas and me, guiltily, and embarrassedly, avoiding the staff. By now I am living the life of a retiree.

Evenings when Jordan invites the other senators around, they eat and I pour them drinks. I pour them drinks even when he says: Helena, we have people for that.

I think that being a good old-fashioned farm girl is my appeal. But I leave him to it, always with a pretty young server, and I watch as they go into another room to talk business that I have no keen interest in.

Secretly I am glad to go to the bedroom and take off my makeup and not have to listen to these men who are older than Jordan, except for Leslie Clifford, who is a similar age. They bore me, honestly.

Their wives only attend formal functions with them at this stage. There is not much I am needed for. So I think about taking the Cadi for a ride, maybe to Rochester ... to see Mitchell.

No! I bury that thought deep.

I lie on top of Jordan's bed and put on the movie I started watching after lunch to see how it ends, while there are perfectly spaced waves of laughter coming from downstairs that I would think are canned if I didn't know better.

Later, Jordan gets ready for bed. From the back he looks good, though his back is a pink and brown atlas of sun damage.

When he turns I see his scars, though they are not as bad as I'd always expected.

He has broad shoulders, burls of reddish chest hair, and his waist has maintained that muscle memory of his years on the field even though he cannot work out properly, since he is still recovering from his hip replacement. There is another scar on his side. His midriff is splotched with red crepey tissue. Still, I can look past it, I've done it before, and boy does he ever look good for forty-seven.

Truth I have not yet slept with Jordan, this time. I don't push it. I have offered to straddle him, to make love lying side on, to do the work.

When I bring the subject up he uses his hands on me and I guide him. He claims he doesn't want anything in return. Nothing feels mutual in the house in Nemo, but I'm not sure I should be complaining. Here is a man who wants to take care of me, and slowly. So I am deciding that maybe I should slow up, let life show me how it should be lived.

*

The year before I met and moved in with Jordan Pinault, I met and moved in with Mitchell. I was camping out to get Shawn Colvin tickets when I saw this foxy boy with beseeching eyes, and we got to talking, being next in line.

And you know how it is when you stand for long times with other people. You get to know them. You stop competing. After a while I forgot about tickets and instead studied Mitchell's freckles, the color of barely-there scabs, like he'd been scratched in a bramble bush, like give it a day and his skin would be bitterly clean.

And those red patches below his eyes that made him look like he'd been crying. Those patches were my favorite part of that face of Mitch's. I couldn't tell you why.

He was from Duluth and had just been fired from his job and I had just been promoted, and that was the magnetic force, because I was always drawn to deadbeats and deadbeats were drawn to me.

It didn't take long for someone to hook him up with a job working 4.30 a.m. until route completion as a vending driver for Pepsi. It took even less time for his first paycheck to get spent on meth in that hotel room in Rochester.

He never lied about it. He told me, because I had told him about growing up with wide-open spaces and little to do, that drugs were my thing when I was a kid. Prairie sunsets and ecstasy. Prairies yawning on and on. Back home we had to break that ennui up with pit fires and drugs and parties with people who liked to live, I told him.

Maybe I wanted to seem cool and understanding.

Tell me what's changed, Hel. It's no fun alone, said Mitchell.

We shot H together a couple of times, but I'm not big into it. Klonopin or Xanax, just about. Good weed – on occasion.

Then Mitch started staying out all night, hanging with people in the park.

I'd find him with track marks up his arms, then blots of dried blood between his toes.

By the time the concert floated up, we had wed and separated. The day of the concert itself I was pulled over on the way to the airport, on the way to a business meeting. I got caught running a red and the State Trooper gave me two options: pay a fine or take a speed awareness class.

I'm mean. I chose the class, in which a female facilitator showed a group of us some road signs we should have been able to identify. Getting back-to-basics, if you please.

Then the facilitator whipped around the room. What was the maximum speed limit set at in the place you were caught? she asked. And what speed were you caught doing?

I kept my eyes on her as I heard the replies. So far, I had been going the fastest; I'm now a little ashamed to admit that I was proud of that.

Then I heard someone outdo me; the voice as familiar as my own feet. When I turned there was my husband of three months, my almost ex-husband: Mitchell.

The facilitator must have seen how we stared at one another because she started reminding everyone how her speeding awareness classes held a confidentiality clause, yet we'd signed nothing, certainly nothing like a contract, and Mitchell and I clearly didn't put much importance on contracts, anyway.

Remember, anything you hear today cannot be repeated, she said, staring at Mitchell and me like a world-weary mother trying to break up her two fighting children. It was another hour before I could leave my seat for a coffee break. Cue the itchiest conversation ever: Were you trying to kill yourself, Mitch?

And he asked, Were you?

He said he was in a hurry.

I knew he was dying, or killing himself more like.

We had to slip the conversation into something more comfortable, so we took it back to mine, where we took it underneath the sheets. Lying in bed after, intertwining fingers, we both declared the marriage was back on and that we would each contact our solicitors the next day, call a halt to divorce proceedings.

*

I am relieved to have changed my car when soon after I pull up to my mother's house Mitchell appears. I hide in the back room while Bess opens the front door to him, declaring she has not heard from me. She does not invite him in, even though she thinks he's the absolute sweetest and still calls him her son-in-law.

Her vote – if she had one – would be for Mitchell.

The couple of times he came to Rapid City during our marriage he would don a cap and sit over cans of Pabst with local ranchers, shooting the breeze. He enjoyed Bess's art, which convinced my mother that they were kindred spirits. Not that any man I have been with was arty, maybe in temperament but not in talent, and that was where I was kidding myself.

Mitchell doesn't look so good around the mouth, Bess says when he is gone, and she resumes peeling acrylic paint from pieces that have not worked out. When they dry out as much as their color will allow she will make the most beautiful mosaics. She won't like them as much as I will.

I don't know, Ma, I say, he must have signed himself out of rehab.

I can't mention the word *meth* to Bess, and I'm not sure why I can't when she was an artist in the fifties and sixties, and has lived her cut of bohemian life.

Well then, Bess says, he'll have to try harder if he wants to see you. Such a pity, he was my favorite of all your husbands.

I laugh. Then, with the coast clear, I go to the window and watch my one and only husband drive away until he is only a pinprick on the horizon.

If guilt has a landscape this is it.

*

After his second hip has been replaced with plastic, I am helping Jordan get out of the shower and into the bedroom, drying his skin with a towel when he catches me looking good and hard at his scars.

Good thing I was in the bath, he says, when she did that.

66

He is talking about MJ McCord. I saw her sing in Rapid once or twice, and once at a party also. So unearthly gorgeous she was, and so fragile-looking. Maybe it was obvious that there was something unhinged in her. Not that I'd ever spoken to her and now when I think about that there is regret. Especially since we were linked: her father Chad and my father Dale becoming forever entwined through both their friendship and the proximity of their deaths, leaving behind another fatherless daughter around the same time. And their women. MJ's mother then mine. Another little widow.

Bess has told me about Chad McCord, how he and my father were scooping silage from a wagon when Chad's sweatshirt got caught on a moving part – the beater, I think – he was tangled in the machinery and flipped on his back and cut up badly, requiring that too-common emergency flight to Sioux Falls. Doctors tried to save him but he'd ruptured the femoral artery.

Then two days later, same farm, my father went into that grain bin.

But she seemed so sweet, I say to Jordan picturing MJ, almost hearing her voice.

She wasn't sweet, Jordan says. We were told in the NFL that you never mess with anybody's play, and MJ did. It's like pulling someone's mask, Helena, you just don't do it.

I was always so distracted back then, I say, pulling his Tee-shirt over his head, even though he can do it himself, but he is vulnerable right now after getting his operation and having sent his staff home, and only having me.

Now he is opening up, I do what I can to lengthen this occurrence.

I remember the feeling I used to have around him, how obvious it was that he had his mind on someone else and had it bad.

Did you love her? I ask him.

No, he answers quickly. But I wasn't careful of women's feelings, sure, that was part of the problem.

She fell for you and you couldn't give her what she wanted back?

I wasn't ready to settle.

But you are now?

I was ready a lifetime ago, I was ready shortly after MJ did this to me.

Because she did this to you? I say it gently.

No ... I don't think so, because I wanted a good woman to have to be a good man for. I didn't respect women much when I played football.

That's standard practice, isn't it?

Maybe it is, he says. I saw what Ricky had with Natasha; she wasn't a model or singer nor did she have any ambition, but she had his back and is a good mom to their boy.

And you wanted that? I ask, believing that my ambition has recently up and left.

Sure, he says. Who doesn't? Takes a while to realize these things are important.

Sounds like me now, I admit aloud. Coming out the other side of all these bad relationships of trying to fix people.

Thisbe wasn't like Natasha, that's for sure, Jordan mentions his ex-wife for the first time. Thisbe was brash and loud, she was nutsy ... psychopathic or something.

I've had my share of people who need fixing.

You can't do it, I don't think people change.

Thisbe cheated on you? I ask.

68

Yes, and here's the kicker, Helena, she did it publicly, and knowing how I value my privacy.

I suppose that when it all came out about you sleeping with MJ behind her husband's back it must have felt like that for him. For MJ's husband.

Karma? Is that what you mean? Jordan asks.

Not exactly. Empathy, I say.

This is the sweetest, most vulnerable and lucid he has allowed himself to be. The most he has allowed me in to understand that there is a softer heart inside that big body, but it is also the longest that I have gone without intimacy. I know he is unable right now but I need a connection, I wrap my hands around the back of his neck.

I can't wait for you to be back to new, I say, kissing his ear.

Not sure if I like girls initiating that anymore, he says, removing my hands from him. I probably never have.

Sounds good, I say though I feel like he has put me in my place. Let me know when you are ready.

*

In April, Mitchell comes back again, Bess calls to let me know. He was motorcycling, she says, and he had flowers and chocolates for your one-year anniversary.

Did you send him away? I ask.

Oh, Helena, he looked adorable, your mother says. You wanna seen him.

I sigh. When Jordan leaves I'll come over, I say.

For all of half an hour I think about the passion there was in that relationship, an abundance of it, and I'd liked it.

69

There was no disconnect, until the meth. I miss our conversations. I would say something and Mitchell would respond. It just isn't like that at home. Not only is my brain rotting in Nemo, there is also no culture. It makes me nostalgic for my childhood when Bess would invite her friends to dinner and their conversations about art stimulated me, then we'd go to the Dahl Arts Center or enjoy the free street theater.

Then I chose an analytical path because of course fees and trying to get myself a career with a backbone when I would have loved to study something in humanities. Now I am hurtling toward forty, separated and childless, and after always seeing myself as this career woman with a husband and three kids, maybe.

Jordan has three. All daughters. He has very few photos of them about the house. The eldest must be the image of her mother. The middle one has Jordan's stern brow and the little one has his curved mouth. I wonder about asking to meet them again, but he refuses to talk about his children, I understand the pollution in relationships.

Mitchell is staying in the Super 8 Motel, says Bess.

Do you think I should go and see him?

How could it hurt? she asks, but I know all the ways.

Bess likes how he has remembered our anniversary and I'm surprised he remembers anything. But I go. I'm on my way to the motel when I need to stop for gas. At the gas station, waiting for my car to fill up, I see the Sheriff staring at me. I look away and then back but he remains staring. I smile at him and he keeps the stare.

I feel like saying, hey, what gives? Is it the car? Do you have a problem with me driving a ninety-thousand-dollar vehicle? Instead, I mutter some swear words under my breath.

I recognize that dumb face too, back in 2002 he shot an unarmed Lakota boy and wormed his way back into the force. So now he's a Sheriff. I guess that figures.

When I am in line ready to pay, the Marcach Gang roll into the forecourt on their Harleys. Green is their color, the color of cash. The sheriff tos and fros, like an anxious deer, then he sidles over to talk to them but I can smell his fear.

I'm coming out to get in my car when I hear him say he has got a call from the highway patrol. Ephraim Shea is at the helm, and – damn! – is that Mitchell on the sidelines? He is wearing a white stocking cap and a green bandana over his mouth but it's him alright.

I climb into the car and slump down in my seat. It doesn't look like he is missing me too hard right now. Looks like he has found a new crowd to fall in with, like the bums in the park and junkies in hotel rooms. Like his tore-up brethren from his soldier days.

In my rearview mirror, the sheriff watches me drive away, still watching the gang with a shifty side-eye, hand never far from his holster.

Mitchell doesn't even realize I was there.

*

If I hadn't seen him with the Marcach Gang, I wouldn't fill with dread when, in May, there's a turf war in Verboten Clubhouse that spills into the hills, killing nine people and injuring many.

Initially it's unknown how many are killed by bikers and how many are killed by police.

The police were gathered to monitor the meeting of the Marcach Gang when the Chevaliers came out of Texas to avenge one of their members being killed in the week prior.

Soon the victims are named but not soon enough. You bet I'm relieved when Mitchell is not one of them.

When the police find meth, they arrest close to one hundred and sixty people, and confiscate hundreds of weapons. Mitchell is one of twenty people who haven't been let go. All at the same time, my hair begins to escape my scalp, leaving an intricate nest on my pillow each morning I wake up in Jordan Pinault's bed.

*

Your man will return from prison and he'll need your nursing, Bess says when I tell her I've received a letter from Mitchell, in which he asks me to visit him in the county jail.

Jordan says I must be fucked up in the mind to even contemplate agreeing. He explains that I can refuse to go, like I don't already know that.

Jordan, I say, sometimes you talk to me like I have no brain.

He looks insulted.

He is surrounded by yes-men. And once I was probably guilty of being a yes-person, but not anymore.

I am not a kid anymore, nor – and this is not false modesty – do I believe that I am anyone's great prize. But I am loyal and have never made an enemy of an ex.

Seriously, I say, I married this man because I loved him and he isn't a bad person. Mitch must be afraid.

Considering he looks so angry, it is a surprise when the date comes to visit Mitchell and Jordan is sweetness and light.

He says he wants to take me out somewhere for the day. To the theater … in Chicago, he says. He has massaged his schedule.

I say I appreciate the thought but no, and he says: How will that look, the senator's fiancée going to visit a gang member in the clink?

But I'm not your fiancée, I say. I'm still his wife.

C'mon, says Jordan, at our age people don't wait. And his meaning is unclear, but still I remind him that our ages are quite different.

People like us don't wait, then, he says.

Is this a proposal? I ask.

Could be, he says.

Is it?

Sure!

Smooth devil, I say.

I've done all that, romance and trying to impress women, he says. We are too old for that.

Maybe I'm not, I say.

We are family, he deflects.

Then let me meet your daughters, if we are family.

I can't even see my daughters.

Why ever not? you ask.

Their mother is a crazy bitch and liar, he says – which I have already heard, and this is the liposuction of his storytelling.

Thisbe is not a good historian, how so? I ask. I think I might hear the whole story this time.

Well, let me ask you this: why do you think the leader of the Marcach Gang isn't in the clink with your ex?

Jordan, tell me.

Because Stone Shea was screwing Thisbe when I was still married to her.

How would that work? I ask, and to clarify what I mean, say: How would that keep him out of jail?

They had a fling, says Jordan, and she – feeling guilty, probably – accused Shea of rape. Shea was sent away for sixteen days. Thisbe was fudging the truth the whole time.

Holy moly.

Didn't *Bess* tell you?

I don't like the way Jordan says my mother's name, but then again, she is not a yes-man, she asks him plenty, therefore he questions her in return, even if just her name. But I don't like it. Everyone loves my mother.

My mother doesn't gossip about people, I say, that's not her style. You know she doesn't judge.

Yeah, seven marriages later, sometimes you need to judge, says Jordan.

It's six, I say, and that's not very nice. You had two, I remind him.

The first one doesn't count, it lasted a week, a piece of ass was all she was; a Vegas blowout at the end of the season.

I'm not happy to hear him talk about a woman that way, but the NFL mentality dies hard, I guess. I know Vegas was a rebound thing afterward, quickly annulled, and that Jordan had been engaged to Miss Ohio before that. Once I would have cared, but I don't care now.

Where would we be if people believed every story they heard? I ask. No one would trust a single person.

That's true, he admits.

So I'm gunna see Mitchell.

Okay. And I'm gunna do it better next time.

Do what better? I ask.

Next time I ask you to marry me, he says.

Fine, you do that, I say smiling, and next time I marry I'll do it differently too, and not marry a man who sends me prison visit requests.

*

It is hard to look into Mitchell's eyes when he sits at the other side of the glass in his faded black and white stripes. His eyes look the clearest I've seen them, yet he looks so lost. His hair is longer and unrulier than I've ever seen it. I want to wash it and cut it.

What in the world were you doing, Mitch? I ask him.

I came looking for you, he says, holding the phone against his mouth.

You didn't look awfully hard, I say. How many times did you call at my mother's?

I'm not someone to push someone to be with me.

And you're also not someone to carry weapons and fight turf wars, so what happened to you?

You know me, Hel, I follow crowds. I have to stop following crowds.

I'm sad to see you in here.

I just got in way too deep and maybe I needed this to happen to get out.

What are you gunna do when you are released? You need to get away from the gang.

I'll go back to Rochester, lay low.

Where was Stone?

Mitchell looks around, then says: He was there.

What happened?

I can't say.

Who started it?

That doesn't matter does it, aren't none of us children.

But Stone is out.

He's Teflon, babe, on account of he knows a few things.

What does he know?

Stone Shea was pinched along with the rest of us that night, but I heard he is out there. Like, just scrubbed off the rap-sheet.

At least I know where you are now.

Yeah, you know where to send the divorce papers.

Mitch …

You aren't wearing your rings.

The metal detectors …

You serious with Pinault?

Pretty much.

Some people think he's great and all because he played football.

You think I care about football? Or that he's a senator … our politics are worlds apart, you know that. I'm not with Jordan because of who he is.

Just watch him, Hel. There are stories going around, and you don't know him.

Who told you these stories? Stone Shea?

He and Stone are like two cheeks of the same ass, Mitchell says.

It's not like I expected you to be happy for me. I sigh.

Our arguments often go on and on until we end up in bed and that is clearly not going to happen here. It is not going to happen anymore.

I go home to Nemo, to Jordan, where he doesn't ask me anything about the visit, just guides me through to the kitchen where he has prepared us a meal of lobster thermidor, which is another overrated thing.

We eat and we drink until we are full and we are drunk. And maybe it's the alcohol, or the nerve tablets I took before I went to the jail, or maybe it's having just seen Mitchell, and wanting him, or it's all down to Jordan's jealousy that I won't make an enemy of a man I once loved, but he finally acts loving towards me.

We make love for the first time. And the next morning, I attempt to do it again but he just can't. And I can't help but remember a couple of decades ago:

I had been looking out of the wood-framed windows at the canyon at one of his parties at his old house in Colonial Pine Hills, when a much younger Jordan Pinault came over, grabbed me and we started to make out. Then he asked if a friend could join in. When I saw it was Ricky Nwafo I nodded. I was pretty lashed on ecstasy.

Then they were both kissing on me, it was late and the party had mostly trickled out of the house.

Ricky led me to the bedroom where I let Jordan undress me, methodically and roughly. Ricky undressed, pausing to ask if he could fuck me and rolling on a rubber. His politeness was killer.

I remember saying he could, then Jordan was pushing him away, saying: Yo, man, you think I like to watch that shit, and I don't. Amber is mine. I had her first.

Helena, I corrected them – it was work to even talk – not Amber.

Helena, I apologize, said Ricky unleashing a wicked smile. He pulled me to him and we kissed.

Fine, said Jordan unbuttoning his flies – he never wore underwear and still does not – taking his erection in his hands. Ricky had me arranged on the bed with surprising tenderness when he asked who I wanted behind, and who in front.

You, you fuck me, I told him, while Jordan held his cock in front of my face and tried to put it in my mouth, but it softened. Every time I've remembered it, over the years, I've thought of him as the weak arm of our triangle.

Stop staring at me, he said to Ricky, and Ricky just laughed. I mean it, man, Jordan said. Stop.

Jordy, said Ricky. Just shut up, enjoy yourself.

I was their connective tissue, bracing myself on Jordan's thighs until the glad shudder of Ricky's body made Jordan give up trying. I pulled the bedsheets around me as they carried on the discussion.

When Jordan left the room, Ricky said: I feel like you want to kiss some more, Amber, but you'll understand why I can't.

I only remember saying, My name is not Amber.

*

I love this red stream of wine, the glass comfortable in my hand, sparkling, the fit of a ring on this finger again. My nails look great and I am grateful Natasha booked us both in for a manicure now that everyone at the party wants to see my hand, and have an opinion, or give a compliment, even a back-handed one, that such a big colorful rock suits me and would look awful on small hands.

I'll save any insecurities about my hand size for after the wine and pills have left my system.

Natasha has a glass of red too. For Ricky, just water. I wonder if he – like Jordan – really does not remember that we had that night together, that original, indelible sexual encounter. He is friendly, maybe suspicious. He puts his arm around me at one point and says he is glad to see Jordan happy again.

You look beautiful, he says.

And inside me, a lightning-bud. All the ingredients are present: a drink, a beautiful and sensitive man that I realistically cannot have.

The party room in Buffalo Plains Casino is quivering on its head, in my silvery-red heart of wine, but I don't feel very beautiful. I have taken to wearing my hair up to hide the empty patches. My head is trapped in meticulous detail of which strand goes where.

There is a mumble from the table where a raft of congressmen sits drinking beer, playing cards. The owner, a man from the Lakota Sioux, is watching them with obvious contempt.

What time of year will you marry? Natasha asks me.

Soon as we can, says Jordan, then goes to order drinks when he sees Bess arrive wearing a patchwork tunic and stylish white pants that I always think only postmenopausal women can wear with confidence. My ex-stepfather Alf is in tow. They are back together and soon to remarry.

Well isn't this kinda fun, Alf says, directed at me. Very interesting friends you have, Lennie.

I nod as Bess says: Yes, indeed. This might be the perfect time to ask them what they are gunna do for the Lakota people regarding their water.

I addressed this in my proposal, go read it, says Senator Clifford who has overheard what Bess has meant him to and has now joined my party within *our* party.

Senator Clifford is also exactly how he introduces himself alongside his bone-breaking handshake, which my mother hates, I can tell.

In return, he can call her Ms. Russo, she tells him. Times like these I sure miss Beverly Burgess, she adds for effect.

He was my old college professor, says Alf. Beverly was just out of college himself, a great guy by all accounts.

Indeed, says Leslie. Bev's missed on the campaign trail.

And the arts, asks my mother with her glass of chardonnay. What are your plans? Do you know how important they are here?

Everything you want, says Senator Clifford, let's have a meeting. We'll change it all around for you … since you are family now.

Leslie thinks it's a game but my mother doesn't play.

Isn't that beautiful, she says, that's all it takes, for you to fall in love with someone you wouldn't have imagined yourself with, that's all it takes to change your view on the world and who you want to help.

Ain't that the truth? says Clifford.

Probably not, my mother says, but don't you think that lies are much more beautiful to the ear, that's why we all like 'em so much.

Clifford's wife, Jami, with her pink face and purple western boots, comes and stands by his side. Jami looks interested, she smiles and watches between her other half and Bess.

You're Helena's father? Clifford detracts, speaking across her, and me, speaking to Alf.

Helena's father is having a nice long rest, my mother explains in her dry, mordant humor. Has been her entire life.

Right. Sorry to hear that.

He died in a grain bin accident.

Right. Sorry to hear that.

That monumental upset of hers has long become something Bess tries to belittle and in turn widen, like an accordion, when she feels the need.

Maybe farm safety is something we should talk about, too, she says piling it thick.

My mother is poking fun now but he eats it up.

We have tried, Mrs. Russo, we have tried, he says.

Ms., she corrects him.

Some politicians have unsuccessfully tried to legislate farm safety on a state level, explains Leslie, like a proposed bill in Washington this year that would have strengthened safety training for farmworkers. That bounced between the House and Senate, you know, the bill has yet to make it to a final vote, Mrs. Russo.

Ms.

Leslie Clifford looks frustrated. Well, are you or aren't you married? he asks.

What difference does it make, Leslie? says Bess. It feels like a distraction. And of course, I know about everything you've already said. All I care about is that children of farmers stop being orphaned. And, you can call me Bess.

Farmers do not like mandates on their livelihood, agrees Alf – who is a nice honest man but will never be honest enough for Bess, too afraid of causing offense to people who are not afraid of doing that at all.

Leslie Clifford says: Mrs. … Bess … If nobody is insisting on it, we let the sleeping dogs lie.

My mother says: Boy, do I know that.

It would seem many legislators recognize the difficulties in requiring farmers to adopt new behaviors, says Leslie. Now, what else have you got for me?

And I hear the man in Trump Towers is gunna announce that he's running for the main job, says Alf.

Is that some kind of a sick joke? Bess says.

Are you excited to soon be related to such a star? Jami asks her, nodding at Jordan.

I wouldn't say I'm a football fan, Bess says, doesn't matter what a person's passion is as long as they have one. I suppose I do love that. And Helena says she loves him, so I'm sure I will grow to.

I think why Jordan and Leslie get on so well is the football thing, to be totally honest with you, says Jami. Leslie majored in Business Administration but he played college football. That was until he got an injury.

And what about you, Jami? says Bess.

What about me?

What did you major in?

Jami nods. I like your mother, she tells me. And I love your tunic, she tells Bess directly.

I know, I say. Ma just has flair.

But it's hard to say, my anxiety tablets have way kicked in and by now I'm feeling satisfactorily woozy.

I'll get you the name of the fabric artist if you tell me where you found those purple boots, my mother is saying when out of nowhere Leslie Clifford begins to tell everyone the Super Bowl story about Jordan, I'm fuzzy on how he starts, but the gist is this:

Pinault blew through the competition all game, he says, then he drove the team 90some yards downfield, and threw to Eric Nwafo, Nwafo scored the touchdown, and naturally the game-winning touchdown, in that final minute, Leslie says, but Pinault was instrumental. Instrumental, Leslie says coming to the end – I hope it's the end – It's all down to the law of possession – maybe it's not the end just yet – and boy did he possess that ball. Pinault burned himself alive, and you can't do that forever. That's why he is walking like an old man these days. But you'll keep him young, Helena.

I glaze over till he gets to my name, so does Jami, Alf too. My mother lights up.

While you were sitting in the lights on Friday nights, freezing yourselves, she says. I was at the Dahl, hosting our emerging artists' evenings. No blow by blow accounts of that, I'm afraid.

Senator Pinault is the most gifted artist you'll have ever seen, just look at YouTube, says Leslie.

Leslie, my mother says, there are a lot of old male poets who like to write about old male sports stars and remind us all that they are ordinary, in the end. Particularly in the last line: they set out to choke you good and they usually do. But I don't think that any one of us is exempt.

I suppose at least Jordan *had* the glory, says Alf. Once.

The correct answer, says Leslie.

But don't you really think that's harder? says Jami. No one can prepare you for coming back down off the mountain.

Yes, I say. Plus, I heard climbing down mountains is bad for the hips.

My mother and I exchange a little smile. And I think of Mitchell, and I wonder what he is doing right this minute. I wonder, does he know this is happening, that I'm going to marry another man? I wonder, has he stopped taking drugs, and is he better for it? I wonder, for all his faults, why was life so much better with him?

The Cute Response

1995

That night the three of them sat around the table. Mary Jane had her dog, Lucille, on her lap and was feeding her tidbits of chicken alfredo.

Please don't let the dog do that, MJ. You're making a rod for your own back, her mother said.

Mary Jane smiled and carried on. Her husband poured wine for them both, bypassing Marjorie, who was on the wagon.

Did you hear from the promoter? Mary Jane asked John.

We'll talk about it later, he said.

But did you? What did he say?

They aren't gunna go with you, I'm afraid.

John wished she would not talk about work in front of her mother.

It's okay, I'm good, said Mary Jane.

Maybe she was – they had a chunk of money, ate out and vacationed well, had a nice home and nice cars.

But John so hated to see a talented person seem settled before she was twenty-five. He wanted more for Mary Jane than stasis. John had used his hospitality contacts to book gigs for his wife in the first instance. Now he had located a promoter he hoped would take her on tour. The promoter said she was good but not original, that she sang too many covers, and John didn't see the need to tell her this. Mary Jane worked every Tuesday night as a Stevie Nicks tribute act swapping her short plaid skirt, Army Surplus boots and furry crop top sweater for flowy ethereal layers, bracelets and scarves.

When she first learned the lyrics for *Landslide*, she said: Nicks was a whole year older than me when she wrote this. There's time, there is.

But Mary Jane's time was now, he just knew it.

Maybe her set wasn't wholly original but she certainly had a range better than Nicks, and around the house when she sang Karen Carpenter's *We've Only Just Begun* he was blown away.

What's this now? asked Marjorie, studying her daughter.

Oh, just singing stuff. Mary Jane looked at John and smiled. On a good note, she said eagerly, John is bidding on a new restaurant. He's found a business partner, haven't you, sweetie?

C'mon, let's not talk shop at the dinner table, he replied.

Oh honey, I want my mom to see how well you are doing. I'm proud.

He squeezed his wife's hand and smiled.

85

What restaurant is it? Marjorie asked before she stuffed some lettuce leaves into her mouth.

John cleared his throat.

Will we tell her? Mary Jane asked him.

Not yet. Sorry, pardon me, John said as he left the table. He went outside to his car and searched for the bag he'd had in the back seat for the last couple of days, forgetting to bring it indoors until now. Inside was a bracelet he had bought for his wife, and now seemed as good a time as any to produce it. From the kitchen, he could hear the women talking as he rummaged about to find a pen to write on the gift tag.

When he wants me to tell you, I will, I promise, he heard Mary Jane say.

I don't like how he talks to you, Boo.

He talks to me just fine.

Marry a man your father's age, said Marjorie, and he'll treat you as his child. He's already made you quit smoking.

John didn't make me do anything.

And still you don't smoke anymore.

Isn't that a good thing? What was the point, all it does is cost you. One day it might cost me my voice … my life even.

Jeez Louise, MJ!

John came back into the room with a pre-emptive cough. I forgot I had this for you, he said and handed the gift bag to Mary Jane.

What in the world is this for? she asked.

Reason: immaterial. He kissed her forehead and sat down, he could feel Marjorie's eyes on him.

Mary Jane opened the bag then opened the box and looked at the bracelet.

See, it's pearl, said John, your birthstone. I had it made especially.

She asked him to clasp it on which he did and then she leaned in and hugged him before getting up and planting a kiss on his mouth. John rubbed her sides and told her she was welcome. He felt self-conscious.

Maybe he could pretend that Marjorie wasn't there, twiddling the turquoise stone on her junk jewelry necklace. No, impossible.

He smiled at Mary Jane, tried to relax as he said: Let's book a vacation, honey.

But we have so much work to do, shouldn't we wait?

I don't see any reason to. Just one week away.

Where to, do you think? Her face shone. Marjorie knocked back her water and poured herself some wine. Mary Jane interrupted her excitement for a moment to look at her mother with disappointment.

How about Turks and Caicos?

Mary Jane looked back at John. Sure, let's do it.

Marjorie got up. Excuse me, she said and went to scrape her plate into the bin. John remained behind as Mary Jane followed after her mother. He had not seen Marjorie since April, when she last had a drink. Well, he assumed she'd been drunk then, but who knew, she could be a liability sober too, phoning him, and telling him what she was wearing.

If he were to keep track – which he was – the tradition was seeded back in '90, the day before the wedding, which also doubled as the day before Mary Jane's twentieth birthday. That day her mother came to the house on West Boulevard knowing he was alone.

What she did not know was that John was to fly out to Phoenix that day to meet Mary Jane, who was actually having a bachelorette with Celena and Grace. Nor did Marjorie know that the Garbers were already there.

As was Jack, a brother of John's whom he had not seen in twenty years but had surprised John with his willingness to cross two states to attend the wedding.

When Marjorie came through the door that day, at first John thought she had found out and come around to make amends, to beg him to bring her to Arizona.

She was not invited since she had caused a scene at John and Mary Jane's engagement party, getting drunk and calling him a pedophile, which broke Mary Jane's heart and made her decide to not have her mother at the wedding, *and* to skip town to avoid her finding out.

But Mary Jane did want a shindig. She wanted to pretend to her mother after that they had simply called into the old brick courthouse and got it done, let her mother huff it out. Which five years on still hurt Marjorie despite believing the weaker *courthouse* version, so maybe Mary Jane had been right to leave Phoenix out of the picture.

That day, John decided he could spare Marjorie a little time and kindness, he wondered how he would break it to her. He had visions of the three of them patching up things up at the wedding. Surprising Mary Jane with this new, accepting interpretation of her mother. But she did not want to go. She had not found out.

Is this really what you want? Marjorie said. This is a child.

Her words reminded him of the engagement, just not quite as harsh.

More than anything this is what I want, I love your daughter very much, John said.

He was still surprised because before he asked for Mary Jane's hand in marriage, her mother had seemed to like their relationship. Marjorie was amused by it at least.

He had no tendency to trust the woman, knowing how she had used Mary Jane like boy-bait since she was a child. As personable as she could be he often remembered it. And he remembered it the day before the wedding, the day she called her daughter a child. Marjorie tilted her head at him.

What does that look mean, Johnnie? she asked.

What look? he replied.

You are looking at me like you have something you want to say, so what is it you want to say?

You are the one looking at me strangely, he said.

Oh, Johnnie, you are a funny man.

Thanks, I think.

I don't know, I just think about you and her, said Marjorie.

Is that a good thing?

No, not really.

I know there is an obvious age gap. And that ...

Johnnie, hear me out, she interrupted, I know you top to bottom, and I often think that many May-December relationships are cute, I do.

And this one?

Honestly, not so much.

Not much we can do to fix that, said John, Mary Jane's young and I'm not aging backward.

No, you aren't, more's the pity.

Mary Jane is very happy, he said, hopefully you can see that. Her father gave me his blessing.

Oh please! cried Marjorie. You make Art Garber look like a kid. Her *father* hit a home run that's all. Please don't confuse his orgasm with parenthood.

Marjorie, I want your approval, too. I do. I know it's important to Mary Jane.

Mary Jane, funny how you call her that.

It's her name, isn't it?

Yep and I should know, I gave it to her. Almost twenty years ago to the day.

Then he thought about Mary Jane's birthday coming the next day, which could also have been the reason for the visit but he realized that it was him Marjorie wanted to see. C'mon, you're a man of the world, Johnnie Kloster, she said.

Thank you, I think … he uttered.

So how come you never married before?

Never met the right person.

That sounds funny to me.

Did you ever marry?

No, but I had options. And I don't like MJ taking the first option, do you know what I mean?

Sure, I get that.

So, we're on the same page?

Which page is that?

That you should just cool it a while. Let her live a little.

And then a pang of guilt hit John that they were to wed without her mother's knowledge. She'll live plenty, he promised. I'll help her … anything she wants to do. You say you know me and you should know that about me.

Do not get her pregnant, said Marjorie shakily.

That's not really up to …

I mean it. Her eyes pooled.

Marjorie! Come on. What's making you upset?

You are.

Why?

Can't you see it?

What?

I'm effing … in love with you.

John laughed. Now, Marjorie, that's not a bit funny. You shouldn't be saying things like that.

—

90

Saying things like that is exactly what I should be doing, no one else is gunna say them. Everyone else hides under these things, can't tell someone the truth because it will upset someone else.

Mary Jane would be upset, very upset, to hear this.

And you're not gunna tell her, Marjorie said, her voice offering roses.

How do you know?

I know men like you, John, you are a secret-keeper.

Why do you say that?

You have led this spick life and no one has any dirt on ya.

Gone looking for some, have you? John lightly laughed.

You're not right, you're not right for my baby.

I know there is an age gap. I know we are from different backgrounds, that we shouldn't work, but we do … and I'll look after her better than anyone can. I know that. So please don't worry, Marjorie.

You are making a mistake. But don't make a mistake, I'm begging you.

You shouldn't be saying all this, not now, said John.

Then when? When she has your kid and you've deserted her, is that when? When she's back with me and I have to look after them both.

I can't decide if you hate me or if you … you said something you can't take back.

I don't want to take it back, Johnnie, I won't take it back.

When have I ever given you the feeling that I like you, like that … in return?

Oh, Johnnie, shut up! It's there, it's undeniable.

You're wrong, I don't have feelings for anyone but Mary Jane.

I have enough for both of us. I would make you so happy.

What are you proposing?

I'm a woman, still young compared to you.

And you would do that to your own daughter?

It's for her own good too. She'd get over it, go have a career, meet someone down the line who is better suited to her.

And you'll try this again, any man she meets, you'll do this.

Johnnie, you aren't listening when I say that I am in love with you and that if you marry my daughter I'll be destroyed.

I think we need to calm down. Take some time out.

It's the truth.

You'll get over it, Marjorie, meet someone down the line …

You're what I should have been looking for, all this time. Boy, we could have it good. She grabbed his hand and put it on her face, she put her head in his neck and kissed him, he held her back by the shoulders. Allow yourself this, Johnnie, she said.

It's not what I'm interested in at all. He walked to the other side of the room. I think you should go, Mary Jane will be back soon, he lied.

He would have to leave to catch his flight. His bag was already in the car, his wedding suit too.

We've nothing to hide, we're consenting adults.

You're on your own with that.

Fine. She walked towards the door. You've had your chance.

A day later and he could still feel her body against his. If he could have just focused on Mary Jane and not that, and not how much his brother Jack looked and spoke like a stranger, he would have been fine.

After the ceremony, they ate with the paternal side of Mary Jane's family, yet more strangers, and John thought again about Marjorie's proposition.

He looked at Art and his young wife Forde, his third wife, who looked like Grace, who looked like Mary Jane, who did not look completely unlike her half-brother's wife Anne.

John blushed at the thought that he had joined some puerile rich man's club where people married their own daughters, or at least the feminine part of themselves at a younger age. And Celena looked like nobody but like a place – their place – and a past, his young bride's past. Celena, who slept through the wedding meal.

She's fine, Mary Jane said. She just gets a little tired.

Forde, who was a student nurse, declared that this was not normal behavior, and drummed up a conversation that was much too medical for a wedding party.

And instead of carrying his wife over the threshold that night, it was Celena John carried to a bedroom in a hotel in Phoenix, Arizona. It was then he realized that you do not marry just one person but all of their people.

And again, he thought about Marjorie, and again he tried not to.

It was important that Celena liked him now, he thought, since Mary Jane's mother did not. Or, as it turned out, she did, she liked him too much. But Celena scared him.

John knew as little about the drugs revolution as he knew about the sexual one, and he did not want Celena to think he was a square. And in another life and time … yes, he could have been more laid back, and been more laid back about love, too.

He even supposed that in that life Mary Jane's mother – because from that day forward Marjorie would only be his wife's mother (his mother-in-law) and he would no longer be her *Johnnie* – might have seemed like a good option, if he'd met her before he'd met her daughter.

Marjorie was fun – she could be – and a good-looking woman, but it was not about looks for him, thought the man who had gone on to marry the most beautiful woman he had ever seen.

Mary Jane's mother, unlike her daughter, did not have a beautiful soul, and that's what counted. She was living back where she'd started out, in an apartment in downtown Rapid City. She'd been done with the farm, unable to find a buyer during the crisis, she gave it back to the bank. Marjorie had wanted John to buy it and keep her there. What good was a rich potential son-in-law who would not become her surrogate husband too? He thought this now, and he thought about how she had admitted to going looking for dirt on him, and the reason she could find none was because there was no dirt to be found.

John's life was no whirlwind of passion, nor had he ever followed the bad religion of unrequited love. He had learned his lesson at the full height of the 60s, after working his twenties and most of his thirties away, he decided to complete the set and make himself part of a two.

He was running his first hotel when John had met her. Susan managed a hotel too. Despite working unsociable hours, they would meet up once a week to dine out or cook for one another, to make love habitually and conventionally until it turned out that Susie was *dating other people*, as she put it.

———
94

And having made the rookie mistake to believe they were exclusive, John felt his first, albeit delayed, episode of heart-hurting that he was not keen to repeat.

That had been square of him, to expect a wonderful independent woman like Susan to be backward-thinking during a revolution.

He tried to be fine with her seeing other men until he could no longer be. Which was fine too, Susan understood.

Everything was uncontaminated, courteous and pleasant until Susan got lonely, then she would call John at night to see if he was home.

And he, hating to be thought of as an ill-disposed guy, would let her stay over. Maybe something in him wanted to feel wantable, to be comfortable with a lovely woman like Susan again.

So, they continued like that for a few months, John telling himself that this was what other men his age were doing, but it never felt good to be left in the morning, nor did making love to a woman he did not have this urge to look after and make the world better for. Without love, he wasn't sure what he was making, except for making himself miserable.

In his forties and fifties, John Kloster dated here and there, so preoccupied with work and making a little empire. His drive to climb the ranks through the hospitality business was his main priority, and first he'd acquired a restaurant, then a motel, then a hotel. He didn't even notice he was missing something in his life until Mary Jane appeared at the motel with her big eyes and expressive mouth, one tatty suitcase by her heels and a headscarf around her confusion of white-blonde hair.

When Mary Jane asked if he needed a worker, she had worry written all over her.

John could not turn her away, so he told her to come in, gave her a room to stay in, telling a customer that the receptionist had made the mistake of double-booking the room, all because he could not let Mary Jane walk out of his life. He had worked in the service industry long enough to know a good apple from a bad, and Mary Jane — when she set her suitcase on the bed with a welcome look in her eyes — was as beautiful inside as she was on the out.

Over time, they clicked like nothing had ever before. His time with Susan seems like a flat facsimile now that living with Mary Jane was like living in color. Every color. She was quiet when she was sad, and chatty when she was excited, chattier when she was nervous.

She had no gameplay. You asked her a question and Mary Jane told you the answer straight. John supposed, in that way, she was like her mother, but only in that way.

*

Something changed after Turks and Caicos. Her life got a little bigger, inflated. He heard from the promoter whose idea it was to inflate her circle. No harm intended, John, he said, but MJ's not gunna meet anyone influential under your wing, in your hotel bar!

It began with a party and the elite of Rapid City. Musicians and sports stars overlapped and the brightest and best in South Dakota hung out at these parties.

One night John drove her to a mansion, which was the home of Jordan Pinault, who was an NFL player whose nice chunk of money made John's nice chunk of money seem paltry. A younger, poorer man might have been intimidated. Or unreasonably jealous. Not John.

John whistled with admiration as he pulled up outside, went to the door and shook Pinault's hand just to have met him. They had a little small-talk on the stoop, then John drove away feeling like a father must feel when he brings his daughter to her first party. Then he went to the hotel to oversee the renovation work, had a burger before collecting Mary Jane at the end of the night, who came out buzzing.

She had been talking to a producer in the business of hunting for truffles and he was going to give her a call and maybe have her come by his studio. She said she sang at the end of the night, and some people at the party had verified that Mary Jane really could sing.

That's excellent, baby, John told her as they went out for a celebratory drink.

At the bar, he looked at her face over the table and they held hands, she lit up from the inside.

You think this is gunna work out for me? she asked.

Oh yes, absolutely. This is your time, he said asking if she wanted him to drive her to the producer's home, which was where his studio also was. John wanted to be protective of her, music producers were notorious for taking your money and selling your dreams up the river. He had already paid someone a thousand dollars to make a modeling portfolio for Mary Jane and then never saw the photographs. That day, the photographer kept turning around and looking at John and saying: You really got to be here?

But John was only there because the photographer could have been a charlatan, and was. He was not planning to leave his wife with someone like that again, but she insisted she wanted to go to the producer's house by herself and she didn't need any money. She had been invited there, after all.

Suddenly she had a life outside of their marriage that John had pushed her to have but now he worried about her terribly. Though he needn't have to begin with, Mary Jane was extra happy when she came home from the producer's. After a few days, the producer called her back to listen to the tracks and extended the invitation to her man. John and Mary Jane sat in the studio listening to a new track she had put her vocals to, and the three of them grinned like cats.

Isn't she so good? the producer said.

The best, said John, lifting Mary Jane's hand and kissing the back of it.

She wrapped her arms around his neck and carried on listening to it. They left that day with the song on a little compact disc and had to go buy a machine to play it on.

*

By July, Mary Jane was touring in Houston, having been asked to open before an up-and-coming band. When she returned she was different, easy to tear up, upset. She was crying in bed one night when John asked her what was wrong, it was then Mary Jane said what her mother had told her, that John had made a play for her.

You can't honestly believe that, said John.

It's not that I want to, she said.

He tried to submerge it but the longer it went on, weeks of her being upset and barely looking at him, John stressing, thinking they were done. Eventually, he sat her down in the living room. Please listen to me good, Mary Jane, he said. Before we got married your mother made a move on me. The day before we married.

She wouldn't, Mary Jane said.

How can you say that when look at everything else she's done?

But she's my mother, John.

Mothers are just women who have had children, they get it wrong like anyone else.

I'm gunna get her to call over here and we are gunna go through this, together.

Mary Jane, don't, he said. Forget it. Your career is taking off, forget this.

Do you want me out of the way so you can be with her?

Not a chance!

She said you look at me like a child.

I love you because we're family, he said, like she should love you.

Are you saying my mother doesn't love me?

Some people find it hard to show.

Like you? asked Mary Jane.

Don't I show you love?

You do, but ... you don't want me the way a man should.

Not everything starts in the loins.

Oh, John. I'm so confused. Her eyes glittered with tears.

You never need to confuse my feelings for you, he said. I never wanted you to feel hurt, so I never opened up to you.

The next day she phoned her mother to relay what John had explained, and when he arrived home from work she told him what her mother had told her, that they had phone conversations often, and often when Mary Jane was at work.

Mom got the bills and showed them to me, said Mary Jane, looks like you spoke from here.

I'm not hiding the fact.

I went to look at them with my own eyes. Long conversations, John.

I know, and I ask her not to speak to me like that.

So why don't you hang up?

Did you ask her that?

I did.

What did Marjorie tell you?

She pleaded with me to leave you be. She says you say revolting things to her, and she pleads with you to let me have my life to myself.

She does plead with me to leave you, but only so I'll be with her.

You always say this and I don't understand. Mom says you're using me for everything and I said: But I have nothing to give him. See, he has you devaluing yourself, Mom said. Youth and beauty, MJ, are everything worth having in this world.

They are wonderful things, said John, but what about love, about trust?

That's what I said.

And what did Marjorie say to that?

She said: If you find that, you'll be the only person I know who has.

*

John tried to repair the telephone conversations with another new puppy. He called it Mary Jane II, like Audrey II in *Little Shop of Horrors*. Mary Jane loved that musical, she could sing like Audrey, and Marilyn Monroe, and anyone else, if she put her mind to it.

If you were born in the twenties you'd be a movie star, John told her.

Why the twenties? she asked.

He tried to explain that she was an old-fashioned beauty, that they didn't make girls like her anymore. He would think this when they watched a movie and he would glance sideways at her face and think, God, she really could be something wonderful, wondering if he was holding her back like Marjorie had always claimed.

He knew Mary Jane could not hide things and therefore could not hide that she was seeing someone else, someone from the NFL parties. He didn't care who. These guys had wealth on another scale. Maybe John Kloster was the starter husband like Monroe had had, then Mary Jane would move on to the heartthrob, the intellectual, the sportsman. But he knew two things for sure:

someone in Pinault's mansion was pulling her away from him;

and secondly, that Mary Jane II would be their Band-Aid or remind her of their love.

She kissed the little dog all over its head and it healed her heart and strengthened their family – Mary Jane, John, Lucille, and this new dog – but it was a passing phase. It passed.

*

One night before she was about to release her first record, she was gazing into space.

Mary Jane, he said, what's wrong? You should be doing cartwheels right now.

Why couldn't you just hang up on my mom? she said. I can't trust anyone.

You can trust me, I guarantee you can.

I don't even know if that's real.

I only kept things from you to protect you, said John.

Because you do see me as a child.

No, Mary Jane, I don't, and I trust you, with my life.

She cried. You shouldn't, she said, because I fooled around with someone at the party. I didn't sleep with him, but I've been contemplating it, I have. We talk, we talk together in a way that feels like cheating and that's bad enough. I feel just disgusting about it, John.

He looked at her sympathetically. Mary Jane, that's fine.

Really? Then you couldn't love me.

I love you enough to forgive you, that's what it is.

So that I'll forgive you in return?

I haven't done anything to need forgiveness. Listen, I'm speaking to you like an adult now. If you want to end it, do it now, Mary Jane. Do it now and everything will be fine, in time.

You want out of this marriage?

No, I don't. But I want you to be happy.

She hugged him. I'm so sorry, John. I know you wouldn't hurt me, I just can't stop trusting my mom. She's my mother.

I understand, he said.

Then you're too good for me.

No, you are too good for me, he said and they rubbed noses.

*

A week later, having come home early to surprise her, John found a notepad lying on the bed and the bathroom door closed. Before he could read what was written, Mary Jane came quickly out of the bathroom and straight to the bed.

She pulled the top page from the pad and creased it before stuffing it into her purse. He looked at her and saw that her eyes were red-rimmed, and she asked John if he could really forgive her, and John said he already had.

She tried to talk about the fling but John did not want to hear the details. Mary Jane tried to insist that she tell him, but he had put a line under it all and told her he would rather not know.

But what if people are laughing at you and me? she asked him.

Let them, he said.

Then he never gave the note in her bag another thought. Not ever.

Not two weeks later, while crying on to her cremation urn. Not twenty years later, when John Kloster still wondered how he never saw the signs. The note was *that* inconsequential.

*

By the start of August, her song was released and made the top twenty. It had taken years and suddenly she was an overnight success. They had a party at Jordan Pinault's house in her honor. She went alone, John feeling too embarrassed to stick around. Jordan asked him to come in but John wanted to get out of there. There were local congressmen there, Celena Ghost Bear, Ricky Nwafo, and a bunch of girls, and the music producer. She was not alone. These were her people now.

The thought of being in the company of some man who had touched his wife was too much. John buried that thought as he shook Jordan's hand.

Yeah, I'm real proud, he told him. Then John drove around Rapid that night before finally going home to wait for her call.

It was Officer Heath Noteboom, a thirty-year-old policeman, who came to the door and asked to come inside.

John, he said. I'm sorry to bother you, sorry to bother both of us.

It's Mary Jane, isn't it? John went to grab his car keys.

No. Noteboom put a hand out. Stop there. Don't move.

Am I in trouble, Heath?

Take a pew if you would. It is Mary Jane. She is … for want of a better word, she is dead, and for want of a better word, she has done herself away.

John's knees almost gave way. No, this can't be.

She's dead.

How?

She … Officer Noteboom looked at his notepad but John could see that there was nothing written on it. She shot herself.

Mary Jane doesn't have a gun. We don't keep guns in this house.

No, but she found one. You can always put your hands on a gun easy enough.

I'll have to call her mother.

Her mother knows. I swung by there first.

Is she okay?

Officer Noteboom looked puzzled.

Marjorie? John clarified.

Well no, sir. What do you expect?

I need to talk to her.

Mary Jane's mother burst through the door.

My baby, she said throwing herself at John, so he had no choice but to catch her. He held her quietly.

Why did she do it, John? Marjorie asked.

Seems there was a lot going on over there in Jordan Pinault's abode, said Officer Noteboom.

What like?

· Seems she was having an affair with him. Hate to say that to you, John, you being her husband and all.

Jordan Pinault? asked Marjorie. Did you know she was sleeping with Jordan Pinault, Johnnie?

She never slept with anyone, said John.

Maybe he imagined the glimmer of superiority, or was it jealousy, in Mary Jane's mother's eyes.

Not like she'd tell you if she did, Marjorie said.

I don't understand, what happened? John shook his hands and ran them through his hair.

It seems that there was an altercation, said Officer Noteboom. Firstly, there was a party, then it was only MJ and Mr. Pinault.

A party? Marjorie asked.

For her recording contract, John said roundly.

So why weren't you or I there?

She needed space.

Well, she had it with Mr. Pinault, said Noteboom.

So, it was Jordan, muttered John.

What was? asked Marjorie.

She had a small … friendship with someone, said John.

You knew? Marjorie looked aghast.

It wasn't full-blown. That's not the point now, Marjorie! Excuse me.

Marjorie shook her head. You see, Johnnie, I knew this would happen. You couldn't just let her be.

It didn't go far. I'm not explaining this to you, this is not important now.

Oh really? Seems very important.

They had an argument, said Noteboom, a tiff between … you know … and it seems that everyone left. Then Mr. Pinault took a bath, thinking he was alone, at home alone, and Mary Jane walked back in with the deep fat fryer. They'd been having a cook-out.

Can we get to the point? said John.

She threw the oil over Mr. Pinault, who is currently in the hospital. He beefed it outta the bathroom pretty quick and went into his bedroom – tryin' to stop her doing something silly – but, too late, she'd located Mr. Pinault's gun, put it to her head and shot herself, dead: Mary Jane.

Good grief. Marjorie cried hysterically. Booboo!

No, that's not right, said John. Not right at all.

Is Jordan Pinault alright? asked Marjorie.

In the hospital right now, might need skin grafts.

Have you spoken to Jordan, Officer? asked John.

Certainly have, briefly before he went into the ambulance.

What did he say?

That Mary Jane was a real nice kid and he was sorry for things turning out the way they did.

What? asked John. I need to speak with him.

Won't bring her back, John, said Officer Noteboom.

I want to hear with my own ears why she attacked him, why she killed herself.

Oh, I can tell you that, John. Mr. Pinault says she was shouting, she was a very angry woman, MJ. Quite nasty. At her wit's end, really, because he wouldn't marry her.

No, Heath, said John.

Officer Noteboom, sir. I'd appreciate you calling me that.

Mary Jane is married, Heath, said John. She is married to me. Why would she be angry with someone else for not wanting to marry her?

Mr. Kloster, I know it's difficult to accept, but she had written a suicide note saying she was gunna do this, and it was found at the scene.

Who found it?

I did, in her purse.

When would she have time?

It's open and shut, Johnnie, said Marjorie, who made her way to the drinks cabinet.

Yep, said Officer Noteboom. Sadly yes. Shut.

Crying for a Dream

2015

With a red thread, Nova ties dried sage to a clump of prairie grass then fastens it to the rearview mirror before she and her brother take their aunt to a doctor. Not a Shaman, like their uncle, but an American doctor this time.

When they reach his office Nova helps Wanda out of the car and closes the car door behind her knowing that when they return to the automobile and open the door again the world will come spilling out.

And so it does.

Wanda slumps down in her seat, she asks: What is o-var-ion? The word *cancer* she knows.

Nova is here to be strong for her and now she is crying, she cannot stop herself, she pats the tears and looks at Aunt Wanda.

She is glad Akecheta asked all the questions: like, how come no signs? and how come all of a sudden? These gruff interruptions of his.

Ake shook the doctor's hand on their behalf, which was thick with psoriasis. Nova does not trust a doctor with such a condition himself.

Wanda looks already resigned. She will not have American medicine, she will have herbs only, herbs are all she needs. In Akecheta's car, Wanda says that even when her time comes – now she knows there is a silent killer inside her: the white man doctor's term – she will still be with her family in spirit.

Nova has rarely known a Lakota woman to live as long as her aunt, and never on the rez. At forty-five, Nova herself is an old woman on Pine Ridge.

Herbs will do, Wanda repeats and Akecheta stares directly ahead, angry.

Always so angry, even when he is happy and laughing like a turkey. That strange rare laugh of his that Nova loves to hear but rarely does. Like when he is serving dinner for the family in his home and is laughing at the funny things her daughters say. Even then, Nova catches glimpses of her brother's anger.

Their mother knew what she was doing, for once, when she chose that name for him: Akecheta means *fighter*.

On the car stereo Senator Pinault is talking. Who is he talking about? asks Nova.

Trump. He's on the Presidential campaign now. Akecheta turns the radio off again.

From the reality show we watch? asks Wanda.

Yes.

The rich can do what they like.

His hair looks like shit, says Nova.

And there's the fake tan, says Akecheta.

It's not fake, says Nova, it's from a bed, you can see the goggle marks around his piggy eyes.

Beverly Burgess, says Wanda, that poor man, now he was a good senator. A Democrat.

Akecheta sneers. He was not a good man, and just because he is ill now does not make it so.

Nova catches her breath. Those seconds of talking about something else have stolen the news that her aunt is ill, and now the fact falls back on her like a sledgehammer.

Burgess is like every other honky, Nova says. He is full of big words. Big promises. Even though he is a Democrat, I never liked him, this continues.

I always liked him, Wanda laments.

By the casino is Akecheta's home. Inside Nova's girls are sitting: Alexa, slipping tiny glass beads on to a thin needle, Candace wrapping herself up in blankets, doing nothing at all.

They have well-neigh moved in since Akecheta took Wanda in, and he says he doesn't mind, it is a big house for one man alone. Many times he has offered that they might all come and live here.

Alexa and Candace gather around.

You okay, Unci? Alexa asks.

Fine, fine, lil mama, Wanda says, shuffling across the room in her soft leather moccasins.

Nova takes Alexa home to the trailer but leaves Candace. Tonight she is working in the Buffalo Plains Casino and Hotel scrubbing dishes. At least there Akecheta can watch her.

Lately Candace has become a risk-taker, getting into trouble for doing silly things. Usually she is chained to Nova and is forbidden from posting anything else on social media.

But Nova has to let her go, knowing self-direction is important. She teaches that anyway, at the preschool where Nova works, where their motto is: receive the child in reverence, educate her in love, send her forth in freedom.

A motto that Nova tries to use for home but it's not easy. And besides, now there is her aunt to consider.

*

Every summer night on the rez, Old Park is open for sports. The girls are basketball crazy, they play with the other kids until curfew. But the place is emptying. This year so far, only halfway in, and they have lost twelve of their young people: some friends, some cousins that Americans might call *distant*, just kids though, ranging from twelve to fifteen years of age – one year younger than Alexa and one year older than Candace. Lost them all.

Tonight Nova wakes from her nap and walks to the park where she calls Alexa back to their single-wide trailer. Alexa is bugged that she has not got the same autonomy as some of her friends, whose parents are otherwise engaged in drinking and fighting and don't keep tabs on them.

Alexa pouts as she walks past her mother and ahead of her back to the trailer. She is inching taller since May, her neon-colored hoop earrings are swaying à la Miley Cyrus. She shouldn't really wear them when shooting hoops. Nova could turn it into a joke: No hoops for hoops, but it wouldn't be well-received and she picks her battles. Makes sure Alexa doesn't hate her.

*

I am dreaming, Nova tells herself, but she is also skiing. Something she has never actually done, but somehow she knows how it feels to glide across ice, how light the snow flutters around, knows how the cool sensation around her body feels. How it is to be bodiless. Nova sees MJ before her and realizes that maybe she is not the one skiing, but that MJ is the one.

MJ, with her hair white and frosty, and her smile, when she smiles, is also white and frosty.

MJ turns, skates off into the dazzling cleanness, and Nova can't stop her. Or won't. She makes the decision that next time she will. She will at least try to speak up.

When she wakes from this exhausted fainting vision, Nova writes it up in her sleep diary. No one has ever told her to do this, it's something she just likes to do, and in her diary she sees that she has dreamed about MJ every day this week, which is not surprising, considering the date.

Nova brings a plate of food and sits with her aunt as they watch TV on the flat screen.

Holy crap, I haven't slept so hard in forever. I guess I needed it.

I guess, says Wanda.

You sure you don't want to come and stay with me and the girls? It would be easier than this.

No, her aunt says, reaching forward and grimacing, lifting some buffalo, mushroom and wild rice on her spoon. Wanda has always said that a woman with many children has many homes, she has none, though she kept her sister's four with her when they were removed by the authorities. So Wanda counts the two that are left as her own, and right now she is at Akecheta's home, but he works a lot.

Ake leaves you here alone though, Nova says.

You and the girls have school starting soon and then I'll be alone anyway, says Wanda.

For me, it'll only be till twelve-thirty.

Uh-huh, Wanda says. You have children too. One day they look after you. For now, take care of yourself.

I do, Nova says. She has lived with narcolepsy since she was fifteen years old; lived with it for fifteen years before she knew what it was she was living with.

She'd had enough of people thinking she was a no-good bum like her middle brothers, since deceased. Wanda took to drinking heavily then but who could blame her? Another decade of this, Celena (her old name) thought on the eve of her thirtieth birthday, and a new millennium, downing a fistful of pills, a razor blade tucked into her purse always.

She had no true friends left since MJ died, there was a spate of suicides both in the reservation and out of it. And it was contagious.

Aunt Wanda found her. And her uncle, the shaman. He gave Celena herbs to try, but Celena could tell that he too thought she was on drugs, the same way everybody always did.

It had been Akecheta who took her aside and told Celena she needed to stop what she was doing, that it was going to kill Wanda, because their aunt relied on the two of them, lots of people did, and Celena realized she needed to seek help and went to an American doctor and was put on medication.

By thirty-one she met Jacoby, whose people were Poor Bears on his mother's side and Last Horses on his father's. She was thirty-two when they married. Another year and they had Candace, another year and Alexa was born, another year and Jacoby decided he was a roaming skin and was gone.

Celena stayed on the reservation, became Nova — meaning *new* — chose her own identity, got her degree and a teaching job in the preschool. True, once she had her daughters she could leave. Now it was important not to. Lakota was who she was, even though she'd been raised Catholic by her boarding school aunt.

Later Nova learned the Lakota language without the stigma that hung over it back when she was a girl.

Celena had not been raised to know it.

Nova was a half-blood who envied the old fork-tongued generation.

Now she wants to get them young and get them proud to be Oglala Lakota.

But despite the diagnosis of narcolepsy and the medication, the tiredness remains, and short working days suit her. Sometimes a colleague will ask if she needs a nap, but at least the little kids don't think any differently of her. And during the months of summer, she is lost with nothing to do but rest and recall.

Nova cuddles up beside Wanda on Akecheta's guest bed as the warm red flush prickles over her head down her face and asleep she falls.

MJ is back. Nova asks her where she has been, skating? This whole time?

MJ pulls her ski goggles up so Nova can see her eyes, but they are now not blue but iodine brown.

Just on vacation, MJ says. Can you guess where?

When Nova looks down, MJ is no longer standing on a white mash of snow but instead on sand, and she is dressed in a grass skirt, and she is wearing a lei around her neck.

The sun comes out in the dream. This brown-eyed MJ is smiling. Hawaii? asks Nova.

There are men in the distance, block figures against the sun. There is noise, splashing, a water spray. A dolphin in the ocean. It is blurred and pausing mid-jump, glitching like a frozen computerized image.

Now Nova looks at MJ closer, now her face is not hers at all, it cannot even be mistaken for it, or be thought to bear any resemblance. Because it's been so long, thinks Nova, I forget her face. *This* face is longer, the nose stronger, this face has the look of a lioness, and this face opens its mouth and says: You left me.

And now she looks familiar again.

Now she looks like a woman from the girls' high school basketball team. The coach.

And she is covering herself with a white robe. She is saying: Let's stay here and see this thing through, and Nova is saying: Brown-eyed MJ, I am not the one who left, why did you leave me? and she starts to cry.

Nova feels the sobs inside her chest, there may be tears but they do not wet her face, because she does not have a face in this dream. She never does.

There is arguing in the background, there is a man shouting, and Nova can hear the real MJ shouting too. This brown-eyed girl in front of her is staring at Nova with a look of defiance.

Nova says: How do you know about Hawaii when you've never been?

I've been before, the girl says.

With John? she asks.

With him. The girl nods sideways.

Nova opens her eyes and sees her aunt asleep and she lies there, holding her. Nova has to remember to write this into her dream diary, she cannot bear to let this one slip, it is the fullest yet. But she does not want to move. These times with Wanda lying beside her won't last, she thinks.

Nova recalls when Akecheta first built this house, she and her aunt lay on this same king-sized guest bed, Nova was pregnant with Alexa then. Wanda had rubbed her belly and sang, beer lightly lacing her breath.

Now Nova lies still and has a very real and lucid sense of the life MJ could have had. Seeing it, or rather thinking it, because she has lost John Kloster's face somewhere behind her eyes too. Nova knows their marriage would have ended, the tear was already visible.

She once imagined she and MJ would get that flat together they'd always said they wanted until John came along. Nova would have lived a life outside of the rez. A white blonded American life.

A deafblind life, like Akecheta would say. She'd have become a city Indian for the love of her best friend: the first white girl to look at Nova (Celena, back then) without a racist remark, and no one was racist to her with MJ around.

*

It is a hot shiny August night when Akecheta drives Nova to Rapid, convinced that she is trying to distract herself from Wanda's illness, saying that there are Lakota women and children who are missing and murdered, and that going to a vigil for MJ McCord is a waste of time. Nova doesn't care what he thinks. She'll pretend to listen as long as he drives, and sure she worries for Wanda, and the missing and the murdered, more than any man could ever know, but there are so many people's burdens to carry, and right now her spirit has been called to act.

MJ was her first intense relationship, like teenagers have. Preparation for lifelong partnerships, and much more special than what Nova had with her ex-husband.

Celena Ghost Bear loved Mary Jane McCord more than Nova Last Horse ever loved Jacoby Last Horse.

In Main Street Square an ancient John Kloster hugs people as they arrive. Everyone who wants one is given a candle, burning. MJ's song is playing on the loudspeakers, but there is no one else from back then, except for Eric, the Pastor, who shakes John's hand.

Nova stands beside a woman who seems familiar but Nova is not sure. She has patchy hair, and Nova would like to ask if she has cancer like her aunt does but she has learned the hard way that it is too personal a thing to say outright. They talk about the weather and about the news, but they barely mention MJ.

Nova begins talking about herself, though she hates how she talks, so glacially slow with strangers, afraid of sounding uneducated. The woman with the patchy hair is pleasant, she says she lived here in Rapid, on a farm near MJ's at the time and then moved away to study, and now she lives in Nemo. Nova fights the fatigue.

She watches out for Marjorie, but she does not show up. Nova has not seen her since the funeral service twenty years before. Marjorie had been too drunk to stand. She had been wrapped around John like a wet black shawl.

Now the music melts and it is a quiet remembrance, no speeches. Eric says a quick prayer. They say the lord's prayer and then, emotionally, he sings *The Lord is my Shepherd*, as MJ's bright white grin smiles down from a signpost, like she has this last month, advertising tonight like it is the concert she never got to give.

I miss you, my girl, Nova says to that poster.

Pastor, Nova says afterward. I'm so glad you could be here, for MJ. She was my best friend. Remember?

Vaguely, he says.

I feel I should explain, says Nova, that I have narcolepsy. I was only diagnosed at the age of thirty. I'm nearly sure people thought I was always drunk, or drugged. Who knows, who knows what is going on with people?

Ricky nods, totally disinterested, but she would rather be honest than impressive.

He says to the woman beside Nova, the woman with the plain sympathetic face and patchy hair: Tell Jordy I got his call and I've been real busy. I'll reply though.

Then Akecheta brings Nova back to Pine Ridge through the copper earth of the Badlands, past pinnacle and buttes, and graveyards for automobiles, and slow-moving ravines.

Nova thinks about the woman, and Pastor Nwafo and Senator Pinault. She thinks she has a memory, but Nova never can tell.

Sometimes she fought Wanda's clutches and managed three hours or four with MJ. It started as a singing, networking project for MJ; they hung out like groupies of these ex-NFL stars. As Celena, Nova would not have been accepted outside of her friend's shadow. And she hated Rapid City usually, the white people always had something ignorant to say to her. Despite that, she had what she liked to consider was a flirtation with Eric.

He used to kid her: Hey, what are you on? Most certainly does the job, can you score me some?

She never saw him take drugs, which is not to say that he did not take them, just that she never saw him.

There were wood panel ceilings in every room, Persian carpets, custom fireplaces – six of them – and a little coffee machine in Pinault's kitchen that Nova called R2-D2. She would hug it and rub it. Talk to it.

They all thought her kooky. That kooky Lakota girl, they called her. Kookota, Eric called her affectionately. She'd thought affectionately, but he was one of those men who would flirt with a door.

If Eric Nwafo was made of chocolate, he'd eat himself, MJ used to say.

And she said that with affection.

Nova thinks she remembers the woman with the patchy hair now, she remembers waking up on the couch, and the woman – only a girl then, definitely at high school, perhaps a senior, but years younger than her and MJ, seven years younger, probably – would be standing self-consciously in that awesome, expansive custom-built log home in Colonial Pine Hills, and Nova would feel bad for her.

She was like a lap dog around Jordan and she never had any attraction in speaking to the other girls. But also, she didn't stare Nova up and down.

The more she thinks about the woman with the patchy hair the more Nova remembers her, and a younger girl with dirty blonde hair. Nova can see the face of the lioness. The girls' basketball coach. Coach Rackin.

Nova remembers someone rolling their mouth and that she left the house before the police came, that when they were talking on the TV about MJ's death, she did not go forward, even though she knew there were things that did not tally. Nova did not think too hard about it when thinking hard was so tiring.

But the night MJ died, Nova remembers hearing shouting. She remembers hearing a girl's voice. But Nova has never used her memory much, moreover her intuition and understanding. Memory is a muscle she is afraid to use in case Nova remembers something she shouldn't.

119

*

After a morning speaking Lakota, storytelling and painting circles with the children in the kindergarten, then trebling up on her medication and caffeine. Nova drives to the house where it happened, past the gray statue of a cardinal bird upstanding on an oval island of lawn that is enveloped by a sweeping arch of a driveway that holds one car and one Harley, and now, her car.

Though Nova has expected servants when the door opens there is a young black girl behind it.

Can I help you? the girl says.

Hi, Nova says, yes, maybe, can you get your mom?

A woman, the mother, appears. Tall and elegant, and confused.

Hi, Nova says. You don't know me but … Could I use your restroom? It's just, I'm pregnant, and my bladder is really not what it was – Nova lies, thankful, finally, for the potbelly her medicine has given her and the round youthful face, Nova could pass for a woman ten years younger.

I don't think so, the woman says.

The little girl looks at her. Mom, she pleads.

Okay, real quick. The woman ushers her to a bathroom down the hall.

Nova goes in and sits, running the water. The décor is different but the ceilings are still wooden. It is still dark.

You could still wake up in some corner and believe that you are in the neighboring National Park. Nova tries to collect her thoughts.

When she comes out she looks at the hallways, where the woman is waiting, putting her cell phone into the pocket of her jeans, trying to guide her to the door.

Nova remembers the door, and the girl in the bathrobe. The lioness. The basketball coach! She looks into the living room; so often Celena woke up there. The Persian rugs are gone from the living room, and the walls are lighter, brighter. She tries to see past it. Squints a little.

Would you like a drink? offers the girl.

I shouldn't.

It's good for you to keep hydrated.

Reluctantly the woman – Pinault's ex-wife – gestures for Nova to enter the kitchen where that coffee machine would have sat. R2-D2 is gone. Nova smiles as the girl opens a carton of grape juice and pours her a glass. Very sweet of you, she says.

Nova has a feeling of déjà vu, which someone once told her meant she was living her life right, and Nova tries now. She really does. She is trying right now.

Ephraim Shea, road name Stone, enters the room. You need me before I go to the meeting? he asks the woman.

Where is your phone? asks the woman in a monotone voice that is trying to keep bigger emotions under wraps.

I hate that thing, says Stone, that anyone can just expect me to answer right there and … He stops and glowers at Nova.

You know each other? the girl asks, catching an atmosphere.

Nova shakes her head, she does not, not really, only from what Akecheta and Wanda told her he had done to them, and to her alone.

Nope, says Stone and he says: That looks good. I'll leave in a little while, I've developed a thirst.

Stone, says the girl, pouring him a drink. Do you remember what happened back in May?

What happened?

The massacre.

Of course he remembers, Ever, says the woman. Let's just see our new friend out and then we can talk.

It's not private, says the girl, it was on KOTA, on the radio.

Oh yeah? What? says Stone.

Just a warning from the RCPD that there will be – she adopts a radio voice – an influx of Chevaliers in the Black Hills area Thursday through Labor Day weekend.

You remembered all that? says Nova. Smart kid.

Thank you, says the girl, smiling. Are they the guys you don't like, Stone? The ones that killed your friends?

Ever, says the girl's mother. We'll talk about that after, Nugget.

Are you ready to go? Stone asks Nova.

Nova takes one sip and thanks Ever and her mother, Thisbe.

*

But by October's warm days and cold nights, Nova's fragmented memories won't leave her alone, nor will thoughts of the woman with the patchy hair, nor of Senator Pinault and Pastor Nwafo, and MJ, and the lioness. These thoughts, she can't dead them.

It is raining hard when Wanda sucks her teeth as she looks out the window of Akecheta's home out on to the lot, and says: Mother Earth is disappointed in her children.

Well, says Nova. I'm proud of mine, you know that?

Her girls look at her. I'm not going, so don't try that emotional blackmail with me, says Candace.

What are we gunna do when we get there? asks Alexa.

I know, says her older sister. We'll make flags and voter buttons. It's hella babyish.

Babyish is where you need to be right now, says Nova.

Anything to keep Candace off Facebook and away from the things she wrote. She wouldn't accept her mother's friend request but her page was left open once and Nova read from it.

To think no one would have told her otherwise.

I never claimed to be no one but who the fuck I am, she'd written.

Life is like a dick, sometimes up, sometimes down, it won't be hard forever.

And taking suggestive selfies with her nipples showing through her underwear, and posting the images.

Her friends didn't help with their replies – Frickin hot! And Wanda liking all her pictures.

Unci, Nova had said, she's too young. She needs some toughness and boundaries.

President's Day is such hot garbage, says Candace, face it. Our *founding* fathers? That's bullshit. Plus, I hate Rapid City, it's the most racist city on earth.

What do you have to compare it to? asks Nova.

Maybe don't take them, says Wanda.

No, Unci, they're going. This is a President's Day event for girls, okay? They will be learning about voting, and there is nothing more important than women being in the know.

Nova plans to scope out the woman with the patchy hair while they are there, but she runs errands instead, and when she sees her kids come out of the event with their buttons and flags and looking really cute and patriotic as hell, she thinks, this is it. This seems better.

Hey, she says, there is still a trunk full of girl scout cookies. Let's try to unload some.

Fuck my life, says Candace.

Nova sighs, she does not know what to do with this girl. Not since she vented on Facebook that she'd been raped at the age of five, and Nova hadn't known. Wanda had responded in support: My gorgeous and tough, loco great-niece, candy bug!

To think no one would have told Nova if she hadn't snooped.

Candace said she couldn't remember who did it when asked. It was an older man on meth. It's why I hate meth-heads, she said. He was a visitor to a friend's trailer. I can't remember which friend, and why you mad with me? I was five!

Nova had cried and screamed. I'm not mad at you, Bug, never, she said.

After that, she struggled to manage the girl. They were working through it, but how did one do that? It brought all sorts back to Nova, so she wasn't just dealing with the present, not just her daughter, but all her kindergarten and first-grade students, and all the people of her past. That her own assault happened at the same age. That some girls survived them and others did not. Then there were her memories, half-memories, dreams and imaginations.

Let's go to Senator Pinault's house and sell him some cookies.

Are you for real? asks Alexa.

I'm for real.

In Nemo, she sees the car the patchy-haired woman got into the night of MJ's vigil back in the summer. Nova holds an umbrella over her head and a box of cookies under the other arm and goes to the door. The girls are behind, afraid of the huge barking dogs.

Oh no, they are teddy bears, teddy bears, says the woman.

She is now painfully thin and wearing a fancy real-hair wig, and her face looks almost frozen like she is full of fillers. Are they still selling girl scout cookies? she asks.

Helena tells them all to go into the living room and she pulls the dogs into another room before appearing with drinks for the girls and a bowl of pretzels each. A maid brings Helena and Nova coffee. This is the opposite of what Nova envisaged. She pictured the door being shut in their face; Nova has to admit that Pinault is attracted to women she does not find to be small-hearted, but of course, this makes sense.

Nova tries to remember why she even came, but Helena is so chatty she cannot screw her thoughts back on.

Helena does not want them to go back out in the rain. Stay until it eases, she says. I was watching the worst movie.

The house is huge, bigger than Akecheta's at Buffalo Plains Casino. But not bigger than Pinault's old house by the canyon. Nova is yet to see another house as big as that one.

You have kids? Nova says.

My fiancé has three.

They must love it here.

Their own house is nice though, says Helena.

Nova thinks she should take Akecheta up on his offer and move in. Give her girls a chance to be with her aunt while there's time.

Do I recognize you from MJ's vigil? asks Nova, trying out her best acting.

That's right. That's where!

So, is this Senator Pinault's house? she asks, seeing a photo of him and Helena, her hand on his chest showing off a huge sparkler that is on her finger right now.

Then Nova feels uncomfortable, she is expecting that Helena will feel some kind of way, that she and her girls must be there to steal something.

Even the maid gave them some kind of look. But Helena only smiles and Nova breathes again and relaxes.

There is a wooden dolphin on top of the fireplace.

I recognize that dolphin, Nova says, he had that in his old house.

When were you in Jordan's old house? asks Helena.

He had parties. It was the nineties.

Do you remember those parties?

Candace lets out a burp and everyone looks at her. She eats another pretzel.

I don't really remember them, says Nova. There's the problem. I have narcolepsy.

Poor you, gee! Helena says. I've always worked in hospitals. Not the medical side, managerial, but I know about the condition, and … guess what? I used to go to those parties, too.

Yeah, really? says Nova. There were a lot of people.

That's true. They were pretty wild at times.

Gee, small world, says Alexa. Nova looks at her, the shimmering plastic rhinestones around her neck catch the light.

Badass, badass, says Candace. My mother is actually a badass.

Helena laughs. Girl, everyone's mother is a badass, she says. My mother takes absolutely no shit.

I hope you hear this nice lady, Nova tells her girls.

Helena nods. So, that's a given that I'll buy cookies. Don't worry about that. But, you know, why go? You girls are so fun. I'm bored as hell. Do you ever get like that?

Nope, says Alexa.

I do, says Candace.

So stay, tell me all about yourselves, Helena says. Nova, what have you been doing since those days?

Just trying to stay awake, you know.

Oh, I know, says Helena. I hear that! Let me get us some more coffee.

Pieces of People

1995

i

Growing up, Akecheta Ghost Bear always worked jobs.

From chopping wood in his boyhood, to making small amounts of dough doing odd jobs for neighbors and ranchers and his uncles, to running errands for his aunt Wanda, who received disability checks from a botched operation.

And, on top of it all, keeping his three younger siblings out of trouble, who did not work jobs, but survived the first two weeks of each month on food stamps.

It was his job to ensure they ate the rest of the time.

At thirty years old, Akecheta began working at Buffalo Plains Casino and Hotel, in Oglala, with Abraham Rounds: a man who had not wanted to give him a job at first. Abraham had a fixed idea of *Natives*, as he called them.

He'd planned to ignore Akecheta, who had been standing over him, as Abraham – an old man, even then – sheltered his eyes from the cold January sun, breathed some heat on to his hands, and swung the heavy wooden door of the casino and hotel as it jarred once more, then cracked like a dropped pane of glass.

The old man solemnly cussed.

Heard there was a job going, Akecheta said to him.

He'd worn a baseball cap and had tucked his butt-long braid into his coat but the old man looked at him just the same is if he hadn't.

Heard wrong. No job goin' here, Abraham said.

But Akecheta would not be deterred.

There was a flier on the window that stated that they were looking for staff, a flier that Akecheta knew the old man was going to try to overlook, and Akecheta did not wait to hear the lies about how the post had been filled already.

I'll take an application, said Akecheta all the same.

Abraham Rounds bunched up his face as he tried to look closer at the hinge, his lips crimping.

You can see I'm busy here, he said out of the corner of his mouth.

Abraham had not showered that morning and his short gray hair sat bouffant at the sides but flattened on the top from his sleep. Under his bottom lip was a line of caked blood from a dry shave he'd rushed that morning.

Akecheta looked him over then walked off to the pickup and returned with his toolkit.

He set the galvanized metal box on the ground and gestured for the old man to move out of his way. Then he noticed that the door had dropped down someway off one hinge, and he realigned it, using all his strength to hold it and hammer it.

Then Akecheta opened the door, closed it then opened the door again with smooth ease and no cracking sound this time. He put his hammer back in his box.

Had trouble with that door for months, said Abraham, testing the door for himself.

You need someone around who knows a thing or two about such things, Akecheta said.

Well, thought I already had. Had two carpenters call already, and our foreman here at Buffalo Plains. He insisted we needed to buy a new one.

You don't need a new door just yet, said Akecheta, he placed his hand on the flier. What's the job you have goin'? he asked.

Abraham looked at the flier then back to the young man standing in front of him. We just let a barman go, Abraham said, but I feel that would be a waste of your talents.

No, sir, said Akecheta, I can put my hand to most anything.

Well, good, said Abraham slowly and coldly. Say, won't you come on through.

They sat face to face across a table in the corner of the blackjack room. What kind of clientele do you get here? asked Akecheta.

People who like a good time, Abraham replied with a smirk, like he found it amusing that the young man was matching him question for question.

What do you do when someone has had too much of a good time? asked Akecheta.

There is no such thing, said Abraham.

I disagree, I do, said Akecheta. Which led Abraham Rounds to put his hand out, spit in it, and say: Alright, alright, that's quite enough. Put it there. Job's yours, fellow.

*

Akecheta was draining a beer barrel behind Buffalo Plains Casino when Senator Beverly Burgess came out into the parking lot in his metal-tipped boots and took a parcel from his inside suit pocket. Akecheta knew Burgess was around a lot and that he never came to gamble. He watched him hand the parcel to a young man in leathers, who then got on to a Harley and rode off.

A week after, sometime early February, Akecheta was coming home from a shift when he saw the same biker on the same Harley talking with his brothers, Eugene and Freedom. Akecheta slowed his pickup, stopped, and called out: Everything good?

The biker stared at him and said nothing.

Eugene said nothing.

Freedom said, Yeah, everything. Good.

ii

That same week as he drove to work he saw the little girl out on the rez, no coat, her hair unbrushed, she was walking, carrying a little pink backpack like a shell. He stopped and wound down his window.

Hoka hey, watcha doin'? he asked the little girl.

Goin a school, she told him.

Where's your mom, or your dad?

131

Sleepin'.

Holy hell, he said and the little girl went to walk on.

Get in and I'll take you.

She was so little he had to go around and lift her into the pickup and buckle her in.

You got your own car, man? she asked.

I sure do, lil mama.

You got a job?

Yep. Where do you live? he asked.

On the rez.

Yeah, I know that. I mean wherebouts.

I can see it … but I can't say it. She pulled a cute, exasperated expression then smoothed down her hair.

You must like school, huh?

It's alright.

Yeah? Better than home?

They're sleepin', she said.

Sleepin', huh.

Been druggin' all night and fightin' and I gotta get me some learnin'.

Akecheta laughed.

Why you laughin'?

No reason.

Stop that. She pouted.

You're funny, is all.

You don't want me to smack you, do you, mister? The little girl made a fist.

No. I don't want to be smacked, he said setting a foil-wrapped sandwich on her lap. Put that fist away and eat up.

The little girl unpeeled the foil. Woah! she said.

It's yours, he said. Bet you haven't eaten.

Oh, no, I eaten, she said.

Then take it for your lunch.

I made lunch, she said.

And you are what age?

Six, last month.

Hell, he said.

What?

You're tough, that right?

Yes, I am, mister, she said.

Ake, you call me Ake. He smiled to himself. He always found kids to be surreal.

You can call me Jace.

Well alright, Jace, he said, pulling in at the school.

You gunna come pick me up later? she asked.

I don't know. I have work.

She pouted and gave him her best sad eyes. Figured you were busy, she said.

He scrambled under his seat for a poncho his little sis had left in his pickup and he handed it to the little girl. You'll be cold during the walk home. Take this, he said.

No.

Why not? he asked. Should I go in and talk with your teacher?

Why do that? Jace asked. It's just an ugly color.

It is? He looked at the poncho. Want my jacket instead?

She stuck out her tongue and pulled a face.

That's ugly too? he asked.

Gross city! she clarified.

What time do you get out of school?

Be real! said Jace. Can't tell the time yet, mister. You're so stoopid. She returned the sandwich to him.

That afternoon he came back and stood at the school. Jace's mother collected her, practically about to fall down drunk.

Akecheta thought about stepping in, withholding the child and scaring the mother, but in her he saw his own mother and he found forgiveness that he was not sure was his to give. And anyway, the child ran into her mother's arms and they hugged and looked happy together, normal, as they walked away.

*

Their trailer zone was hidden behind a row of trees, on a road dotted with rusting automobiles. On better days Wanda would have sat in a plastic lawn chair, wearing homemade scrubs, sipping on a can of beer, watching the sun light everything dusty peach then disappear behind the hilltops.

There was a horse head painted on the sidewall of their trailer and inside a dirt floor and cardboard in the windows. At no point had the local authorities ever connected the community to an electricity grid or running water.

Indoors, Freedom's girl, Katrina was standing over Wanda, who was sitting under her picture of the Holy Mother. But I love him, Katrina was saying: She had dyed her hair blonde and was wearing an electric blue top. Wanda, I love your nephew, and he don't care. He has children and he don't care.

Oh Trina, said Wanda as she nodded hello at Akecheta. What you want me to do about it? He's an adult.

Akecheta went into the only other room where his two brothers were sprawled out on the bed listening to 2pac. Budweiser empties scattered on the floor and a bottle of lemon vodka sat on the table.

Why has Katrina bleached her hair? Akecheta asked Freedom.

Told her I only like white girls though, said Freedom, laughing.

Who cares about her hair? said Eugene.

Tits and ass. No teeth, though. Freedom laughed.

Who cares about teeth? Eugene said then kicked Freedom who was still laughing.

I swear you both drank lighter fluid as babies, said Akecheta.

Wanda came into the room.

Free, she said, go talk to your girl, she's talkin' crazy out there.

Freedom ignored his aunt, turning around on the bed. Ake, he said sitting up, bring me and Gene to the meat factory.

For another handout? asked Akecheta.

That sweet Puerto Rican lady hates to see anything go to waste.

Or Delma probably feels pity for you, thought Akecheta, in your patched-up oversized jeans and undersized head. And Eugene too, with his pitifully big eyes. Gene took to seizing on the ground once in a while; usually, it was sincere but also it was something Gene could switch on to get himself out of trouble.

I'm just home, man, said Akecheta, hanging his coat on the hook at the back of the door.

Wish I was gifted with money to get the meat, said Freedom, lying back down again and tossing a pillow in the air.

Get off your ass. Gifted! said Akecheta.

Strange world of progress … said Freedom. Some of us have been to the moon, while some of us are still throwing sticks at it.

Keep talking, said Wanda. Katrina's gunna kill you if you don't go and help her with those kids now.

Freedom shook the cans on the floor, found one with some in it and shook a few drips into his mouth. Akecheta never saw him or Eugene without a can of piss in their hands, and it made him mad, especially since one of their little cousins had just been killed by a drunk driver in a head-on collision a half-mile away, along a dirt path in Oglala.

Time to face the music and dance, sang Katrina as she thumped the door.

Freedom groaned as he got up and followed her outside.

For a half-hour, Katrina screamed at Freedom. When she stopped, Akecheta went outside to put water in his jets. By then Katrina and Freedom were leaving arm in arm.

That blue looks dope on you, Freedom was telling his wife.

Akecheta shook his head and watched them walk on. Their uncle rode was riding in on horseback, smoking a cigar, his faded homemade tattoos blackening his hands.

Akecheta lowered the hood on his pickup when his uncle sidled up beside him.

You need to talk to your brothers, he said staring straight at the burning tip of his cigar.

What about now? asked Akecheta.

There was a biker gang that tore through here earlier. One had a bag I saw him give to Gene.

A bag? said Akecheta.

Large gym bag.

Describe the biker, Atéla.

Green shirt, leather jacket.

I know him. Know of him.

Who is he?

Called Stone Shea.

Stone? said his uncle. Be careful, Ake. Heart and mind!

Akecheta tinkered about with his pickup and once Eugene went to a friend's trailer for more beer, Akecheta went back into the trailer.

Under his bed, he located a gym bag full of weapons: sawn-off shotguns, a semi-automatic .22 rifle and baseball bats, a pouch of bullets included, all wrapped up in the American flag.

iii

Burgess and Stone made their regular dealings in the casino's parking lot under Akecheta's untrusting eye. Then Burgess drove off to check in on a golf course he owned, and Akecheta approached Stone, who was getting back on his bike.

You had better stay the fuck away from the reservation, he said.

Stone laughed with corrosive enjoyment. He slid his leather vest back to flash the gun in his holster.

Just stay away, you heard me, Akecheta shouted.

When he got home that evening he could hear his aunt crying from outside the trailer. Inside their animal pelts were burned and black. Wanda's handmade vase collection was smashed in shards around the floor.

What happened? he asked.

They tied her up, these bikers, said Celena handing a beer to Wanda.

Where were you? Akecheta asked his sister.

I was here, said Celena. Freedom's children were here, too.

Your sister was asleep, like she always is, Cheta, said Wanda.

It's not my fault, shouted Celena, her voice quavering.

They didn't want to hurt anyone, liberate anything, they wanted to ruin what little we have, said Wanda.

Where are Freedom and Eugene? he shouted.

Out. I don't know.

The children clung to his legs. Celena pulled them over to her. Hush, it's fine, she said. They're gone now. Ake, who do you think has done this?

Americans, leather vest and motorcycles, said their aunt.

Celena looked afraid. The Marcachs? she said.

They are bad news, said Wanda. Why would they do this, Cheta?

Ask Freedom and Eugene, said Akecheta, ask your other nephews.

*

He did not know where Stone lived, but he asked around at the casino and was able to learn that Shea lived on Moonlight Drive in the Custer highlands.

That raw March, Akecheta took off hot. He found the house, the porch, the horses his colleague had described, and he snuck around to the back door and looked in the window at a cabinet of knickknacks, landmark postcards, steamer trunks, files and crystals.

He wrapped his rope over his shoulder and checked the gun in his waistband, palmed the baseball bat in his hand. Then Akecheta burst the door in to find a woman in her sixties sitting at a round table dealing tarot cards to nobody.

Get on the ground! he shouted at her.

Akecheta started smashing the place up. Family photos, he smashed them on the wall, smashed a hole in the TV with the baseball bat. The gun stayed in his waistband. He thought about liberating something but decided not. He was here for revenge, to let Stone know what it felt like to have his family hurt and scared.

He told the woman to get on the floor again, he pulled at his rope but he could not bring himself to tie her up. A young girl, his height but really young looking, dirty blonde hair and the face of a lion, came into the room.

Grandmother, she shouted.

Elijah, the grandmother called, do anything he wants. Anything. Then she started to whimper.

Akecheta told the girl to sit down, as he smashed plant pots and anything else he could reach, but his anger had cooled down. These people did not deserve this. The old woman reminded him of his aunt, which made Akecheta wonder if she had cried the same way. He had never heard his aunt cry until after Stone tied her up.

He remembered his mother crying the day they took her to prison for meth and ripped the family apart. And the girl – Elijah – he expected to cry but she did not. She just looked at him undaunted.

Far from afraid. Suddenly it felt like his retribution did not work. This is for Stone, he spat.

When he arrived back at the trailer, this time the outside was painted green and there were gunshots through the eyes of the painted horse. This time his aunt Wanda was cold with him, she would not accept a hug. She could not cry.

Did they hurt you? Akecheta asked her.

Your sister, they pissed on her, she was asleep.

He pulled Celena outside by the arm. Aaaahhhhh! he roared. You need to grow up!

It's not me you are angry with, don't take it out on me, she said.

You are worse.

No, I am not.

You let white men piss on you.

I did not *let* them.

Where are our useless brothers? Akecheta asked.

Where were you? You are a useless brother, too.

I was getting revenge.

They knew you would, Ake.

No, they didn't.

They did. That's why they came back. It's something to do with you, she stated. I asked Freedom if he was getting drugs from the bikers and he said that it was not a deal gone wrong, that it was you they wanted. You, Ake.

iv

He saw Stone pull into the parking lot of Buffalo Plains Casino with the girl on the back of his bike. They both got off. Akecheta heard Stone tell her to wait while he went to the door where Beverly Burgess handed Stone an envelope, no doubt thick with greens. Stone hopped back on his bike and steamed on out, his engine rumbling. Then Burgess came outside and Akecheta stepped back so as not to be seen.

Good to see you, Bebe, said Burgess.

The girl did not reply.

There were always girls, always young. A different one for every day of the week. But Akecheta knew this one from the house in Custer.

This one, he was certain, had been called Elijah by her grandmother.

He watched from a short distance as Burgess put his hand out for the girl and she took it, walking a step behind him. At that point Akecheta made his presence known.

Can you spare a moment? said Akecheta, and Burgess reddened angrily and told the girl not to go anywhere. She was trying to cover her face with her dirty blonde hair. With her thumb, she twiddled the South Dakota state ring on her finger.

Akecheta followed Burgess indoors into the lounge as he said: Bebe, wait there, and she sat down on a sofa, lifted a cushion and hugged it. *Now* this girl looked terrified. Akecheta followed Senator Burgess into the office. What's going on? he asked.

None of your goddamn business, Ghost Bear, don't you need to clean a barrel?

Excuse me, did I say: What's going on? I meant: I know what's going on here.

This guy's in Mensa, said Burgess, as if to an audience.

Akecheta had long sussed out that Rounds was a manager and not the owner, he got a good read on that from the get-go. The real owner was Senator Beverly Burgess, who had the place set up in Rounds' name. Being a jack of all trades, working a bit on security, placing orders with breweries, Akecheta got eyeing up the books. Burgess was the eighty-percent owner and NFL player Jordan Pinault was the silent partner of the remaining twenty. Plus, Akecheta could tell by how the gears shifted when Burgess was about; they were not crooked in their workdays, that he could tell. Just at night, like jackals.

I want in on it, Akecheta said.

She doesn't eff with Indians, said Burgess.

Everything is transactional with people like you. Drugs … girls. Buy me.

I don't want you.

Buy my silence. Buy Mrs. Burgess not finding out that you are taking drugs and dealing drugs, and fucking minors. Not telling your wife is worth something, right?

You wouldn't have the balls.

I like Olivia, she's a sweet person, and so is that girl's grandma. I've met her, real nice woman, reads cards, likes crystals. She would like to know.

Just tell me what you want, Ghost Bear, said Burgess, starting to sweat.

A good living wage.

Alrighty. Done.

Rounds' management job, and jobs for my brothers.

Better and better. Rounds is done, are you?

This was too easy, he thought. This secret was worth far more than that. He had to chance his luck.

My aunt was right about you, Akecheta said. You do have the Lakota people's interests at heart.

Always did, said Senator Burgess.

Okay, I have it. The transaction. I want half of your share.

You're getting out of hand now.

Is it worth more than your reputation, because look at me, Senator, I don't have a reputation, I just know that I respect the land and others and I don't hurt anyone, unless …

Is that a threat to expose me?

More of a promise.

Fine, chief. Fine. We'll get the paperwork drawn up tomorrow, now enjoy your evening!

Another thing.

Anything, darling, he said facetiously.

Tell Stone Shea to stay the fuck away from my family. It starts with me, it stops with me.

That I can't do. Stone's his own man.

Well, you're gunna have to make it worth his time.

Akecheta left the room while Beverly went to write a check.

I'm sorry about what happened when I came into your house that night, Akecheta told the girl. How is your grandma? She good?

She's fine, the girl said, her shoulders shaking.

It was nothing against you or your grandmother.

The girl nodded.

What are you doing here? Akecheta asked, he wanted to flip out but instead he tried to comfort the girl but it was as if she was high or could not talk, she had shut down.

If you ever need anything, I'm here, he said and the girl looked away, trying to hide the tear in her eye.

Ghost Bear, shouted Burgess. That paperwork you required.

Akecheta went into the office and looked at a letter that stated Burgess was giving half his share to him, and alongside it a healthy check.

We'll get it made official tomorrow, Burgess said. But then … it's done.

Akecheta dusted off his hands and held them up to show surrender. He lifted the contract and the check, and watched Senator Burgess leave with the girl. Akecheta felt in two minds, as usual.

*

Jordan Pinault and Beverly Burgess were bickering about politics in the private room when Eric Nwafo entered.

Yes, Senator, Nwafo said pulling up a chair. I can't get through to Jordy that Democrat is the way to go. Tell him, please.

We are pals, said Pinault, aren't we? Aren't required to vote the same.

So, said Nwafo to Burgess, you are business partners but he won't vote for you?

Business is business, said Burgess.

Akecheta watched intently as he served them all whiskey sours.

Yeah, said Pinault. Business.

He took a drink and ignored his barman.

We work well together already, Burgess said laying his hands on the table, as if to say, here. We work well together *here*, investing *here*, taking our profits from here. Letting others manage the day-to-day so we don't have to really work together.

We mostly work well together, said Pinault. Did you hear the news? We have a partner now.

Silent partner, said Burgess, pointing in the air.

Akecheta began tidying up behind the bar so it did not look like he was paying attention.

Him? asked Nwafo, quietly.

Yep, said Pinault.

How come? he asked.

Never mind, said Burgess, he works harder than anyone here.

Even Rounds? asked Pinault, developing a tone.

It doesn't come out of your percentage, said Burgess, so worry yourself not. You should be thanking me, Jordan. You should definitely be thanking me.

He'll probably drink us clean, Pinault muttered.

Listen, we have an agreement and we are both happy with that. Anyway, he's teetotal.

Nwafo looked at the barman and Akecheta's eyes touched him.

Alrighty, then, what are we doing tonight? Nwafo asked.

Partying, said Pinault.

I can't keep up with you two. Burgess laughed.

Hey, we're off-season.

There's a pretty little filly you want to see, isn't there? said Burgess.

Hmm. Pinault looked at Akecheta again. Maybe.

She legal? asked Nwafo, lifting a deck of cards and staring at the Buffalo Plains logo on the backs.

Is anything legal? asked Pinault.

That's not the nicest thing you could say, said Nwafo.

Don't throw a strop, said Burgess. Just like Jordan doesn't try to convert me, you shouldn't press your holier-than-thou shtick on us. Try being more like our mutual friend.

Are we having a game? asked Nwafo, shuffling the deck. He dropped one card and went to pick it up when Pinault spun around in his seat and grabbed him by the throat. Rage burned in his eyes. He held Nwafo like that, until he gradually released his grip, put his hand on his knee and frowned.

What was that all about? asked Nwafo, holding his neck and staring at him in shock.

Nothing. Apologies. Pinault took another drink and frowned.

Good lord, you need to look after them brittle nerves, said Nwafo.

Yep, said Burgess, I always tell him the same.

Nwafo shuffled the cards again, slowly, watching Pinault sidelong, a frown deepening on his face.

Listen, Bev, said Pinault, avoiding looking at Nwafo. I grew up with this dude, we're brothers.

Brothers don't ever put their hands on each other once they're grown, said Nwafo.

Take a joke, said Pinault. He looked at Akecheta, who was ready to kick somebody's ass. What the fuck is his problem? he asked.

Hey, said Burgess, simmer, Ghost Bear. A little brotherly tiff, that's all.

Akecheta went back to drying a glass and holding it up to the light, so he was looking at them all.

Nwafo exhaled as he dealt the cards. Intermittently he looked at Pinault as he was trying to recognize him.

You good? asked Burgess.

I think so, said Nwafo, lifting his hand of cards.

Akecheta knew that brother or *like a brother*, he could not see Pinault grab another white man by the throat, and he poured three more sours, bent and spat in one, and brought them to the table.

Another round, he said, to let you all know that there are no hard feelings, and that I will do my best for this place. Okay, partner?

He put his right hand out for Pinault to shake it, but Pinault took the glass that was furthest out of reach on the tray, as if he knew, always seeing the worst in people.

And Nwafo, smiling weakly, accepted the closest one and took a sip of Ake Ghost Bear's spit. Burgess gave Akecheta an appreciative wink and moved the conversation away from politics and onto football. Safe ground.

*

146

Free and Gene – in their late twenties – had never tried to get a job. Akecheta offered them jobs at Buffalo Plains Casino but they refused, drank while his family went hungry and Akecheta got even angrier.

There is a custom his tribe is supposed to observe, that nobody eats if one does not, and so he was furious with his siblings. They all looked after themselves only.

Celena was not just as bad as Eugene and Freedom, but she was bad in her own way. Aunt Wanda would be asking her for help, to help the women and children of the village of Oglala, and she would be curled up asleep on a chair. You could be talking to her and she would let her head fall to the side and her mouth droop open, and she would close her eyes to you. Sorry, I tuned out there, she'd say, when she came to.

Celena had been smart, tied the Lakota part of herself to the American part. Her best friend was a blonde-haired white girl who had wound up marrying a rich old codger, and while Akecheta did not want that for his sister, he did let her drive the pickup and would be just the amount of rude to her if she went without asking, until that rudeness of hers thickened even more.

When his shift was done, he went to the meat processing factory where Ricky Nwafo's mother Delma worked, which was what made him like her so much, that she had kept her job even though her son had mad wealth. Which was the same thing that made him hate Nwafo, that he did not tell his mother she did not have to work now he was rich as cream. Delma was always good to Akecheta and his brothers when she could be.

Sorry, she said tonight, they're cracking down on how much we can ditch at the end of the night. The staff, some of 'em, they're taking it.

Akecheta opened his wallet. No. I'm gunna pay you, he said, and for everything the last few months.

No, no, she insisted. Clean slate, buddy.

A man working there stood up. Who's this, Delma?

A friend of ours, a longtime friend, here to buy some meat.

How much you tryna spend? he asked.

Akecheta took his wallet from his shirt pocket and dished out a wad of greens then they helped him pack up the bed of the pickup with sides of beef.

He headed out for home and Akecheta went into the trailer. There was his aunt and Celena, both on edge. They had developed a knock, like a password. As if the distinctive roar of the pickup was not warning enough. And as if the bikers would care to knock; they hadn't before. He had tried to warn Stone off but the contents of the gym bag had doubled. His brothers had to go.

Akecheta waved his aunts and uncles over, the little kids too, and got them all to help unpack the beef. His sister said: This is too much, half of it will go bad before we have the chance to eat it.

Then go down to the next village, share it out, he said.

Then he told his brothers he'd take them to the source: White Clay, Nebraska, where most of the alcohol was smuggled in from since the ban was put on alcohol by the tribal government.

After eating, he wended through the rez, over the bumpy gravel roads, stopping only for a tank full of Regular.

Over the next state-line, he plowed through the shadows and whispers of the automobile graveyard, on to the dusty streets of White Clay with its two columns of decrepit stores and buildings, most of them shuttered, and the boarded-up bars making the place look like the set of an old Western movie.

A town with four beer stores and a population you could count on your fingers and toes. Now the place had two more inhabitants.

Here you go, he said as he gave his brothers a few dollars apiece and they disappeared into a store and came out with their cans already opened and sizzling in their hands. Akecheta was in his pickup and outside it, on the curb, was Eugene's gym bag.

Your clothes are in there, said Akecheta. Since you won't do better for Wanda, and your kids, I'm making the decision.

He left them there, where they drank themselves into oblivion, winding up in a fight.

It was thought that Eugene first attacked Freedom, and thinking he had killed him, killed himself.

Two days later, waking, coming face to face with Eugene's death, Freedom made his final journey.

Like some West Side Story shit, thought Akecheta, when he could clear the water in his head for long enough to let the thoughts rise before pushing them back down again, and getting back to his job of being a man. A man with many jobs.

Passing Game

2015

Put the menu down, son, or we'll never get served, the father tells the boy, thinking that they have waited long enough already. But the boy is only looking at the menu because his father forbids the iPad at the table, clearly values time spent in conversation. But for the boy, their conversations have become so one-sided they always circle back to the starting point.

And, for the father, it is hard to know what else to say that hasn't already been said. Maybe it's down to the boy's age, him being fourteen, being born on the 12 September 2001, and named Phoenix: not only for this city that has always been special to his father – where father and son are now spending time together, where the father has just had a stint commentating on the Super Bowl.

But the boy was also named Phoenix as a nod to their broken post-9/11 nation rising up from the ashes in those bleak days.

They are sick of Mexican food the past few days, they have burritos coming out of their ears, and so Ricky has brought his boy to this nice Italian he used to frequent when he was at rehab camp pre-season. The restaurant has gone downhill, granted, though it never was anything special to look at, with its chopping ceiling fans and dusty chandeliers, black and white prints on the walls and specials up on the chalkboard that now look incredibly cheap. Yet, the food, as Ricky remembers it, is exquisite. The service has definitely waned, though.

Ricky remembers a few young waitresses who were as cute as corn. Now, however, the staff is male and middle-aged, unmotivated. They wear white lambent dress shirts, black matte pants, and vests that highlight their generous love handles.

The waiters prefer the female clientele. It doesn't matter the age group, or if they are groups of college girls getting together, or perhaps a birthday, or colleagues out for a business meeting, or just mothers and daughters grabbing some lunch.

This one waiter, who is particularly irritating to Ricky, toys with all the women no matter their appearance, calling them *lovely ladies*, saying they don't need dessert, that they are *sweet enough*. Acting extra corny for his service charge. Ricky would love to know if it is a successful approach. He just can't see it working. He and his boy are in no rush, but their invisibility is starting to bug Ricky. So he calls the waiter over, who now has an entirely different demeanor. He has no time or focus for Ricky's charm, nor does the waiter seem to recognize him.

Ricky is trying to ask the waiter about red wines since he has his attention, when the man abruptly tells him that they are on the menu.

I'll give you more time, the waiter says, trying to walk off because a woman has entered the restaurant, an abnormally skinny woman.

No, says Ricky, just bring your finest, and get my boy a drink, too. We'd like to eat sometime this year. Ricky rubs the jagged scar that has landed in a faded lightning bolt across his knuckles.

This year. Good one! It's only one month in, says the waiter. And your boy?

Tell the man what you would like.

Orange pop, sir, says Phoenix.

We don't sell sounds. The waiter laughs.

Fanta, says Ricky.

Are you sure? Not a sound? The waiter puts his finger in his cheek and makes a popping sound. For you, young man. Enjoy.

The boy looks confused and Ricky smiles, though he is very unhappy.

Orange Fanta, he says, and anger rises in him because this grown man is trying to make his boy look silly, and when the boy is worth twenty of the waiter. He walks off, approaches the skinny woman who has a wild head of dark hair and a young daughter in tow, who is roughly four years old.

Ciao, she says.

Ciao, the waiter replies.

The child wears a polka dot tutu.

The mother is in a sweater dress adorned with the print of a painting: a naked, red-haired woman standing in a shell. She is using her hand and hair to cover her body. The waiter seats the mother and daughter at the table beside the father and the son.

The daughter looks glum. She does not return Ricky's smile. He has always liked little kids. The girl is cute but not cute enough; she must look more like her father. Maybe this is a disappointment to the very attractive but excessively skinny woman, Ricky thinks.

The waiter is about to talk to her, Ricky is sure, so he says: Pardon me, those drinks, right. They won't get themselves.

Pissed off, the waiter gives him a hairline smile and leaves the order at the bar, then he returns to fawn over the woman.

I lived near Florence for years, she says. Do you speak the dialect? the woman asks the waiter.

No, he says.

Then I'll not waste it on you, she tells him. I'll have a carbonara and a little plate. I'm not being cheap, but she is not a big eater.

She nods at the daughter.

The waiter leaves. The little daughter sneezes, and they search the table for it. The mother searches her clothes, then she sees Ricky watching and sits up, adopts an air of disinterest.

You'll find that later, she says to her daughter.

Dad, says Phoenix. He nods at the waiter who is finally standing over them.

The waiter pours Ricky's wine and waits for approval. They do the same routine around the food. The waiter's attention is brought back to the woman again. She has a glass of white wine and the child a glass of water.

Chin-chin. Okay, chin, the woman says until the child lifts her glass and clangs it off her mother's glass. She begins to talk to the child. This is – she holds up a spoon – cucchiaio, she says, and this is – holding up a glass – bicchiere di vino.

The daughter corrects the mother's pronunciation and the woman laughs with biting self-consciousness.

Dad, says Phoenix, you think Brady is gunna play next season?

Umm, hopefully, Ricky says. Brady has had another fine season.

He's a machine. Did you see his execution?

I did. I didn't love their chances going into that fourth quarter. But …

He's my hero. Besides you, I mean.

Ricky laughs. That's sweet.

Were you ever that good? asks the boy.

Different position, says Ricky. Apples, oranges.

The woman is crouched down looking at the wall until she locates a socket, where she plugs in the cell phone charger she has taken from her bag, then she sets the phone on the seat beside her and places her coat over it. After a while, the waiter offers to take her coat.

No, that's a very expensive coat, she says. I'll keep it where I can see it.

Ricky feels repulsed.

What are you gunna study in college? he fumbles to say something to Phoenix.

I told you yesterday, Dad: Football.

And what if that doesn't work out?

I can commentate, like you.

That's not my real job. It's a rarity.

I know, but I don't want to get into the ministry.

Ricky has always told the boy he doesn't have to, he doesn't even have to join the youth corps. He can miss Friday nights to throw leather, and any nights he has practice.

But Ricky does want the influence of religion on his son like he has had on him.

He wants him to feel that church is always an option, yet the boy has not even been baptized, and he knows that the congregation would be unhappy to hear that.

Are there any girls you like in school? he asks Phoenix, not wanting to look at the woman again, who is now quiet, but Ricky feels will get loud again the moment he or Phoenix allow a mist of silence to fall on their table.

No, Phoenix says. But I know what you're gunna say.

Whadda you know?

To choose a woman like Mom.

How do you know I was gunna say that?

You tell me often.

Yeah, I do? he says, concerned.

Phoenix listens to a lot of music that Ricky does not like: Jay Z and Kanye. Bitch this and that. While these days Ricky likes Kid Rock.

Have some fun first, won't you? he says.

Is that what Jesus would do? says Phoenix trying to be rebellious, but he is really a good kid, and Ricky appreciates that he must feel preached at, at training, in school, plus, Natasha is tough on him, and so are his grandparents, demanding manners all the time.

What's a boy to do to let off a bit of steam?

I think Jesus would have fun and that he wouldn't hurt anyone, Ricky says. He looks at his son in his coral-colored Pull & Bear hoodie and is struck by how beautiful he is. How beautiful he is pangs. It is a long beautiful ache. He is the most beautiful young man Ricky has ever laid his eyes on.

Okay, Dad, says Phoenix, playing with a napkin.

And pick someone who won't hurt you either. That's the secret, look after each other.

Alright, I'll remember that … when I'm old.

Ricky laughs. The woman looks over at him and fixes her hair. Once she has his attention she begins a conversation in Italian with her daughter.

Is that ceiling fan annoying you? Ricky asks his son.

What ceiling fan?

Lift your drink, I think we'll just move over here, he says, lifting his wine bottle and glass, and going to a table where he cannot hear the woman anymore, or see her, putting his back to her.

Although he feels compelled to look when he hears the waiter bidding her arrivederci, because she has finished her lunch before he has even got his. And the painting on that dress of hers really is mesmerizing. He must find out what it is called.

*

Years ago, after football, and grounded in Rapid once more, he walked into Firehouse Brewery feeling like flirting with the manager. Natasha had an attentive nature, and a fixated stare that showed confidence, and a tiny martini glass tattoo just under her elbow, which Ricky thought was a little sign of a wild past.

His father had taught Earth Science at West Jr High School, and Economics and Sociology at Rapid City Senior High School. His mother was a meat factory operative who, for a long time, worked on production. Natasha came from a similarly modest background.

It was all very ordinary. Ricky and Natasha dated. He began to attend her church. She adored his parents and they totally respected her. This was the girl they wanted for him. This was the girl Ricky the NFL star needed. Natasha was strong and caring and had good values.

She looked after him, put his pajamas on the radiator on those luminous but frigid Dakota winters. Then Natasha became a great mother. And through her, Ricky became just a regular man, which was partly what he wanted. And to get away from the old crowd. To immerse himself in all that was good.

You have been blessed with two wonderful existences, says Brian Schumer, a recent divorcee and church friend of Ricky's. Brian has recently admitted to a bout of uncertainty and loneliness.

It is February, during a mild spell, when the Nwafos have a cookout, and alongside two of Phoenix's friends, they invite Brian.

My time in football was a sweet spot in my life, but this is sweeter, says Ricky, nodding at the table where the three boys chat quietly between looking at their iPhones.

His mother Delma stands over them on the fumed white oak floor, a look of perplexity on her face. She sets a bowl of Cajun shrimp salad in the middle of the granite tabletop.

Damn straight, this is sweeter, says Papa Ken.

Ricky's father's pride in him is immense, though he is not the kind of man who will ever show it. His pride kept him and Delma in Doolittle Street, in their little blue-painted house until lately, when they eventually moved into the house Ricky had constructed next door to him and Natasha.

Before they eat, Papa Ken gives thanks, and the kids wince. Neither Parker nor Kincaid come from Christian families, not that Ricky objects, but he knows his folks do.

They had always liked their kids, Julia, then Eric, and now their grandchildren, to keep good company. But these are good kids, Ricky knows that.

And what is he going to say, that his son must only befriend other children from the church, children who are not compatible with Phoenix's personality? He cannot, especially not when he hears how some kids in the boy's school poke fun at his spiritual side, calling him Flanders, after the irritatingly upbeat neighbor in *The Simpsons*. A show they have banned in the Nwafo house for its anti-religion message.

Ricky once heard a visiting Pastor from Illinois tell the youth corps that when they reach heaven, they won't miss the people they knew who were not saved, and Ricky had not agreed. He takes issue with a lot of the church's teachings. He'd tried to explain it to Phoenix.

I know, Dad, Phoenix said, it's all out of whack. You just cherry-pick what sounds right and forget about the rest.

What could Ricky say to that? It was how much of the congregation worked. They could justify anything if they wanted it badly enough. Someone could visit and deliver testimony on how they had murdered someone in the past, and then say: But God called me, and I asked his forgiveness, and he forgave.

Ricky honestly didn't know how that was enough. In truth, God had never spoken to him that way. Maybe He had never spoken to Ricky at all.

As Pastor Nwafo, he would go to funerals of youngsters and say it pleased God to take them young.

Like the girl with the tumor on her brain.

Like the unarmed black boy who was killed by the police the year after Ricky's boy was born.

Back then he thought of his son, with his African-American grandfather and Puerto Rican grandmother. Though Phoenix is light-skinned. He has a white mother, Dutch grandparents on her side.

His experience is not the same as his father's. Phoenix's friends are white, mostly of German descent. It pleases Ricky that the boy has friends who are like brothers since he is an only child.

Thinking of brothers, Ricky feels bad; he would have liked to invite Jordan to the cookout, but Natasha can't have him around. Jordan is silent around her, secretive. He will call over but dial Ricky's cell phone and have him come sit with him in the car, talk for hours if you'd let him. Even when Jordan had Thisbe and the girls, he was never a man who enjoyed family days together. Which maybe was no bad thing because Natasha thought Thisbe too *showy*. But some girls are just like that, and Ricky does not believe that Thisbe tries to be that way, more that she is just very effortlessly beautiful. He knew a girl just like that once, which was why he chose a girl like Natasha. He wanted loyalty.

The last time Ricky heard from Jordan, he wanted him to meet his new girlfriend. Ricky said he would love to meet her but was really overloaded. He failed to mention the cookout. Brian Schumer would have loved to see Jordan, but Ricky doubted Jordan would have been up for it. He had lost a lot of that old charm he used to have. Now he was somewhat blistered. That's politics for you! Sometimes the Senate is in session. Sometimes he is cagey. Plus, Papa Ken has never liked Jordan. He's gunna lead you astray, he'd say. What about his own folks?

But Ricky didn't know. He'd always kind of felt responsible for his friend. They were brothers, always had been. Even when they were two kids playing ball in the road that led to the highway. Try to break that up. No one or nothing could. Though sure, they had drifted, they now mainly kept in touch by phone. Nearly every other day, they would chat.

The last Ricky had heard from him, Jordan told him that he'd taken dear ole Bev Burgess out of the care facility for icecream.

He's a piece of shit, said Jordan.

Hey, that's not nice, said Ricky.

No, seriously, said Jordan, when you think about it, he is the ultimate piece of shit, and you can say anything to him now he's stroked up and doesn't react.

Bev hadn't been the same since the stroke, and although he probably deserved everything he got, Ricky had a hard time with it. He'd rather not know that Jordan was pulling anybody's mask or accidently letting him fall from his wheelchair and scuffing the whole side of his face or letting him sit for hours in piss-saturated pants. Ricky would rather not have these details. And it wasn't his place to judge Beverly Burgess, who was in his own purgatory now.

*

In late February, the principal of Thornhill does the honors of an introduction at the end of season game. The Lakota girls stand on their side, then the visiting school come into the hall in their long shorts and vests, and the crowd begins foot-stomping and booing. Music begins and they stand to sing the national anthem and then sing it in Lakota.

Then the principal nudges Ricky to step forth, and he steps forth, out on to the bleachy court, waiting for their silence. The principal takes the mic to regain the crowd's attention.

Now a few words, like I said, from Pastor Nwafo: a true sportsperson himself.

Ricky takes another step and the room quietens. His shoes squeak on the floor.

I want to talk about how we treat each other, he says, staring across at the teams. He tries to look up and down each team and find them in their eyes. What I want to do is read a passage from the bible, he says.

Ricky has felt *her* watching him ever since he got to the school. He remembers her without remembering her. Ricky doesn't know exactly why, but he feels uneasy. Her face, although she is scowling, is not why he feels uneasy. Now, as he fumbles through the passage, stumbles on the words, and for the first time, maybe ever, loses his composure, Ricky is trying to look at the girls and the people who do not want him there. He is of a kind, he feels, as he reads his passage and the whistle blows.

The booing picks up again while the game is being played. The girls holler and run, hands praying around the pimpled ball. There are hoops that go in, hoops that kiss the rim and fall back over, and throws that wind up at the other end of the court, taken there in gliding dribbles, to layers of applause and whoops from the crowd, but more and more boos.

Ricky watches the game, he sees the elbows, dirty play. This surprises him, though it shouldn't, that girls are capable of bad tactics, but it is nothing he didn't see in the NFL.

Though he can use this, he thinks, if he is allowed the chance to give a locker room reflection afterward, he can tell them that he was ejected just once in his whole career. Only once, and while sticking up for that hot-head brother of his, Jordy Pinault, and never again after. It's a close game all the way until a Thornhill girl buries the game-winner with a jump shot and the scoreboard reflects it. Then boos ramp up again, on both sides.

The coach, the woman who has been watching him the whole time, with dirty blonde hair, and brown eyes that look black, goes and stands by her girls, encouraging them to shake hands with the opposition. Some of the handshakes are barely there; some are a slapping away of fingers.

Ricky makes a point of shaking everyone's hand. Including the coach's.

Thank you, Coach, he says.

You're welcome, Ricky, she says with no return of his gratitude.

He is thrown by her over-familiarity. Her bad tone. Then he knows who she is, at that moment. It's been decades but it's here.

I hope that helped, he says, looking around.

This was the principal's idea. We don't want the police. This time.

It's better to forge mutual respect somehow.

The coach laughs, baring her teeth.

Anyways, you're doing a great job with these girls, he says. Good for you.

She turns up her nose. The room is emptying.

I better hit the road, Ricky says.

You better, she says like a threat. She looks like she might pounce on him.

He has always been the same, if someone doesn't like him, if he senses that they don't, he must try to make them like him. He knows *her* and knows he never did anything wrong by her. He has to let her see the good man Eric Nwafo truly is. Everyone else can see it. One ejection in his career.

So, you like doing this? he asks.

Yes, she says. Always loved basketball. It saved me from some horrible things that happened to me when I was a kid. Really vile matter, when I was a *kid*.

162

That's the beauty of being in a team, he says, trying to smile, and make the best soup of sympathy and positivity that he can.

Do you see him much these days?

Who? he asks.

Jordan.

Jordy Pinault? His guts churn.

She barely nods.

No, not really, says Ricky. So that went well. At least you got a win.

My girls are still smiling, win or lose. No one needs to get sick.

I hope you're smiling.

Oh, I never smile, she says. Don't you remember?

Look, if you're ever down to talk, I'm here, he says, backing away. About the team… Anything.

The coach crosses her arms. He notices that her fists are tight, and hatred shines in her eyes like wire.

He is still thinking about what she said when, a couple of weeks later, he cannot put off meeting with Jordan any longer. He has had an operation, so Ricky goes to visit him. He sits in a chair at Jordan's bedside in his house in Nemo. Ricky asks him if he needs anything, and Jordan shakes his head.

Do you? Jordan asks. He seems kind of dazed.

Me? No, says Ricky.

Jordan lifts a cup from the bedside table and throws it against the wall.

What are you doing, man? Ricky asks.

Everything okay? Helena asks, appearing at the door. She looks at the cup lying in two on the carpet and the staining cold tea weeping down the wall.

He tried to get out of bed, Ricky says – feeling he must lie for his friend. There was a little … droppage.

I'll get you more tea, says Helena, crouching as she picks up the pieces and cradles them in her hand.

She looks familiar to Ricky, something about the back of her head, that thick wavy hair. Ricky says he does not want any tea but that Jordan maybe wants some.

Jordan moves restlessly in the bed and looks away, toward the window, seeing nothing outside. Ricky again feels like he should say something kind in this uncomfortable spot. He thinks of asking Helena to come back to church, she seems nice, and Natasha could use her help at the Sunday crèche. Then he thinks better of it.

No girlfriend of Pinault's could ever be nice enough to allow Natasha to tolerate his company ever again. It is still tricky there since the text exchange, and he suspects it always will be.

No, he will not have Helena, or Jordan, in his home any more than he needs to for his wife's sake.

You're Bess's daughter, Ricky says.

That's right, Helena says, going red in the face.

I officiated when she and Alf had their backyard wedding, says Ricky.

Jordan laughs.

Well, Helena says, they might need you again. He's back.

Alf and your mother? asks Ricky. Are they back on?

Helena nods.

That's sweet news, says Ricky.

Old Nam hippie, says Jordan, he's not like you and me, Ric. We fought our war.

Our war?

Against the other team. All those teams. Jordan grimaces as he moves.

Oh, football, you mean.

Ricky pulls a confounded expression at Helena, and she smiles a small return.

Of course, man, says Jordan. What else was there? Except getting ass.

Ricky curls his lip then laughs. He has to question Jordan's IQ these days. He no longer has youth to blame for his stupidity, his crassness. Maybe those knocks to the head … It happens.

Can I … starts Helena before Jordan snaps – You're excused. Go away.

Helena leaves.

Ricky sits back in the chair and looks out of the window at the wonderful scenery, the trees: ponderosa pine, aspen and silver birch. God's work. He knows Jordan won't appreciate it all. And that is the difference between them. Well, one of them.

He tells Jordan that he has brought a flask of soup from his mother, and his father has sent over a bottle of whiskey. Despite not being his biggest fan, they have always looked out for him and still do.

Jordan's own parents were rich, uninterested guardians, much richer than the Nwafos, and yet they were feeding the Pinault boy for years.

My parents told me to pass on their regards.

They can't visit? says Jordan.

They wouldn't dream of imposing. And won't you be up and about before no time?

I hope so, says Jordan.

It won't be as bad as last time. Last hip, says Ricky. And you have Helena now to help.

Yep, I have Helena. Dumb bitch.

Ricky bites his lip, then he says – Lot of robins this time of year, doncha think?

Jordan looks deeply sad. It is a look that Ricky remembers when he goes home.

165

A look he thinks about when Natasha asks him what this new girlfriend of Jordan's is like, and he replies, Oh, lovely. Yes. She's Bess Russo's daughter.

Her? She's not his usual type.

I guess not.

Ricky remembers how he, Natasha, Jordan, and Thisbe used to go on double dates when Thisbe first moved over from Texas. Ricky had enjoyed her company a little bit too much. She was a sinner that could not be redressed. He enjoyed trying. Thisbe had this no-filter attitude, which was refreshing to listen to for an hour or two, here or there. Entertaining for a couple like him and Natasha, who prided themselves on always being the best, kindest, most righteous versions of themselves.

Thisbe was beautiful and feisty in the beginning. And Ricky remembered how Jordan had liked feistiness in girls when they were younger, how it always wore thin.

She's not like Thisbe, Ricky tells Natasha. He has this one eating out of the palm of his hand.

Natasha shudders. She clearly remembers the text where Jordan called her *low-key sexy* and stated that he wanted to *eat her out*.

When she showed Ricky, she seemed disgusted, but he was proud, in a way. Then hurt and betrayed. Then proud again. But only because, perversely, the texts became the remedy for her lack of self-confidence, which had recently taken a double hit when she found herself helping Phoenix with research. Their boy was writing a report on his hero, and as a surprise, had chosen his father as his subject.

That same day, Natasha Googled her husband's name with their boy, and found the first article, titled: *What are Old NFL Stars Doing Now?*

166

In the comments, someone said of the photo of Natasha with her husband, that she looked like a random person picked off the street to win a meet and greet with Ricky Nwafo.

The second confidence-denter came in the form of an article titled: *Beautiful Famous People who have Ugly Spouses.* Accompanying the text was an old photo of the couple; Natasha had just had Phoenix, her hair was hard to work with post-partum and stuck out everywhere. She was still carrying the baby weight, though naturally was always kind of slim-thick. Natasha has prominent unblinking eyes that were cruelly set upon in the comments section that she later read alone, and later again showed to Ricky, but he insisted he loved those eyes.

However, he did not admit that he was less fond when she used eyeliner to highlight further her best features – as she had always thought them, until that article. Nor Ricky did not like – for her sake, and his own – that some troll in the comments called her Beetlejuice after the whacky Michael Keating movie.

Natasha cried about that reference for two days straight. He noticed that her black and white pantsuit with the vertical stripes was gone from her closet.

After the discoveries, she considered liposuction, got depressed and needy, always asking him for reassurance. But she was beautiful, to her husband, in a way he now appreciated beauty to matter.

Then the smutty texts arrived from Jordan, which Ricky occasionally remembers with anger, but when he noticed her insecurities wane, he was almost thankful for them. Then it flipped, and again, Ricky felt the betrayal.

Before she told Ricky and showed him, Natasha replied to Jordan's message by saying:

This would really hurt my husband, and Jordan had replied: Then don't tell him.

All their boy code had worn away. The traffic light system they had lived by since their late teens clearly no longer worked. Red. Green. *Amber.*

Ricky went to his father, and his father told him to ignore it but don't forget it. He went to God, but God never replied, so Ricky answered himself on God's behalf, and his answer was this: Pinault is Pinault, and what are you going to do?

He set out to be a good friend instead, but he would not invite the guy around his family. So when Jordy split with Thisbe and things got hostile, Ricky found himself punishing Jordan by saying he was busy.

If you need anything, I'm here for you, bro.

But Ricky was not.

Then Thisbe dropped the charges and changed the locks, and Ricky kept his distance.

I'm here, he'd say, but he did not offer Jordy a place to live. He had money and his Republican comrades.

Plus, he knew Jordan better than anybody and how he just could not help himself. Natasha wasn't the first person he'd propositioned.

One day Thisbe came to Ricky. He met her in his pastoral capacity. She was by far and away more vulnerable than he'd ever seen her. She was meek and humble. Humble, broken, and beautiful, as she told him about the passion she had found with this so-called *hot biker,* in that open, honest way she has.

Ricky may have been a man of the cloth, and a friend of her husband's, but he was still a man. When Thisbe told him about her loneliness, and her craving to be touched, and about her being touched, Ricky found himself getting hard under the table.

Then she pulled an expression, and his stomach flipped, or dropped, he wasn't sure which, because a thought came into his head then that she looked a little like him. More like him than his own sister, Julia, who had Papa Ken's permanent somberness. Or maybe he just saw a little of himself in Thisbe, which started Ricky wondering if Jordan had been first attracted to her for this reason.

And in that instant, sitting across from Thisbe, as she talked about fucking a stranger in a biker club storeroom and what her life had become as a result, what buoyed up in Ricky's head was the thought of that drunken night that he never liked to think about, twenty-something years before, when all the girls had gone, and Pinault knelt at his feet, and offered to blow him, and how that soon turned into an argument, an embarrassed, aggressive argument, on Jordan's part, who argued with Ricky, asserting and insisting that he'd like it.

Try it. Close your eyes. Sit back down, goddamn it.

And Ricky remembered looking at Jordy's face and thinking, no. Another man or not. No.

Best friend or not. No.

This human being has an ugly, angry view of intimacy. And Ricky was through meditating Jordan's desires.

That day Thisbe came to Ricky, she talked about rape accusations, and violence, and silence, and the RCPD, and Ricky knew the score: That Ever – the eldest Pinault baby – though no one asked, was not Jordan's. Yet Jordy overcompensated and spoke about her as though she was. He would get tetchy if he thought someone was saying otherwise. They never were. Nobody truly cared. They all had their own stuff to consider.

For a while, fatherhood looked to be the making of him, biological or not. Then he paid a stranger to have the following two girls. His. And after the divorce, he never mentioned any of those little girls again. Only Thisbe, and how much he loathed her. But not the little girls to whom he'd been a father. It was like they had never existed, which Ricky attributed to Jordan not knowing his own father much, who always worked away, making money to be spent by his son without consequence. Football was the perfect art for people with nothing, but Pinault had everything. Thought he was entitled to more.

The day Thisbe came to Ricky, she confided in him what her marriage had become – though he wouldn't take sides because Jordan was his brother, and let he that is without sin … and whatnot – and he went home, and that night, made love to Natasha, but then he flashed-back to the Ricky/Jordan/Amber triads they so often had. *Amber* meant: you can jump in, too.

Come meet Amber.

Oh, you're not called Amber? I apologize. Sincerely. Coy smile. Flirt, seduce. Get her onboard, join in.

Jordan enjoyed being watched. Sometimes he took it too far.

Then he became friends with Beverly, and there were the girls Beverly found him, and that was where Ricky had to draw the line. He had no time for such things. And he didn't hurt anyone.

The day Thisbe came to Ricky, she said, Violence thrives on silence.

But if it was a crime to be silent about what had all gone on, that he was not a part of, Ricky was a tiny bit guilty of that. And sorry for it, too. But not sorry enough to speak.

The Value of the Remainder

2010

Three babies, Thisbe! said Lori Butler. You don't, I hope you don't mind me saying, have a single stretch mark. And how old is the baby? One, if even?

Almost one, yes. But I've always been tall and snaky, said Thisbe sliding her arms into a kimono that was hung on the wall in the dressing room at Lori's home.

What is your secret? asked Lori before reeling off a list of cosmetic procedures.

None of that, said Thisbe.

She could not take full credit for any post-baby body since the only one of her three daughters she had carried was Ever, that being five years ago now.

After that instance, she and Jordan hired the uterine services of Jessi: a little Louisiana woman who had already completed her family of five boys.

Despite stipulating that she was only prepared to give the gift of life to a childless couple who could not naturally conceive, Jessi's embargo was soon unblocked by an in-person introduction to – lo and behold! – Jordan Pinault. Leading to Jessi jumping at the chance to carry Thisbe's egg because it came with the Pinault seed. That egg became Evan. Then Jessi did it again. She was more than happy to host the egg that became the baby: Avery.

But the births had gotten harder and Jessi had gotten older. So she was happy when the Pinaults came, and she was happy when they left.

Jordan told the woman from the surrogacy agency that Thisbe had problems conceiving again, though past incidents and near-misses had proven quite the opposite. Thisbe once joked that she was more fertile than a tomato plant in summer – though not to Jordan. Her old girlfriends back home would say that Thisbe only needed to sit beside a man in a bar and she would get in the family way.

And actually, every part of Thisbe's pregnancy with Ever had come naturally to her: a great pregnancy, what her ObGyn called a *straight-forward, easy birth* – all things considered – with Jordan coaching her through it like he was on the field.

Regardless, Thisbe did not correct her husband at the initial surrogacy meeting when he told his story of Ever: telling of a problematic conception and birth.

Thisbe went so far as to correlate, calling Ever their *miracle*.

Thisbe had been four months along when she met him in a grocer's in Lubbock. She'd been studying the folic acid content in her favorite breakfast cereal, staring at the box, when he came over and pretended he had to reach past her for a pack of his own.

She'd had no makeup on, her hair wrapped in a bandana, her skin was briny with sweat when he introduced himself like he expected her to melt further. Though Thisbe knew to be standoffish, knew to pretend she didn't know who Jordan was. Knew that men like him liked that.

Like her old friends would have said: Thisbe girl, you could faceplant in shit and come up smelling of roses. It was true that she once got away with things. Her old friends said maybe it was because her mother, Glenna Hartfield, had died in childbirth, it meant Thisbe would have a blessed life.

Though this meant that Thisbe had no recollection of her mother. However, she could not choke down the thought that her birth had caused her mother's death, meaning Thisbe was just fine with renting a room in Jessi's uterus going forward.

At Lori's home, the women drank Arnold Palmers and munched on carrot and celery sticks. They were in their forties and older. They had been neighbors of Thisbe's for years though this was the first occasion they had socialized together, and only because Lori had ended up receiving a letter that had been posted in the wrong mailbox. She had returned it in person, along with an invitation for Thisbe to come to a girls' night in. She couldn't resist it.

Seriously, Thisbe, said Linda, the lawyer, as she sipped on her drink, I would kill someone for your figure.

No, you wouldn't, Thisbe replied. You better believe I looked like a boy growing up.

Holy cow! Killing someone for a figure, said Penny Lawhun, a single police officer who lived with her elderly parents.

Penny was poising herself for the needle in Lorcan's hand to iron out her crow's feet.

What a defense that would be, said Lorcan Butler, Lori's husband. They were both plastic surgeons. But you work out, he said to Thisbe while injecting Penny's face.

She noticed he had a way of asking a question as if he was relaying a fact.

She has three young daughters, Lorcan, said Lori. Thisbe has not got the time to work out.

But you run around after them kids, said Linda, the lawyer.

You don't work? asked Penny.

I work. I work like crazy, said Thisbe, the mother.

What at? asked Lorcan.

Lorcan, stop! said Lori.

Don't you have a nanny? asked Penny.

Nope, said Thisbe.

Oh, you really should, said Lori. You need help.

I do fine.

But what about *you*? asked Linda.

What about me? said Thisbe.

Thisbe thought about her father bringing her, her sister, and brother up without a mother, and without Jordan Pinault's money and house, *and* in a place where there was virtually nothing to do. These chicks were privileged and delusional.

Jordan is probably very good with the kids, said Lori. I'll bet he plays ball a lot with Ever.

Thisbe was impressed at how Lori had retained her children's names. She had lived next door to the couple for years without knowing theirs. But Thisbe was also disappointed that perhaps this was why they invited her here, to talk about him. That they only had an interest in her as the woman who slept in Jordan Pinault's bed.

174

Yes, Thisbe had gone and married the man, but despite that fact, she always found it hard to believe that he was a person who people still found interesting. Jordan seemed dull to her, or foolhardy, or forgetful. And when he was none of these things, he was a menace.

Sorry, we're hounding you, said Linda when Thisbe did not reply.

Is there alcohol in this? Thisbe sniffed her drink. She had expected expensive wine or extravagant cocktails.

No, it's just an Arnie, half lemonade, half iced tea. I need to keep a steady hand, said Lori. But if you would like something stronger?

The masseuse came to the door and called Linda in.

No, I'm good, said Thisbe. So, she thought, amused, this is the way old white chicks have fun. Filling their wrinkles in, paying people to rub them down.

I still get a kick out of that Super Bowl, Lorcan said, when Pinault strode down the field, then threw to Nwafo, then Nwafo scored that beautiful touchdown in the final minute. But he couldn't have done it without Pinault. It was a game beautifully controlled. Really was.

Yes, she said. She had heard it from so many men. People would come to their table when they used to eat out to tell him so. They would go into detail about that final minute, that stride, that magnificent partnership between two lifelong pals and their magic on the field, and she would know what they would say next, just not how they would say it, it was different every time, but the essence was the same: Ricky and he were a dream-team. Gods. Yadda yadda yadda.

You probably hate football, said Penny.

There was a time I enjoyed it, Thisbe said.

Lori nodded as if she understood what she meant.

175

Are you getting fillers? asked Lorcan, examining Thisbe's face.

Nope, she said.

She's a baby, said Lori.

It's preventative, said Lorcan. What age are you?

Twenty-seven, she said over the top of Lori, who was saying he shouldn't ask a lady her age. I look a little older. I was never asked for ID in a bar, not even when I was … young. Younger.

But you have great skin, so leave it alone, said Penny thoughtfully.

It made Thisbe think back to college, how many times Thisbe had heard that she was cute – for a black girl. How many times someone had asked to touch her hair. It made it hard to take their compliments, though they meant well. Thisbe was always suspicious of rich white people when they thought they were kind to her.

When Lorcan finished leaving punctures and left, and another masseuse called Penny into the room, Lori said: Do you ever look at the man you married and think, eurgh!

Hmm, said Thisbe. She looked closer at Lori.

Lorcan's a gambling addict, Lori said.

Really? asked Thisbe, sipping her drink. This is actually not that bad, she said.

Good, glad you're enjoying it. Lori paused. But yeah, he can't leave the casinos alone. Especially in Deadwood. And poker websites. My!

Well, he is a doctor, said Thisbe.

What do you mean?

They must be born risk-takers.

I'm a doctor, too. Should I be offended?

Oh, please no, said Thisbe.

So what should I do? Lori asked.

What *can* you do? Thisbe said.

Take more risks. Is that what you're saying?

I'm not saying that.

Before this, said Lori, it was women. Lorcan was a sex addict.

Well, addictions swap one thing for another.

What are you saying? Lori asked, her voice sounded fraught but she looked relieved that Thisbe was not surprised nor shocked.

So, he has an addictive personality. Thisbe gave a blasé shrug. You are way more intellectual than me, Lori. You'd know.

Women always did this, told her their deepest secrets. The first time she met the senators' wives, when their husbands got together and left them alone, and the political spittle began flying around in another room, a wife announced to Thisbe that she was leaving her husband. Another, separately, that she had been in touch with an old boyfriend on Facebook. Another was spending money in some way her husband would not like to know.

Thisbe got the feeling they saw her as free and as someone who would give them permission to take a leap they could not permit for themselves. Or maybe this was the way they all spoke to each other, and she was in no way exceptional. Just a bystander who happened to be in the vicinity during the airing out of a direction-less, internal monologue. Or fantasy.

Does Linda know? Thisbe asked.

About what? asked Lori.

The gambling, and Lorcan fucking these other women.

No, whispered Lori. She does not.

Penny?

Nor does Penny know.

Thisbe nodded.

So, do you want to know what I think?

Lori nodded.

Go place some bets with him, Thisbe said, let rip. Aren't your kids adults by now?

They're in college. Lori chewed her bottom lip.

And Lorcan's not fucking other women any longer? asked Thisbe.

She saw a spark in Lori's eye, like she liked her straight shooting.

Gosh, no, Lori said. He's recommitted to monogamy, Lori said. But actually, I feel like I should forgive Lorcan because it wasn't a love affair, nor was it an emotional … involvement, he swore. We have a healthy sex life, have it once a day. Does that sound normal to you, Thisbe? said Lori, fishing, Thisbe realized.

It's relative, she said, waving a hand, waiting on the, how often do you and Jordan go at it, that never came.

She wouldn't tell. How about never? Not in years. When they did, he was nasty about it, and she was no longer turned on by that.

Lorcan was sleeping with this married woman, said Lori, and others he'd met at a bar, and at the casino. Online, too. No one knows. Not that it's your problem. You're blessed that this kind of nonsense doesn't go down in your home. And what a home. It is gorgeous, Thisbe.

Oh, thanks, she said.

But it had gone down.

Before Thisbe's time, Jordan had been fooling around with MJ McCord, who had been married to an old codger. But that was not before Lori's time; she and Lorcan had lived in the Pine Hills for some time, including then, in the mid-90s.

Thisbe wondered if Lori still associated the house next door to hers with the death.

Thisbe had only found out about it when Jordan got a contractor out to build a neat little cabin that was just his in the garden, and the contractor had said to Thisbe: Gee, would ya look at this palace. Must be ten years since Mary Jane blew her head the fuck off here. Which room was that in? Thisbe was angry to not have been told. Angry that the contractor said it all juicy like that. Morbid as fuck.

Thisbe asked the mystic from the local paper to come exorcise the house. The mystic claimed she'd seen it coming. Read it in the stars years before or something.

Thisbe had even mentioned it to Ricky, but he had looked at her like she was some kind of devil worshipper, though she understood in him this self-righteousness over everything and everyone.

And Natasha, she told Thisbe that a girl had to do what a girl had to do, in that irritatingly deadpan, disinterested way of hers.

Natasha: the only friend Jordan liked her to have, but Thisbe would rather have none.

The masseuse let Penny out and told Thisbe to come in.

Thisbe stood in the beige therapy room and disrobed, lay on the table, and the masseuse stood over her. She poured oil on Thisbe's back, mashed at the knots with her elbows, touched the flanks of her body, which gave her a strange feeling.

It traveled out from her core, it traveled along her arms and her legs, it spread like fire around her groin, and to her very organ of skin, it was as if that skin became a hand that massaged the masseuse's hands in return.

She didn't know what came over her. One minute she was aroused, then she felt a feeling she had not allowed herself to feel, one that she had pushed down into her feet and ignored, like she used to ignore everything. Thisbe felt this great gulp surface through her, and Thisbe burst the bank of her emotions with a huge sob.

The masseuse did not react. She kept on massaging even more strongly. She tamped down on her shoulders, so her face was in the open headrest, her tears allowed to just fall on the cream carpets in Lori's house.

Her nose began to run. Thisbe tried to hide her emotion, but she knew that her body was deceiving her. Then the masseuse asked her if she wanted to sit up, and she gave Thisbe a tissue which she ran along the undersides of her eyes. She then blew her nose into it.

This is normal, the masseuse said, believe me. People who have been through trauma, this happens.

She was fishing too, perhaps, or maybe living a public life had opened out Thisbe more than she could bear. She sniffed and said: I've never had any trauma – well, some – but no more than anyone. I'm a tough bitch, usually. And I'm not a crier.

The masseuse wiped her hands and looked at Thisbe with her head cocked. Something is going on with you, but it's no bad thing. Crying's fine.

Thisbe nodded and said: Maybe. For some.

Are you happy in your life? she asked.

Thisbe didn't think twice when she said: No.

Where did that even come from? she thought. My life is perfect, she thought. She also believed that the masseuse had that same talent Thisbe did; she had always been able to draw people in.

But Thisbe knew better than to be drawn, and that just because the masseuse looked trustworthy didn't mean that she was. That was where people went wrong with her, trusting Thisbe with their boyfriends, until she had no girlfriends left. People opened up and let her in. And she would not let this woman in. She didn't need to.

Yes, there are bad points of my life, Thisbe recognized, but they are few, very few.

But they are also big and they are significant, she thought.

You would really benefit from yoga, the masseuse said.

I would?

Oh, you would. There is a collective for the Black Hills community, and you would be so welcome. I'll leave my card by the door.

*

Hey, Zo,

Something happened the other day and it made me think of you. I needed a photo of a cat and remembered you having a picture of Misty on your Facebook. It stuck in my mind because, c'mon, how long is that cat dead? Yeah, I could have Googled an image but there was a reason it had to be THAT CAT. I thought about you when I printed it off. I also thought about you when I went through your Facebook. Girl, don't be mad! We're sisters after all, aren't we? The closest, at one time.

I put the photo in a frame by my bedside, over my wedding photo. Thought you'd get a kick outta that. Took Jordan four days to notice. One morning, when I opened my eyes Jordan was standing over the bed, he was staring at the picture of the cat.

What in the hell is that? he asked me.

My eyes were hardly open at all.

That's ole Misty, I told him.

Who the fuck is Misty? he said.

Zoey's cat, I said, there was no flattering explanation.

He was miffed why I had this picture, asked if I'd reconciled with you.

It's a pussy shot, I said. Thought you'd like it.

Then I had to go into that story about how you used to feed her back in Hub City, how she left her family and came into ours. Yes, I know, I hated her. But you know ...

Why have you got this photo of a cat your bitch-sister had when she was a kid? said Jordan. (Don't be mad, you've called him worse.)

Because, I said, and I threw my left arm across the bed pointing to his side, pointed at the photo of Karma's big slobber-laced face. (Yes, Karma, the dog we used to have. Karma's been dead since about the time Avery was born. And Avery is now ten ... No, dang! Eleven months old. Born via surrogate, if you want to tell the press about that too.)

I just thought it droll though, to hold a mirror up, shine it back to him, all his ridiculousness.

Misty is staying there as long as Karma does, I told him.

Jordan looked at me with the same look our old principal gave me every time he caught me smoking behind the school gym, and on that occasion after me and Billy Jones had been found horizontal in the photographic darkroom. Anyway, you know the look, it would lead to consequences out of which I could not charm my way. That damn one.

You know how close that dog was to me, said Jordan. More family than family.

But he had this vacant look in his eyes that he gets. Stupid, up to a point. But not dumb. You know what I mean. You saw it before I did.

This is Avery's birth, 2:0, I told him, and he looked really confused, like he'd forgotten all that happened then.

Which was that he was with that punk dog and not with us, and that he looked so depressed when he came to meet us at the hospital.

Keep Karma there, Jordan, I said. Do what you like.

Are you sure, because I thought this was my house, he said. I thought that I paid for everything in here. I thought that I paid for your clothes. He grabbed my nightdress and pulled me closer. I wrapped my hands around his, awake now, understand. Then he let me go. Tell me, did I pay for this? He lifted a silk cushion from the bed and tore it apart. Did I pay for this? He lifted the pillow and did the same.

About then I walked out. I could not watch. I'm a guest in his house and so are the children. He chooses and pays for everything. You know me, Zo, I'm a gutter punk at heart. The old Thisbe would have replied: Yes, you bought it, you bought the most boujie bed linen because it makes you feel like someone to overpay, it's what you always do. You aren't punishing me by taking these things away. I come from nothing. Nothing.

And you know that's true, girl.

You're right, not that I like to admit it, I truly don't speak up when I should these days. He has himself convinced that if he thinks a thing, it makes it true. He's even convinced everyone else. I hear him often enough, when the senators call, or he speaks to Ricky on the phone, telling him that he has just purchased something ridiculous because She demanded he did. (I'm She.) And I pull a face and think to myself, No, boy. I did not. That's on you.

He left the bedroom and followed me to the kitchen. I'm fucked off, he said.

You're not the only one, I said.

Beverly's had a stroke and you're playing silly games. I had a call from Olivia Burgess. Said Bev might die. (This is the old senator — creep, if you want my opinion.)

Suddenly I felt incredibly immature.

I'm sorry, I know y'all are close, I said. And after breakfast I said, promise me one thing.

What's that? he asked.

If Bev dies, no pictures in the bedroom.

I was trying to lighten the mood, and Jordan frowned at me again, real dumb this time. But Karma can stay, that's fine, I said.

All that and for what? I blame you. You and your dumb pussy shots.

Thanks for fuck!
Your sis,
Thisbe H-P

Thisbe selected all of the text and then pressed delete, and closed her laptop.

*

She had just put the girls to bed when she said to him: I'm going to yoga tonight.

Yoga? he asked.

Yeah, yoga, she said. That's good, isn't it?

What if the girls wake? he said.

They won't, and I thought you'd appreciate it, being hella sporty and all.

Fine, he said, you could use some toning up. I'll hold the fort this once.

She walked into the hall and flipped him the bird through the wall.

A cab collected her at the bottom of the boulevard and brought her to Verboten bikers' tavern in Hisega, where she changed in the restrooms into the short red dress she had in her bag. This was how she used to deceive her father, the same trick.

She had two shots and two glasses of wine and did not talk to the punters. She knew they were looking at her like they recognized her, they most probably did, and right now, Thisbe did not care. She felt a thrill creep through her. This was exciting. Nothing had happened and it was still the most exciting night she had had in years.

So exciting, she went back the next week, then twice a week. Thisbe would go out and dance, step up her flirtation with the biker who always watched her like he could eat her up. He kept his distance. He wasn't what she had been looking for, but she was not sure that that was even true anymore. He felt like exactly what she needed.

The electricity in his eyes when their eyes met. She would get on the dance floor, she would walk past him to go to the restroom and she would stand reapplying her lipstick, waiting, more than a bit disappointed when he did not follow her inside and take it from her hand.

*

She had been ignoring the message in her inbox for months, and now the time was here, she absent-mindedly sent through payment for her ticket and sat back wondering what in the hell she had done. She was barely ever at school when it was time to go there, and now, in this life so far away, she had agreed to go back. *Paid* to go back.

She told Jordan that it was a chance to see her father. In Lubbock City, Texas, she sat in a cab and watched him watch TV wistfully alone. He lived for his TV programs and his kids. Everything else could go to hell. Then Thisbe decided that she liked him better on her turf. For him to feel like the uncomfortable one.

So she went to her hotel room where she decided that her difficult life was not a bad one, that it was held up in the center by a pole.

Mostly she was it, the thing that held everything up and together. Rarely she tumbled free into delight or into guilt. Thisbe thought to herself, how hard does life have to be, and how much of the hardness is really self-inflicted? And exhausted by these thoughts, she went to bed.

That night, like a shower of pepper, she dreamed of the leg of the man who had sat beside her on her flight. How he had not said a word to her but slept the whole time, letting his leg push against hers.

Remembering through her dream how she had stopped pulling away after a while, thinking, kiss me, wake up and kiss me. I don't care who you are. And in her sleep, she thought he had climbed astride her, and found her legs tightly swaddled in the hotel bedding when she woke, wishing she could have slept on.

*

You missed the Homecoming Pep Rally and Game, said Katiebeth Reyna in the foyer after breakfast. And also, you missed a nice dinner with drinks.

I had to spend some family time, said Thisbe.

Oh well, we still have the tour and afternoon dinner and catching up. Katiebeth smiled.

I don't know, said Thisbe. Sounds dull.

It won't be. Girl, you have that rock on your hand. Interesting rock …

Boulder opal, said Thisbe. Not really my thing.

Okay, fussy. At least everyone knows you made something of your life.

Katiebeth Reyna had freckled eyes and a head for heights. Her face was on billboards all over town, having her own real estate agency. Her husband Jerry was a local government official.

Who else is coming? Thisbe asked her.

Katiebeth looked at her clipboard and said a few names that didn't spark any recognition with Thisbe, and other names that bored her.

Daryl Rollo.

He's a nerd, said Thisbe, remember how into comics he was? Bet he still is. Bet he's a virgin and lives with his mother. Or not … Bet he has sex with his mother.

His mother's dead, I believe, but yes, he lives in the same house he grew up in.

I didn't offend you, did I?

No. Katiebeth smirked. Jerry and I have our own place now. And, yes. Daryl Rollo is a nerd.

So, who else you got for me?

Sugar Torres …

He was hot! said Thisbe.

Still is. And he's still with Jen. Remember they were high school sweethearts?

Thisbe thought about the encounters she'd had with Sugar while Jenny was at college. About his long dirty hair and beautiful hands. And Jen is coming, too? she asked.

Katiebeth looked at her clipboard. Yes.

Hmm. You know what? Sounds good. I have some things to do, and then I'll meet you there.

I thought maybe we could ride in together.

I know, but …

Oh, okay, said Katiebeth shadily. Look, just in case it is mad hectic later, it's been good to see you, she said and reached out for a hug.

Yeah, you too, girl, said Thisbe. But I'll see you later.

Okay, but in case we don't, stay in touch, okay?

That's a given, said Thisbe, but I'll see you … later. She pointed at Katiebeth and waited for her to leave, then she slipped her rings into her purse and walked aimlessly around in downtown Lubbock in the June weather, her sunglasses on to not be recognized. Still worried about walking into her sister or brother, she eventually slipped into a dark Broadway sports bar.

Thisbe Hartfield. I haven't seen you around in years, said the man behind the bar shuffling ice into a glass. She pulled up a stool, set her sunglasses on her head, and looked at Billy Jones.

I'm back for our reunion, she told him.

Which reunion?

It is all over Facebook, Friends Reunited, everything.

That's another language you're speaking, said Billy. So, when is it starting?

Hours ago. Now.

He laughed. Wouldn't have thought that was your scene.

It's not, clearly.

I don't kick it with the old crew, neither.

Just because people once went to school together, what does that mean? asked Thisbe. That they are friends or something? I'll take a tequila if you're serving.

One minute. He brought a cocktail to a student at the end of the bar.

He poured the tequila for Thisbe. She downed it, he topped it up and she downed another. Then he opened a wine cooler and set it on the counter. He remembered her old favorite. Needless to say, it was no longer her preference, but she smiled, settled and chimed the bottle against his glass of water that he raised in salutation to seeing her, his old friend.

If that is what they were.

She sat drinking at the bar, talking to Billy when a boy from a group of college football players said: Hey, you're Mrs. Jordan Pinault, aren't ya?

What in the world are you talking about? she said in a faux British accent.

The boy apologized, looked tangled and moved on. Thisbe was thankful Billy didn't seem to hear. He was not conventionally handsome – he was rough as guts, sharp in places. But when she was drunk, he always looked picturesque and unsolvable. And she was getting tipsy.

She stayed and had a plate of ribs, then stayed longer until everyone else had left.

You'd think you have no home to go to, Billy said.

Tonight, I don't, she replied.

So, what do you do these days, tell me, he asked her.

I'm a doctor, she said, a plastic surgeon.

Really?

I'm starting my own practice, said Thisbe.

I was gunna have some blow, but now I can't.

You can do what you please.

I won't expect you to join in, now that you are all sensible. Billy looked her up and down and seemed sincere. Next he'd be addressing her as ma'am, maybe… if they had not already fucked all those times. The thought of those times set her lips abuzz. But more than that, the thought that he was not just playing along with her, but that believed that Thisbe Hartfield was someone – someone successful in her own right – got her hot.

Billy took a ten-dollar note from the cash register and waved it over a thick line of coke on the counter. Thisbe almost took the bill, then she remembered that she was a mother and could not partake.

She remembered the first time she had taken coke with Billy twelve years before. He had complained that his head was sore and that he was going out for air, and did she want to come. She'd thought to herself, this means sex. A yes to this question means a yes to sex, even though that had not been on his mind.

She knew that she must only go off with a man if she was prepared that this was the destination. She had learned that twice in her life.

If she said yes and then changed it to no, it was too late. Some guy had his hand wrapped tight around the back of her head (who she punched in the jaw as soon as she could; and a month later, so as not to be the main suspect, put all his possessions and cell number in the Ads for Free, advertising him for gay sex.)

Another guy got turned on when she told him she was not ready to go all the way. She wouldn't give him the satisfaction of saying no a fourth time, so she bit him, scratched him. Then she was lovey-dovey to him after, wrapping her arms around his neck and asking to meet up again.

He had looked at her as if she was insane, the word for what he had just committed forming in his mind. She could tell because he was apologetic, but not for the right thing. He was suddenly tame and trying to quickly get away. She got him back good too; she saw him in a bar with a girl, a girl he liked and treated better, Thisbe could just tell, and she told the girl he had given her friend Katiebeth a unique mélange of STIs.

She had been bold like that. Then Thisbe changed, her heart had been broken, and her mind opened.

She had been expecting her first daughter with a man she loved when he walked out and left her because he wasn't ready for it. But neither was she.

Then there was Jordan. Then life fell into place. Maybe not the right place. To Thisbe, South Dakota was hokey, flyover country. Who was she kidding? Rapid was better than Lubbock.

She initially found the panhandlers fascinating, and the drunk and drugged Sioux men, young and old, they hung around the multistory parking lot. She found the men incredibly beautiful.

And she got why they drank. Thisbe had once stayed in the city for a few days alone, after her first fight with Jordan. She found herself drinking too much just to get through, going to Elks Cinema night after night, just to sit in company. Just to get a laugh out of her day.

Thisbe would walk the streets then, but now it depended on how badly she needed to, and the time of day it was, how dark it was, how deserted.

Now she would only park in clear view and would not take her girls anywhere off the main block when the need arose to go downtown.

And the whole City of Presidents thing! Every former president stood life-sized on the sidewalks, how she hated to turn her back on them. They were always watching her through their bronzed eyes. And the patriotic overload: a presidential pawnshop, the Founding Fathers Museum. Mount Rushmore trickling outward. Thisbe found it all cute, to begin with.

But outside of there, twenty minutes in any direction, and the place was freaking beautiful. Sylvan Lake. How the summer sun hit the mica on Needles Highway and made it glitter and glossed. Cycling with the girls on the Mickelson Trail. Pulling up on the Highway lookout and seeing Nebraska at one side, Wyoming on the other. A day trip east to the Badlands, with those layered rock formations and rugged pinnacles, you could be on Mars.

And if you wanted to shop, and really shop, not art, not vintage clothing, not patriotic memorabilia, but tags, there was always a quick flight to Chicago. Or New York. So she flew, but she always came back to South Dakota, not Lubbock. The place wasn't hers, but she wanted it. It had her heart.

That first night with Billy and with coke, and his wanting to escape the noise and go outside, she weighed up quickly and told Billy she would go with him, and he had stood with his head against the wall, suffering a genuine headache.

Thisbe had been both relieved and disappointed that he had not tried it on with her. Not that first time. After that night, if she did not get a man, Billy was it. She might have lifted his hand and put it up her thigh, and he would know. He needed permission like that, clearance she would not have customarily granted, and this was a quality in a man that she could admire at the time.

How times had changed. Now she wanted a man who could not control himself with her, who found her irresistible, as she had initially thought her husband had, but maybe she had been his alarm to adulthood: this woman is ready, cute, downtrodden, fun, pregnant, she'll do. This was more than likely what he'd thought. And she had thought, Jordan wants me, he's sexy, he's confident as hell. His money doesn't hurt. Thisbe looked at the second line of coke, took a hundred-dollar bill from her purse, and rolled it up.

A Benjamin! Nah, you're fancy now, said Billy.

She ingested the coke, and pulled Billy Jones to her, and kissed him. He smelled sweaty and foul, and she wondered how she had ever made herself fit him or any of these other men in her past. And even the one in her present.

192

She held her face to the side, letting Billy kiss her neck and wrap his arms around her waist. She pushed him gently back.

I'm gunna give you surgery, she said, tell me, what you want done.

Is this a consultation?

Okay, yes.

Why do people not just get old gracefully?

You're not old. You're a baby.

That's cute, he said. Okay. My nose is kinda big. I used to hate it; it's who I am now.

You are not your nose.

Then what am I?

What was he? she thought. She couldn't think.

So, you wouldn't change anything, said Thisbe, is that what you're saying, Billy Jones?

I wouldn't change a thing, no. He stretched out in his seat and looked at the clock above the bar. We aren't gunna fuck, is that correct?

Thisbe laughed. You've got much better at reading the signs.

Why do there have to be signs? Why can't I just ask outright?

You can, she said. That's probably good practice.

I think so, he said, and I don't want to be harsh, but it's late, and if we aren't gunna fuck, maybe you should go home.

So, you don't want to?

I don't think you do.

Oh, I do.

But not with me. They looked at each other silently until the moment was gone. I have a girl I can call, he said.

A booty call? she asked, thinking, God, Thisbe you are missing out on everything.

193

And she burned with jealousy.

*

When she returned home, Jordan asked if she'd been with another man. Thisbe just moved her jaw about and killed the lights behind her eyes in reply. She was starting to learn how to keep secrets from him and found it a good exercise for her. The best one she'd found yet. She had lived through so many embarrassing situations and came home to tell him about them, yet when he went anywhere, did anything, she could hardly get any information from him.

How was the senate's dinner?

It was good.

The end.

She thought that the talk of yoga, of stretching and positions, would make Jordan thirst for her again. And boy, had he.

Once. She often thought that he loved fucking her so much that he wanted her to die while he was inside her. That he wanted to fuck her to death. That stopped being cute long ago.

Then she thought of the Butler's next door, of Lori trying out the Kama Sutra and all sorts of fantasies to lure Lorcan back to her, that they were probably fucking that minute, their wrinkled bodies folding into each other, Lori's plumped-up lips working Lorcan's skinny, gets-about cock while he thought of blackjack.

Jordan hired a nanny so he could go out, or go to bed, or to his study, or his man cabin in the garden, so someone else could do the bedtime routine. And Thisbe went to the bar, sitting where she usually did with Ginger and her daughter Antonya, who were both dating bikers.

Ginger dated Mac, and Antonya dated Armie. And Thisbe sat in their company and drank and the women talked about life, but nothing personal. Ginger with her scaly eyelids, and preference for green eye shadow that together looked crocodilian. And Antonya with her wiry muscled arms, and pruny smoker's mouth. They talked about what they thought of things, about situations friends of theirs had gotten themselves into, friends who may or not be their friends, and may or not be themselves. They ate peanuts and talked about the trouble that the gang was getting in. The Marcach gang filed into the bar. They were raucous, and straight away, Thisbe felt more at home than at home, certainly more at home than she had done that time in Lori Butler's house or any bar in Lubbock, with all the ghosts of her past and her lost promise swarming all around her.

Ginger asked her her name, and she told her she was called Thisbe.

Is that an old family name? Your grandma's or something similar? asked Ginger.

No, she said.

Thisbe always hated her name.

When people asked if she was named after someone, it was their way of saying it was an ugly name, so she thought about that too, how she was even surprised she had given her real name up. How sometimes she slipped up when keeping secrets; she was still an amateur.

Then there was Stone; she learned his name from Antonya. Ephraim Shea, his proper name. Thisbe often stood beside him at the bar. They had still not spoken.

A couple of times she had danced with one of the older men and had Stone watch her. He was a man like Jordan, who you could just not picture dancing.

195

Stone was staring, a look that was so intense it both scared her and thrilled her.

For three months, two nights a week, she and Stone had something. After, she would come home, relieve the nanny, who could tell she was drunk. Thisbe would have a quick coffee, no cream, spray her breath with mint spray and get into her pajamas and roll her dress up, put it into the back of her drawer. She would pretend to be asleep when Jordan would get to bed.

She knew that she reeked of drink the next morning and so started talking pills instead, although she did not need anything other than the freedom to get her off.

One night she was getting a glass of water in Verboten Clubhouse when Stone turned to her and finally spoke. Water, really? he'd teased her.

What's wrong with water?

Thought you were a party girl.

Sometimes you need water, you know. She looked at his beer.

He watched her, they sat side by side, he held his leg against hers. She turned to him and he took her face, and kissed it. She pulled away and looked him in the eyes.

He walked off, and she waited a minute, then followed him down the hall. He was standing in the doorway of the store cupboard. She walked toward him. He didn't have to ask if she was happy to compromise. This was the most uncompromised she had ever felt. She gave in to the temptation with Stone, there in the storeroom, not planning to tell Jordan a thing after.

But finding him awake and reading when she returned home in her dress, so shocked herself by what she had done, Thisbe instantly told him what happened, because she was unsober. And an amateur.

Not even good at keeping a secret.

His reaction was not the surprise. When he got aggressive and nasty, and she apologized. But he goaded her, not accepting that she had been a willing participant in fucking Stone Shea. Jordan turned her past on her. That men had pushed her too far, and that she had not reported them. He did that, made her always sorry for trusting him with secrets, using it as ammunition.

But she'd changed, she told him. He had made her change, she thought. And later, unthought when she considered how he reacted in the bedroom, their girls asleep in their rooms until they woke crying.

He had physically kicked her until she was down, tore her clothing off. Even her underwear. Then he called the RCPD, saying his wife had come home claiming to have been attacked by Stone Shea. Raped, he said, let me be clear.

Then Jordan lay calmly on the bed and exhaled, lifted his book, and waited for a couple of officers to arrive as Thisbe cried and held a towel to her bloodied face, and the girls woke up and came running, screaming, into her room.

Lions, Liars and Bears – Oh My!

1995

There is only this one dog left. Offseason, Jordan flies to South Carolina just to look at him. He has told himself he will not part with his cash if the dog is not up to scratch or a runt.

Jordan gets off the plane and is driven to the breeder's house, a short-ways off the interstate to a modest three-bed in the suburbs. The first thing he hears is the howling coming from out the back as he walks up to the front door. The homeowner, a middle-aged man, answers the ringing doorbell and welcomes Jordan with an ever-growing smile.

Jordy Pinault? Are you seriously Jordy Pinault standing at my door?

The man calls over his teenage son, who looks blankly at their guest.

It's Pinault, Number Eight, quarterback for the Arizona Cardinals, the man says.

The son, who is about sixteen, pauses his Walkman, says hello rather loudly, then walks off, his head bobbing to a tune Jordan cannot hear.

Probably didn't hear me. He's more of a baseball fan, the man says.

I'm here to see a man about a dog, Jordan says.

You are. That's precisely what you're doing. Come in. Come in.

Two girls, maybe thirteen, fourteen years of age, are lounging on the couch in the living room.

Their father, throws a cushion at them, he throws it too hard for Jordan's benefit, and the corner catches the dark-haired girl in the eye.

Get up and make yourselves respectable, the man says to both girls.

You hit me in the eye, the dark-haired girl cries, but the light-haired girl catches sight of Jordan and her jaw drops.

Okay, sorry, the man says, keen to move on but the first girl cries on about her eye until the man snaps, telling her to go and get some ice for it, if it's so bleeding bad.

It is swelling, and watering too. It does look painful, thinks Jordan.

Grudgingly the girl heeds her father's advice and leaves the room.

Hey! Are you Jordan Pinault? asks the older sister, maybe fourteen. She is wearing a tie-dyed tee with white jeans, her hair is dyed an icy blonde with bangs cut in, they are hanging around her pretty little face.

Well, yes, Jordan says acting faux-coy, though he'll never stop getting a buzz out of being recognized.

This guy, says the man, was the reason the Cardinals won the Super Bowl. Truly. You and Nwafo ... in that final minute. Dynamite! Turned everything all the way around. I've never seen a game like it, and I'm a Panthers man myself.

Thank you, that's very kind, says Jordan.

Go fix Mr. Pinault a drink, says the man. What are you drinking, Mr. Pinault?

Oh, Jordan, please.

Jordan, you wanna beer?

Yeah, sure, if it's no trouble.

It is not. Angeline! the man shouts down the hall to the daughter with the sore eye. Get Jordan a beer.

Jordan can hear Angeline tell someone, her brother perhaps: Dad just hit me in the eye with a cushion.

The man rolls his eyes. Angeline, you got that? he shouts.

Yes, a beer. Got it! Jordan can hear she is clenching her teeth.

The other daughter straightens herself up and Jordan lets his smile skim the room. People always remember that after he's gone, he thinks. They remember that he smiled, and they take it personally even if he was just smiling at everything in their vicinity.

The dog starts barking outside. Is that the beast I hear? he asks.

Oh, yeah, that's your boy, says the man.

Karma, says the blonde daughter who is not Angeline.

What's that? asks Jordan.

She gives him some hippy-dippy name, explains the man. Hippy everything. It's a phase, I like to think.

It's a pretty name on him, says the daughter and Jordan nods.

Angeline, shouts the man. Let Karma in.

200

The dog comes bounding into the room, he is as high as Jordan's waist on all fours. Three-quarters his end height already. He jumps up, standing he is almost as tall as Jordan.

Down there, boy, the man says. Karma! He pulls the dog by the collar.

He's good. Jordan laughs. He rubs Karma behind each ear.

Likes you.

So why was he left? He's a brute.

He wasn't the runt or anything, says the man. He was the best, that's why he's more on the expensive side. Folk ain't got that sort of cash, so we held on to him a little longer. His two siblings went quickly, but this stud is top dollar.

The blonde daughter stands up and rakes her fingers through the dog's fur.

Stop it, Lana, says her father. Listen, if you want him to be a guard dog, he tells Jordan, like security, he's still young, he can do it. These girls of mine have him soft as a frog's belly but he can have that knocked out of him. These dogs are like the gods of the dog world. Just look at that majestic face.

Jordan lets the dog lick his face and he laughs.

They're mountain dogs, says Lana.

I did a bit of reading up, says Jordan.

Truth is, he has not. This guy here is the priciest dog you can get and that is most of the appeal.

Lana smells like incense, her hand slides against Jordan's when she strokes the dog. She pulls away and smiles at him.

Isn't he cute? he asks her.

He sure is, she says, her eyes zipping about, looking at his mouth. He could snap his fingers and she would be his.

The dog sits at Jordan's feet. You didn't train him to do that, did you? he asks Lana.

Nope, she says real coy, not pretending.

Karma is Tibetan for star, says Angeline handing him a beer and holding a wet towel to her swollen eye. But you can change the name if you want.

Something that sounds similar though, please, says Lana, or he'll be confused.

No, Karma's good, says Jordan. I like your name choice.

Call him anything you like, says the man, and ignore these two witless horrors. Christ Jesus, Angeline! A bottle opener. How do you expect Jordan to drink his beer?

Angeline takes a bottle opener from her pocket and shakes it at her father. She too turns coy when she has to put it into Jordan's hand, so he gives her a slight smile that is just for her, just for her and her good eye.

*

First thing he does when he gets home is to hire a professional handler. The handler teaches Karma how to behave and takes the bad habits from the mastiff. She advises Jordan to bring Karma to conformation. At his first dog show, the pup can hardly stand still and the handler prances around with him, leash held high in her hand, and everyone is mesmerized by Karma.

He is not a poodle with a bow in his hair, but he is so heavenly.

A good dog beneath his mischievous demeanor and hijinks, he comes third in his category.

At the end of the month, Jordan drives to North Dakota for another conformation show, and prances about himself, leash held high in his hand.

He also stands talking to the other contestants with their possessive competitiveness that he has only ever seen on the playing field before: Men and women, usually much older than him, retirees mainly, but people he would not usually bond with, and they all have stories about their canines. They love them, that is for sure. They groom them to within an inch of their patience. They talk with Jordan about something other than football, with a little bit of football thrown in.

When Karma is awarded Best in Show in North Dakota, Jordan parades that animal with his red rosette and has a goofy smile on his face that he cannot get off. The whole way home, he talks in a sweet baby voice to the dog, telling him he will get a steak that night, that he will cook him filet mignon, that he is the best boy, Jordan's chest swelling with pride.

This night he has a party to celebrate Karma's win, although Jordan is hesitant to have guests around his treasured pet.

This is like your baby. Your son, says Ricky. He laughs. Beverly laughs. They tell Jordan he is smitten.

Then the usual broads come around and they are afraid of the dog, apart from this one girl, Helena. A senior at high school. She walks straight over and hugs the dog as he tells her all about his day, and shows her the Best in Show rosette.

Wow, Helena says, that is pretty neat? Aren't you neato? Real special, she says to Karma, who goes and gets into his dog-bed yawning.

He's usually super spunky and playful, Jordan says.

But it's after his bedtime? asks Helena.

It is. Bless his heart.

Jordan says they should go into the lounge and after putting a blanket over the dog, he dims the lights in the room and lowers the music in the lounge.

He has a beer and looks to his left to find Helena still standing there as if she does not know anyone else at the party. But he is waiting for his girl.

No show? asks Bev.

Jordan says: Not tonight.

I'm gunna hit the road if that is the case, Bev says. But Helena still remains. By the end of the night, Jordan decides she has shown commitment, that counts for something, and when she is in the middle of telling him something utterly anticlimactic about herself, he kisses her on the lips. Afterward, she, like a moron, says: I've been waiting all night for that.

Really, he says, I admire your confidence.

She narrows her eyes at him.

We have done this before, a couple of times, she says.

I know, I remember, Jordan says, but he does not, which gets him to thinking about the years in which Ricky's grandfather Miguel had dementia. Miguel would call Ricky's mother Delma his *abuelita*, and call Ricky his *padre*, and yet he would see his wife Mapy and, with no confusion, say: You are beautiful, estas bella, let me take you out sometime. And he would mention someplace in the old country where he would have taken her, Jordan recalls now, and Mapy would say: At least there's that! Wouldn't it be worse if he now didn't like me?

Jordan must be like that too, he thinks, to still be attracted to Helena even if he doesn't remember her from before.

There have been a lot of girls, especially when he was at school in Memphis. He has lost count. He and Ricky kept tally, competed to see who could get the most notches on their bedposts. Then it was no longer fun and they stopped counting.

Some girl would develop feelings and think they were in a relationship.

But now he has a girl. She is the reason Jordan is performing so well. She is the reason he works out, the reason he thinks of nothing but being his best.

He won't define what they have, and he'd rather she was here, though she is not. There are always backup girls like this one, Helena, who is looking at him with hearts in her eyes. If they have kissed three times then that is two times too many.

I'm sorry, he says after the latest lip-lock. I'm gunna go mingle. See, I don't want to look rude to my guests. And really, this is Karma's night.

He ignores her for the rest of it, even when she gets high and wraps her arms around Ricky's neck, which chicks always do, flirting with one bro to make the other bro jealous. It doesn't work. They have boy code: One can walk past the other and say: Green, meaning: Go ahead, she's yours. Or: Red. Or: Did you see that new *red* sweater I got? Something like that, and the other one gets the hint and stays away.

*

After an early start and too much thought, he spreads himself on the hotel bed and looks at the ceiling. The pillows have given him a crick in his neck, which has crept into his back and around his hips, down his sciatic nerve. It helps to lie flat as he lifts the receiver of the phone.

How are you? he asks when she answers his call.

Just fine, she says.

I know it's early. Actually, no, it's later back home, right?

I don't know where you are … it's 10 a.m. here.

I missed you at the party.
Oh, you did? she replies.
I really wish you could be here.
Really?
Of course.
Thank you.
Guess where I am?
Where?
I'm in Kauai.
Oh, really?
Do you know where that is?
Hawaii?
Well done! An island of. It's really beautiful.
That's nice.
I'm thinking about you a lot.
That's nice.
It's nicer than nice.
I mean that.
Are you thinking about me?
Sure.
I bet you are not.
No, I am.
What are you thinking?
About you.
You're funny. What are you thinking about me?
Wondering where you are.
Now you know.
Yep. I do.
The skies are real blue. Can you hear the ocean?
I think so.
Have you ever been near the ocean?
Nope.
You'd like it.
Yeah, I guess so.
You would.

I guess.

You're funny.

Thanks.

You're real quiet. Are you on your own?

Erm, yeah. Kind of.

Is someone near you? he asks.

I suppose, she says.

Okay, so you can't talk openly?

That's right.

But you can listen?

I guess.

I want to bring you here one day. It's nice. Nicer than nice – he waits for her to laugh and she doesn't – I woke, and I don't know why, but I had the blues. Do you know what I mean by that?

Sure.

What I mean by having the blues is that I was feeling down. I'm here. I'm on my own.

Oh.

Are you relieved to hear that?

Sure.

Sure! You are too much, babe. He shuffles about the bed and rearranges his pillows. I woke up, he says. I heard the waves crashing, then I went for a run on the beach and I had breakfast. I got a dog. I haven't seen you in a while, but I'd booked this vacation before I got him. He's real beautiful. And big.

Oh? He got a name?

Karma.

That's real nice.

Know what I've been thinking?

What?

If you like dogs.

Sure.

He's a Tibetan Mastiff, he's a beaut for real. I think you'd like him. Most girls find him threatening. What do you think?

I think he sounds nice.

I knew you weren't like most girls ... I didn't pick his name. That was the name he had. I didn't want to confuse him, you know.

Is he old?

Only six months or so.

He sounds nice.

He's huge, probably bigger than you on his hind legs.

I am not so small.

No, I know, but he's big, is what I mean. Huge head. I miss him.

That's ... kind of sad.

Yeah. I think that's why I had the blues. Then there is this ... being out here on my own.

Oh.

I thought some time alone would be nice, but there's no one to talk to. It gets lonely.

Uh-huh, she says.

I miss you too, I suppose, he says.

Oh ...

Do you know what I miss?

Sure.

Is he about? Now? Is he listening in?

Oh, not him, someone, but not him.

Her?

Yep ...

You do like me, don't you?

Sure.

I just wanted to hear it, being here, being alone, missing my dog. I just wanted to hear that someone somewhere misses me.

I do.

You do?

Sure.

You aren't just saying that? It's just that sometimes it's hard to tell. Sometimes it feels like I'm someone you'd miss. Other times, I start to question what you're feeling.

She doesn't reply.

Have you anything to add? he asks.

What like? she says.

It's good, isn't it?

Yes. She sighs.

Are you looking forward to seeing me again … as much as I'm looking forward to seeing you?

Sure … I am. Yep.

That's good. I don't feel blue anymore. I feel lifted up now, you know. I can go and enjoy my day. There'll be a party when I get back home, you'll be there, won't you? Tell him, see if he'll bring you. He'll be happy to oblige, I'm sure.

Alrighty.

Maybe I'll call him.

Sure. If you want.

Are you looking forward to seeing me again?

Yes.

You know I'm looking forward to it, don't you?

Sure.

I'm gunna start calling you *Sure*.

She laughs.

See you soon, Sure.

Alrighty. Have a good day … vacation.

Jordan leaves his Princeville hotel room and walks to the reception carrying his pillows. He asks the receptionist her name.

Cher, she says.

Like the singer? he asks.

Like the singer, she says, only wish I could sing like her.

He asks Cher if he can have another pillow. The pillows are made and stacked for short-shouldered people with worry-free heads. He wants something different, at least an option.

Some special treatment.

These are the only pillows we have. Cher goes on typing. Would you like one more?

No, he says. I want you to try one.

She gazes up at him again, her brow pinched with irritation. Anything else I can do for you?

You can arrange me a trip. I want to go at eight o'clock this morning to Kapaa ...

The taxi service will begin at nine, I can book you in then.

No, I said eight.

The phone rings. Excuse me a moment.

He gives Cher her a moment and then he rings the bell. She asks her colleague to come out from the back room and deal with him. When the man gets to Jordan, Jordan tells him: I am dealing with Cher, thank you.

The man frowns at his colleague and says: Sir, is there something I can help with?

Absolutely not, says Jordan.

Eventually, Cher puts the phone down, and the man remains nearby putting letters into envelopes, listening.

Call me a cab now, says Jordan. He looks at his watch, it is seven-thirty.

Okay, she says, but it will not come until 9 a.m. when the driver's shift begins.

He walks back to sit down in the foyer so that he can watch her as she works.

He notices that she does not return his gaze once, and he thinks it rude.

When finally the taxi comes, he goes to old Kapaa town. The taxi driver gives Jordan his personal number and says he can call him directly any time, when Jordan explains the problems he had with Cher.

Oh, she's a grump since she parted ways with her boyfriend, says the taxi driver.

Oh really, says Jordan, tell me some more about that.

Jordan has some lunch out with a few drinks, he watches honeymooners on the beach path, the looks on their faces is gladness. He prickles. He goes to a jeweler and purchases two necklaces, both gold, both with a boulder opal pendant. One necklace has a little offset diamond and the other one a bright pink ruby.

The jeweler jokes with him: One for your wife and one your mistress?

My girlfriend and my mother, he says, lying, putting both boxes in his pocket.

Jordan phones the taxi driver to come get him, and he brings him back to the hotel. The male receptionist is there.

Where is Cher? Jordan asks him.

She is off her shift. She is home, sir.

Can you put this in the safe for me?

I will do that.

I was a jerk earlier, says Jordan

That's fine, sir. The receptionist smiles, nodding approvingly.

Jordan goes to dinner happy, he will call the driver at 6 a.m. to bring him the market in the morning where he will buy Cher a bunch of yellow hibiscus.

He will give them to her just as she comes on shift, and he will say sorry, he will tell Cher to look in the safe, and she will. Then she will find the necklace then wrap her arms around him, thank him in all kinds of ways. She'll go out of her way to find special pillows that he will enjoy.

*

They are in Jordan's home looking out at the canyon when Beverly asks: So, how was Hawaii?

He is leaning on the pool table in the glass and wood-beamed dining room.

Good, says Jordan. Been back a while.

We went to rehab in Phoenix in July, when he got back, says Ricky.

Don't you boys live the life! says Beverly.

Notice he's lost a few lbs, says Ricky.

Yes, you're in good shape, Jordan, says Beverly.

If that shape is an orange, then yeah, says Ricky. I'm joking.

We golfed in the afternoons, says Jordan. In the mornings, we'd have a game of 7 on 7 practice, run the length of the grounds.

Galloping and whooping, says Ricky. Nylon clinging. He pats Jordan's stomach.

Quit that! I lost sixteen pounds.

I know. You're a charging bull now. You know that song, the Elvis one, hunk-a-hunk-a-burning love? He wrote that for you.

They all laugh.

So, you can have your fried chicken later and I'll grill mine, says Jordan.

I went skiing at …, says Beverly, the one up north. Shoot! I can't think of it.

Steamboat?

There you go. It wasn't as good snow as Montana.

We're gunna go, says the music producer, making his way over. South of Billings – Red Lodge. President's Day weekend, kids have a day off either side of the weekend.

Colorado is great skiing, says Jordan.

Have you been to Red Lodge? The town is unique. Everyone brings their dogs in. They work sheep all summer and in the fall they are drunk, playing cards.

I know an eye doctor, says Beverly. She's like, a lot of really big money. Her people like it there.

I would worry about the bears. The Ghost Bears, says Ricky looking at Celena, who is on the couch watching him. She is smiling slowly, her eyes are closing. There she goes, he says. Fast asleep.

I don't know why you let her come here, mutters Burgess.

But you're a huge supporter of them, Bev, or no? says Jordan.

There are answers and there are interview answers.

I'm getting media-trained for the team, says Jordan.

Everything is utilitarian. For your off-the-field issues? asks Beverly.

I've heard both ways, says Ricky, about the bears, some people think, they're there, and that's fine.

It's okay, says the music producer. Mountain lions are like that for me. It's okay to watch the bears, but it's kind of unnerving after dark, waiting for the guide to come back.

They kill you to eat you, says Jordan.

I did not know that, says Ricky. I did not know that.

But yeah … says Jordan looking at Celena. What I could do to her. All bad.

Her? Nah, says Beverly.

Isn't she MJ's friend? says the music producer.

She is, and I think she's cute, says Ricky.

Hell no, says Jordan.

That's not to say I would go there, says Ricky, asleep or awake. I mean, definitely not asleep. But not awake either … probably.

I think MJ's here now, says the music producer.

Jordan looks at Ricky. I'll do the honors, shall I?

It's your home, man, Ricky says.

After Jordan speaks to MJ's husband, John goes back indoors where the music is pumping and people are talking, and everything pauses while Senator Burgess gives a speech about the overnight success of MJ's song. He says she is a sure talent and that she, like Ricky and Jordan, is a star: Names that will forever be associated with their state.

Beverly asks MJ if she will sing, and MJ agrees. But Jordan has to leave the room, thinking he might get the church giggles again, which he always does when he sees her trying to take herself seriously. He hates it when females do that.

Jordan goes and stands alone in the kitchen and Ricky comes to him at the end.

Thanks for hosting this, man, he says. I really do appreciate it.

You know I'd do anything for you, bro, Jordan says.

Their private party starts later, once the ramblers, business-makers and hangers-on have done their day's work and play and fizzled out.

Jordan hears the rev of the Harley and goes outside, there is Stone Shea, his little cousin getting off the back of the bike. She comes into the kitchen and sets her helmet on the side counter. The dog comes over.

Hi, Karma, she says, patting him on the head.

She does not have any real interest, Jordan considers that she looks intimidated. Disappointing. Those leonine eyes of hers are fear-filled.

She takes a flute of champagne from Jordan but jumps when Beverly come in through the back door.

Hello, Bebe, he says.

Hello, says the girl.

You having a good night?

Yeah, she says, pretending to sip the champagne.

I just saw your chaperone out front, settled up. Beverly nods at Jordan.

Trouble out there? asks Beverly.

What? asks Jordan.

Some tiff, or other.

Jordan opens the window and sees Ricky and Mary Jane talking. They look away when they see him. Ricky looks like he is on the verge of tears. The only time Jordan has ever seen him like that.

Everything okay, you reckon? says Beverly.

No, says Jordan. I don't reckon so.

Why don't you go run yourself a bath, sweet? Beverly asks the girl.

Sounds good, says Bebe, pausing, holding out her champagne flute, about to ask whether she is allowed to take the drink upstairs. Jordan is usually particular about such things – mess and whatnot – but tonight he is distracted. Bev misunderstands and tops the glasses up, so she walks upstairs, taking it with her, drinking it rather than spilling it.

After five minutes, Beverly says he will go see how she is. He lifts a bowl of strawberries from the icebox and takes a pill from the medicine cupboard. Jordan stands in the kitchen, he listens out of the window.

Ricky is crying now. You don't care about me, Mary Jane, he is saying.

I don't care about you? I'm only obsessed with you, Eric.

It doesn't look like it.

I am.

Jordan can hear that Mary Jane is crying, too.

Tell me.

I am telling you.

I can't get you out of my mind, Ricky says.

What am I supposed to do?

Do you love me?

Yes, I love you.

Then marry me.

I'm married, Eric.

He'll understand, you said yourself, he only wants to see you happy.

I *am* happy. I love John, I really do.

Mary!

It goes silent. Jordan leaves the downstairs toilet door ajar, so no one will come upstairs. He doesn't trust that Lakota girl one bit, nor Beverly, really. He thinks he had better get upstairs. He raps the door three times and Beverly sticks his head out. He opens the door and Jordan sees Bebe lying in the bath.

Lock that door behind you, says Bev, who gets on his knees and feeds her a strawberry. Her hands are covering her body as best they can.

Jordan watches her in the mirror, her eyes focused on the strawberry.

There is a voice outside; Jordan pushes the window open and looks down. Ricky and Mary Jane are kissing. He has his hands in her hair, she has her hands around his waist. Jordan looks at Bebe in her bubble bath. He sits on the toilet lid and watches, breathless and aroused.

Bebe, says Beverly. You want me to wash you?

216

He hands her a new champagne flute with a pill crushed up inside the drink.

Sure, she says.

Beverly likes to wash her and dress her like a doll. How she looks at Beverly tells Jordan she does not like it. How can she? He's older. Uglier. Eerie to the outsider. Elijah looks frightened again. This is not how she is with just Jordan. Although sometimes, of course, she is fearful, but only when Jordan desires that reaction. So that's okay.

Get out, sweet, and I'll dry you off, says Beverly.

She stands up, still trying to cover herself, Jordan looks away. He hears Mary Jane cry outside, he looks out at Ricky who is repeatedly punching the wall.

After a minute the door handle rattles.

Busy in here, shouts Beverly.

Jordan thinks he hears the person go back down the stairs, his ear is to the door. He opens the door and sees two people, two women. Mary Jane is one of them. She is standing, staring, aghast, at Jordan, then at Bebe who is wrapped in a towel, then at Beverly, who is behind her and has his hands on her arms, then at the bath full of steamy water. The other woman is on the stairs now and Jordan can't see her. She is only a shadow.

What are you doing? Mary Jane screams.

Beverly says: Mind your beeswax.

They could be raping that kid, Mary Jane tells the woman on the stairs.

Probably taking drugs, Jordan hears the other voice say, he doesn't recognize it. Then that woman is gone.

They three head for his bedroom, Mary Jane following. Beverly takes Bebe's champagne flute from her and throws it up the hall toward Mary Jane and it smashes off the wall.

What age is she? Mary Jane shouts, undeterred.

Jordan stops, returns and gets her by the shoulders and tells her to calm down while Beverly turns, passes them, swearing as he walks off, back downstairs. Heads downstairs, too. Her hand held tightly in his. Elijah has no choice but to go where he goes.

If people only knew what you were like, says MJ, following Jordan to the bedroom.

I want to know what you think you saw, he says.

I know, she says. I've known it, heard it, that these parties turn sour. That you and Beverly Burgess are like fruit flies around young girls.

She's not that young and nothing happened.

You are a pedophile, Jordan. Think about it. A real one. A rapist, too.

Those are about the worst thing you could say about someone, he says.

It's about the worst thing someone could be, Mary Jane shouts.

He has never seen her like this. She is usually laid back, mellow.

You are in my home, he says. You have no manners in my home, after I put on a party for you.

You only did this for Eric, she says. We both care for him but I can't sit back and let you do what you are doing. I just need you to stop. Jordan?

Care for him? he says. You mess him around, MJ. You are the one with the secret. A whore like your mother. Do you want me to tell John what you have been up to?

My husband knows, she says. He knows I've been seeing someone. You can even ask John, if you like. And don't call my mother a whore. Don't ever do that.

Jordan turns his back and crouches by his safe and thumbs in the combination. He starts lifting a wad of cash from the back of his safe.

What now? says MJ. You're trying to buy my silence?

He remembers that she has money now, that the old husband has money. MJ is no longer that poor little prairie girl who shopped in the thrift stores. A pay-off isn't going to cut it.

He hovers his hand over his gun.

What, MJ says, what are you thinking? Tell me you'll stop. Just tell me you will and I will believe you.

Beverly's car is starting outside then leaving. MJ looks back at the door. Is she looking for the girl? or Celena? or Eric? She turns back, goes to raise her hands when a bullet strikes her, and instantly, she is dead. She falls on his bed and off, down, on to the floor. Jordan is still crouched, reeling from the kickback of the gun.

He pulls himself up and goes over to look at her lying there, a trail of blood leaking from her head. Her mouth parted and her eyes bright with fear, so bright. He can't help but congratulate himself on a clean shot. He goes to close and cover up the safe.

Then Jordan walks back to her side and kneels down, lifting MJ's hand and prizing the gun into it, her fingers around it, one finger on the trigger. He bends her arm, positions her. Lifeless, gone.

Then it hits him like a train, and he moves away from her, starts schlepping back and forth, trying not to look down, trying to breathe, slower. Slower still.

He walks down the hall, looking into rooms for people. There is no one in the bathroom. Downstairs, moved from the dining room to the lounge, is the native girl. She is lying on the couch, her eyes flutter when he passes by.

Jordan lifts the deep-fryer from the kitchen and brings it upstairs. The hot oil splashes his groin as he does it, agonizing and sickening.

He tightens his grip on the grease, strips off and climbs into the cooling bath, and falteringly, he pours the oil on himself, getting scalded in fits and bursts. Then Jordan clambers back out of the bath water, and sees Elijah in the hallway. She is wearing the white bathrobe that he keeps in a downstairs guest room. He screams at her to get her things and go.

What's happened? Elijah asks, or Bebe, as Beverly likes to call her. I heard a shot.

Mary Jane's killed herself, he shouts. Call Stone to come get you. Tell Kookota to get out.

He goes back into his bedroom, where he splashes some oil on Mary Jane's groin and hands, accidentally spattering a greasy puddle on the carpet, which he covers with a towel.

Then he sits naked at the edge of his bed, takes a deep breath and phones the emergency services to request an ambulance and the local PD. For my … girlfriend, he says. She's just shot herself in the head.

Point of Madness and Action

2015 – 2016

Lately, when we had to exclude a girl from the team for fighting, her father said: Human beings are violent, get over it.

And I said to myself: Hell, yes, they are. We are. Human beings *are* violent.

I don't know how this ever came as a surprise, especially to me, who has been both receiver and dealer.

I told him fighting could not be tolerated, but I said to myself: I am afraid of violence, but I am violent. I also said inside: If I were a man, the people I would punch! And I also said, but not to the father: I am afraid of myself.

The first time I truly knew the violence was inside me, I was twenty and in college on a basketball scholarship.

I was in a nightclub, dancing with friends when someone grabbed my ass.

One minute I was trying to be relaxed, at ease, normal, the next my hand was behind my back, next there was this finger in my hand. That finger was all I managed to grasp. I pulled it back until I felt it pop clean out of the joint. When I turned around, I saw it belonged to this girl from my Phys. Ed. class.

She was standing, staring at her floppy finger, her mouth hung open in pain and shock. Obviously, I apologized profusely for the damage I'd done to that finger. But I was also glad of my violence. I was glad to have caused pain to anyone who thought they could put a hand on me. Even this girl. Even if she had grabbed my ass in jest.

Barely a week before, when she'd been dancing, the same girl hadn't liked it one smidge when another acquaintance from the group slid up behind her and untied her halter top.

Elijah! someone shouted. What have you done?

The girls gathered around me. We stared at that wilted, flesh flower of a finger. I kept on apologizing but for the first time I thought, serves you right.

The girl was mad. I was only having a joke with you, Elijah, she said for yonks after.

But maybe the violence started earlier, with that girl in high school who I flicked a yogurt over after she commented on the graffiti. She never got over that small assault either. My sweater still smells of damn yogurt, that girl said for months after.

And there was Lucie, who I had confided the real violence in, and when someone else told me, word for word, a piece of my truth, I ran from one side of middle school to the other, intent on beating the brakes off my best friend.

As I ran, I pictured her face splatted all over my fist. When I got in front of her, she denied she'd said anything about the real violence. I just broke down.

Again a crowd of girls stood around us. It was humiliating, what can I say? I do stupid things. I apologize to myself. Sorry, me.

But after I popped the girl's finger in the nightclub, I was certainly not remorseful. I was depressed by the feelings the whole episode had brought back. Every so often there were things like that. And Lucie did not understand, no matter how she tried to show she did. What was I complaining about? This was the man they had on their walls, all greased up, smiling away the sun from his eyes.

The Beverly Burgess thing was too creepy to ever admit to, but Jordan Pinault was once *my boyfriend*. Called me for chats, bought me gifts. He was sweet, sometimes. Sometimes not.

Regardless, what on God's good earth was I complaining about?

Lucie had been living this parallel life to me and I could not even tell the full truth to myself, sitting in class, still a little stoned, still a little drunk, my skin red raw from the hot showers I subjected myself to. I hated that skin because it was theirs.

I wanted to cave in on myself. I was weepy, then angry, then ashamed. And these emotions would chase each other, circling around, catching up and starting over again. All these feelings bubbling and welling up, and I did not know how to control them, for they were uncontrollable.

Then Coach Measle asked me what was up. A man, asking me what was up.

Nothing, I told him.

You were good last year, he said. I don't know what's happening with you, Rackin, probably women's things.

Yes, women's things, I'd wanted to say, but that morning I stomped off and later he found me and called me aside and said: You and Lucie, I want to see you both in the hall over lunch.

Lucie had been displeased he'd requested she be there. When I got there, there was another teacher with Measle, a female – I can't remember her name – who asked us what was going on, because we'd been close the previous semester and now we were not.

I shouldn't be here, Lucie said. I've done nothing wrong.

Nobody is claiming that you have, the teacher woman said. Listen, when girls start middle school, they change their group of friends like, three times in the first year, but not you two, you didn't. You have always been really close, and when that happens, well … what happens is, if you fall out of favor with each other, it all feels quite lonesome.

I have other friends, said Lucie.

I looked at the floor.

Elijah, are you jealous that Lucie has other friends?

No, never, I said.

Maybe you should try to make some other friends, too.

Truthfully? I had barely thought about Lucie those few months. Any wonder she left me. And that was only one tiny part of it, there was so much more. But how could I speak it?

The coach told us we were trying out for the team, like it or not, and we did. For a few minutes, I had something else to think about except Jordan Pinault, something else except Beverly Burgess.

Instead of looking all around me and thinking that everybody could probably smell them on me like I could always, and that if the boys knew they would call me *easy*, and thinking that if the girls knew they would call me *a whore*, I focused on the ball. I buried a hoop and ran, dribbling the ball, threw it to Lucie, who took it and ran, and the whistle blew and I went over, took it from her friend (another name since forgotten) and ran off, dribbling again.

Lucie put her hands on her hips; she did not want to be here. She did not want to be this chance to get through to me.

A year later, another girl from a school across county walked into a shooting range, hired a .44 and shot herself in the head. It was then that stories came out she had once been to a party in Pinault's mansion where she had been raped.

There was also another story about a girl who hitched her way out of the county and was never seen again. There was talk that story was a cover-up and the real story was that she'd been murdered. Or that she'd suicided, too.

But what *was* true was they were both my age. They both had blonde hair like me and looked older than they were. And I once knew their names and now they escape me.

I have forgotten many things. I think it is my body's way of hiding the real violence.

But I remember when I heard the stories, I thought, now is the time, but it faded to a scar. Before it turned to pink skin I thought I had my chance to step forward, and so me and Lucie got friendlier again, as we did, on and off. And I told her everything of the real violence, everything.

We were aged sixteen then; the real violence was three years old by then. Then word was I was a fantasist, an attention-seeker. The girls in school decided on it, and Lucie promised she had not told them, but graffiti appeared in the toilets:

Jordan Pinault raped me, Elijah Rackin. If destroyed still true!

I have sex with my cousin, signed Elijah.

Coach Measel says I give the best head, E. Rackin.

Whether the teachers ever saw anything, I did not know. But I have to think yes. I had to check the toilets every day. I could have given up, stayed in bed like my grandmother once told me Ephraim used to do, refusing to go to school. She said that that was why he was trouble, never aspiring beyond janitorial jobs.

But me? I had basketball. And so, I took my frustrations out on the court. Forget teams, I was on no one's side. I shouldered past girls who had tormented me, who whispered: Fuck me harder, you big sexy quarterback. I ran, I threw. I threw an elbow in someone's face, anyone's. I was celebrated, lauded, sometimes. I found some loyalty in a guilty Lucie, but by now I held no importance in loyalty. So I took what I could get.

It was over, as much as I knew it was over, I worried that it wasn't. I was only as safe as the past I had survived.

But since the night Mary Jane McCord died at Colonial Pine Hills it really was over. But I could only see that looking back, with years and years under my belt.

I thought I was getting somewhere, but every so often, out of the blue, there is something new, like a girl on my team at Thornhill telling me how she remembers now that some sonofabitch made her fellate him.

Every so often there are things like that. And a steam of blood comes rising up in my mouth that I just need to spit at someone. And of course I believe her. Every time Candace Last Horse tells me she tells me with the same candor and rigor I don't even require.

I can't forget when Grandmother told me how the boarding school nuns who taught her used to call the Sioux people *Lousy Lakota*, and how they used to get their hair washed in a bucket of chemicals. I'd protest: Don't even say that, Grandmother!

She can't understand why I work in a school on the reservation, why I can't work in a 'white' school.

Remember what that one did to us, Grandmother said, and when she said that she was talking about Candace's uncle. But I remember that day he barged in on us rather differently, he was sending a message to Ephraim, smashing shit up. I can't forget that I did not fear him, and that what I did fear was my grandmother for uttering the words: Do anything he wants. Anything. And how she started to fake cry.

A few months before and I would not have feared her words or understood them. But I did. I had that currency that could save a life, possibly mine, possibly hers, and it was silence and smiles. Appeasing and lying. Lying to survive.

But I could see in his eyes that Mr. Ghost Bear would not harm us, and I only knew what to look for because I was seeing it on a weekly basis.

*

Before his sister accosts me in the parking lot, asking what I remember and what I don't, he comes to collect his nieces from a game. Eyeballs me up and down.

I think not only about the time he trashed my grandmother's home but also the time he offered me help in the casino. He hated Beverly Burgess. He knew what they were doing. And he hated that his sister went to the parties.

Kookota, they used to call her. Sometimes she comes to our games, stands at the sidelines with that same old faraway look in her eyes. She was always one of the last to leave those after-parties. She would be passed out, almost sleepwalking.

A couple of weeks after I see Akecheta, I am in the corner of the lot, wrapping my sweater around me when Kookota asks if she can speak with me.

Certainly, I say.

Candace and Alexa looked bored in the car.

I think their mother might mention that her aunt is sick, Alexa has told me.

I think she might mention that Candace has told her we have spoken about her assault. What I do not think she will do is bring up mine.

My brother told me it was you, she says. I was not so sure.

Who does your brother say was me? I ask her.

You were there, the night Mary Jane passed over.

Where? I say.

Colonial Pine Hills, Pinault's mansion by the canyon. You're Elijah, right?

Well, yes.

My brother, he used to bring me to those parties we all went to.

I stare at her now.

I have narcolepsy, she explains, I wasn't on drugs like everybody thought. When it's like that, everything is hazy: what you saw, what you thought you saw, hazy.

Okay, I say, still dazed with her forwardness in a parking lot.

But I have my suspicions, she whispers, about Senator Pinault and Burgess.

I'm not the person to talk to, I say.

I asked my brother to come take a look at you a fortnight ago, see if you are Stone Shea's cousin. Akecheta thought you were called Bebe.

No, my name is not ... I sigh. Well, it's not that name you just used.

I know that now, says Kookota but I don't ask her hers. I know what they used to do, she says, to you and to others, and what's more, I think Pinault killed my best friend.

She looks at me expectantly. I feel like hitting her. Suddenly I feel like punching her in the face and grabbing her by the hair, tearing out every long black strand of her hair.

You were there that night, she adds. I saw him ... There was a shot, I woke, I sat up. I saw him bring that fryer of hot fat upstairs. I heard him bring it to the bathroom. I heard him scream. I was there.

Her eyes search mine but I give up nothing.

MJ was already passed, she says. You were there, you were in the hallway, coming out of his walk-in closet dressed in a white bathrobe. It must have been his. It was a tent on you.

That wasn't me, I say. I am frozen to the spot. How have I let her say so much? I am angry at her, angry at myself. I am violated again.

You stared at me, says Kookota, and I said: Hey, what's going on, and you said ...

Alexa and Candace are looking out of the car window at me.

I have to go, I tell their mother, but she is insistent:

229

You said: Someone has been killed. So, I panicked, you panicked, we both left out the back door. Then you ran off when the cops came, so did I. I ran off too. Why did we do that?

You'll have to excuse me, I say.

Elijah.

What?

Do you have a best friend?

Not these days. Not in years, I say getting into my car.

Kookota comes to my door. Please, she says, Akecheta just told me and if I'd known sooner.

She looks back at her daughters, gives them the one minute signal with her finger.

I've tried to tell Pinault's fiancée, Helena. I brought the girls to their house in Nemo. She bought their girl scout cookies, and I was right on the verge of telling her who he is, what he did, to MJ and to you, and other girls, when he came home. I worry about her too, she says.

Don't worry, I say. I'm over it.

I drive away remembering things I have tried so hard to forget.

*

We grew up in Custer, on Moonlight Drive, on this ranch that once sold Agri-Supplies. Once Ephraim could go, he was gone, moved in with a girl from Sioux Falls. When it didn't work out, he joined a biker crew. When I was young he would visit on his Harley. Because he was a lot older, I didn't know him well. He worked as a park maintenance supervisor at the grave yard, and typically city employees needed drug screening.

His interest in me started because he needed a cup of clean pee. He started stopping by and Grandmother was glad to see us getting close.

Then Ephraim would take me out for rides, wake me during the night and say: Hey, you want to come to a party? There'll be lots of famous people there.

Who at thirteen wouldn't say yes?

Now I think about Kookota and what she said about sweet MJ McCord being killed and having not killed herself. I used to think there was something between Pinault and MJ, the way they would act. Nice one minute, then they'd snap at each other the next. Like Ephraim and his attachment in Sioux Falls, I can't remember her name. He brought her once to meet Grandmother and Granddad and all they did was bicker.

What did I know? I was a kid, unattuned.

After that night, the last one I spent at Pinault's palace, when Mary Jane McCord died, I went home and saw Grandmother. She was rooting through her button tin. I didn't have the language to say what happened, but I tried. The words sat in my stomach like a cotton wad, expanding, then came out as something totally different.

I don't like Ephraim's friends, I said. Then it occurred to me that I had been drinking alcohol and maybe had taken one of those pills Burgess always slipped me, that I ought to keep quiet. Then it occurred to me that I'd not said no. Even though I could *not* have said no. I would be in bigger trouble if I refused. I knew this.

Grandmother glared at me. What are you saying? she asked me.

Ephraim's friends with people, like Senator Burgess, Jordan Pinault … MJ McCord.

She killed herself last night. It's just been on the radio. Grandmother lined up her buttons on the table. I knew that little girl would die early, she said. Too precious for this world, girls like that. Didn't she look just like Marilyn Monroe?

No, I said. Much prettier.

I pictured MJ shouting at them. Telling them that she knew. She had died for me. Now maybe I would die too.

I ran my grandmother's words over my mind again. *Girls like that*, she'd said. Maybe I was a *girl like that*. I seemed to attract the same people, older men, players. If Jordan liked me and he liked her ... my neck hurt when I thought about it.

A few years later, girls I knew were hiding hickeys with scarves, but back then I was hiding strangulation marks; marks made during *it*. I didn't have the word for *it*. But I knew it was not sex. I did not yet think, this is violence, control. I couldn't when, for a time, he acted normal, even sweet, like he was my boyfriend and not my abuser.

They do things at parties, I said.

Grandmother told me it would stop now, not to keep talking about it.

How psychic could she be? I wondered. Well, not very. She put on a persona and read a palm. She never had people come to Moonlight Drive and the ranch to tell them their future. Custer was the place she kept for her data collection. Mystic was where she donned her kaftans and got creative.

Many years later I had the words. Years after that, Ephraim was jailed for raping Pinault's wife, and I thought of the word *justice*. Grandmother could not understand it really. Not her Ephraim. Not her precious grandson.

Then he was released, he hadn't done it at all, they said. And every past accusation I had, began a long conversation with silence.

*

When I'm angry I come to Custer State Park. It's a regular visitation. I wind down my window, turn off my engine and close my eyes. They come right up to the window, so inquisitive, the males especially, with their huge heads. I look at them in their little eyes, and feel calm.

It's different this time of year. I like best when it is the summer and the park is speckled yellow with sweet clover and you get a scent of it as you drive through. Then, the buffalos' coats are shedding so they look raggedy and mangy. Now it's winter, it's rarer to see them. I still come here and watch them disappear into the void.

I spend Christmas at State Game Lodge, phone to check in on Grandmother. She asks me where I am, she tells me she and Ephraim are having a nice festive time.

Is that so? I ask.

It is so. Why ain't you here?

I'm having dinner in Deadwood with Lucie and Bud – It's not the truth.

Tell Miss Lucie a hi from me, and a very Merry Christmas. And to Bud! And I will see you at New Year, Elijah.

You will, see you in a few.

I go back to my table and wait, the server comes and sets my dinner in front of me, and I eat it.

I drink far too much wine, which is not much, not by most people's standards, and I ask the server what he is doing working Christmas day.

Double pay, he says. Is it rude to ask what you're doing eating alone on Christmas day?

Yes, it is. So rude, I say and he says: My bad. And skulks back to the kitchen.

I think of going to my room, sleeping off my dinner, waking later in the afternoon and going for a drive, try to see the buffalo up close, but I don't. I think about Ephraim instead; he is usually so interested in himself, and suddenly now getting into our grandmother's pockets, just turning up at Thanksgiving, now calling shotgun on her company at Christmas.

He must be in a bad way, I think, if he wants to belong to her. But I have never wondered at this: belongability. Not to Grandmother and not to anybody.

I sit at the bar, where the owner of the lodge eats his dinner. I see his snow-colored hair, his metal-tipped boots glinting. He looks, at a glance, like Beverly Burgess. There is a leap in my stomach, even though I know that Beverly is all but brain dead and living in a facility, he still has this ability to make me flinch, twenty years on.

Nonetheless, I leave the dining hall and go to my room. I look at the bath and the towels, remembering the shape of Beverly's nails, long and tapering, his hands, how, when he spoke, he flailed them around like ribbons, and he would offer to dry me and I would think of his hands like the heads of snakes sizing me up, venomous, head to toe, trying to work out how best to unhinge their jaws and eat me up.

I watch some reality TV for a while and then I pour one coffee, then another, and go out to my car. I drive to Oglala, to Pine Ridge, to Buffalo Plains Casino and find it open. I ask if I can see the manager.

He's at home, the man says at the desk. But this isn't business, I'll wager.

No, not business, I say.

You a nurse? That's Mr. Ghost Bear's house you just passed.

I drive back to the house, hitting a rock and leaving it under the wheel. I go to the door. Candace opens it. Coach Rackin? she says, unsure.

Happy Christmas, I say. May I see your mom?

Okay, Happy Christmas. She walks off and I breathe into my hand and sniff for booze.

Akecheta comes out. Hi, he says, looking at me askance, he looks out of the door.

I'm alone, I say.

Okay, he says.

You told your sister what happened, back twenty years ago.

Oh … he starts.

It's good, I say. I wanted to tell someone, I don't know …

Elijah?

Yes. Elijah.

I'm Akecheta. Ake.

Hi, Ake, I say.

Down the corridor, I hear a woman crying and a man, a shaman, comes out of the door. He speaks in low tones. Kookota turns to look at me. You're here, she says.

Is everything okay? I ask.

Our aunt is dying, says Akecheta, he looks at his sister. Nova, someone should be with her.

Go back in, bro, she says.

The shaman talks in the hall. I have said some words, he says. I've chanted. She knows, Wanda's mind is clear. She has her family and we'll all reunite in the spirit world. She knows …

Holy crap, I say. I'm sorry, I have to go.

Nova comes outside. Coach, she says, let me explain, my aunt, she's like my mother, and she's dying. But she loves life so much she cannot let go.

Your brother said. I'm sorry.

We're trying right now, to say something to Wanda that will help her just let herself be, you know.

This can keep, I say.

You sure?

I nod, feeling choked as I walk to my car.

Is it about Candace? she asks after me.

No. I'll call again, a better time.

She watches me, then closes the door.

I try to kick the rock from under the tire. The shaman appears by my side and offers to help pull it out. Our faces are close when he says: Maybe you should go sleep it off. There is room in the casino. Just go in there, say you are a friend of ours. There are many free rooms today, go in and have some sleep.

Sounds good, I say. I will. A friend.

He puts his hand on my shoulder and it's all I can do not to punch him in the mouth.

I wait until he goes back inside the house and I start the car, reversing back, dinging the letterbox, returning to the lodge.

*

On New Year's Eve, I go out with Grandmother and her friend Laberta to the Gold Pan Saloon. They play pool and penny machines, eat soggy wings and wash them down with liberal quantities of beer. I stay in the corner, feeding the jukebox, drinking wine from a paper cup. I am convinced Ephraim is going to appear, like he always does. Every biker who pulls up outside I am ready to fight. I'm ready. It can't keep.

Grandmother talks it up with the locals and come midnight, everyone but me sings *Auld Land Syne*, turning midpoint to *America the Beautiful*, which is in the same meter.

For days after I turn over the original lyrics they saw fit to take out:

America! America!
God shed His grace on thee,
Till souls wax fair as earth and air
And music-hearted sea!

I am drunk on these words, as I drive home.

Stay with us, angels, says Grandmother as I swing my Dodge around a road made wide enough for turning oxen.

When we get home, Grandmother chastises me for driving when lit.

But you never refused the lift, I say.

Goodness knows how long we'd be waiting for a cab.

Grandmother looks pensively at the photograph she has of Ephraim.

You could have called your grandson, I say, you could have gotten back here on the back on his Harley.

You're killing me, Elijah, she says. I spend one Christmas day with my grandson and you don't allow it. Well I'm the grandmother.

Your grandson, I say.

Yes, my grandson.

Your grandson, I mutter.

Oh, be quiet. Are you through?

Be quiet? I shout. Why did you tell me to keep quiet?

Elijah, she says, I've never seen this nasty side of you, you look possessed, my girl.

I lift his photo and throw it at the wall.

237

For years I've been turning that to face the wall, I say, and every day you fuckin' turned it back, every day I had to look at him. Your fucking grandson. You know what he did, what he let Jordan Pinault and your friend, Bev Burgess do to me. You fuckin' know they drugged, hurt and abused me and you did nothing.

Elijah Barbra! Don't get excited. Sit down real quick.

I collapse on the couch, lift my hand to my nose. There is blood bucketing from my nostrils.

Look what you have gone and done to yourself now, Grandmother says, fetching me a paper towel.

*

One new year in, another one out, Grandmother says.

It's gunna be like that, I say, we are gunna pretend the conversation never happened. Again.

If my head wasn't sore, if I wasn't having one of my weaker days, I would break her face in two with my fist.

I have to go, I say.

I drive straight into Rapid City and to the animal sanctuary.

Helena Russo is there, in her tweeds, bald but a headscarf. I saw them both in the paper, doing their bit for animals. I thought of that dog he used to have, Karma.

He isn't here, and I am set to face him. Helena comes to greet me, telling me that the sanctuary is not open to the public today.

Are you Jordan Pinault's fiancée? I ask.

I am.

Can I talk to you?

Mmm, okay … she says. We walk into the office. Take a seat, says Helena.

I'm Elijah.

238

Hi Elijah, how can I help?

You can listen.

Okay, I'm listening, she says.

I'm thirty-three, I say, sitting on the edge of the desk, and I've been carrying a secret for twenty years. I only told my grandmother last night. I was drunk, it came out … It came out. And not how I heard it in my head every time I practiced, when she stood with her back to me all those times I tried and couldn't.

Uh-huh. Helena frowns.

The only other time I told anyone, well, that was my best friend. And when I told her, this is the way I said it: so I'll say it like I did.

Go for it, says Helena.

I told her that my cousin used to bring me to parties because someone said they could make me a fashion model.

She looks at me kindly, urges me silently to go on.

Then, I say, I said that what happened next, which was that for the next six months, there were two men who would … well, one was strange, and creepy, and the other, Helena, he was different … and he would fuck me. Hit me … I was thirteen at the time.

Helena sits forward in her seat, she holds her breath. And you are gunna say what I think …

I didn't call it rape, I say. I mean, now I know. Over and over. They drugged me, got me drunk. And I used to think that he was the good one, out of the two.

Who was the other one?

Helena, I say, I'm not stupid. Women don't listen when you tell them their man is bad, doesn't matter how many women they hurt. And you … well, look at you. You are a doll, working New Year's Day at an animal sanctuary.

Hmm, I don't know about that, she says.

239

You are exactly the kind of person who only sees the good in people.

You don't know me, she says softly.

Do men like that choose women who aren't good? What would that even look like, tell me.

By now Helena is tearful. Look, you need to stop right there, she says.

I knew it, I say. You are gunna defend him.

No, I certainly am not. It's just that, he's coming. He's on his way. But … Helena stands … I want to carry on this conversation. I really do.

She is shaking, I can see it. So am I. I feel like I'm not even here.

When? I say. I can't wait. I just wanted to warn you, that Ghost Bear woman …

Nova?

She had mentioned that she tried to warn you.

She was selling cookies with her girls.

That's her.

That's Nova. She was great, then she just upped and left. I was enjoying her girls.

Candace and Alexa. They are great kids.

Nova hinted there was something, Helena says.

Then Jordan came home.

You're right, he did.

Well, there is more. There is far more.

We can't talk here. Really, Elijah. I'm not saying I don't believe you, you need to know that to begin with. But tomorrow, okay.

Where?

She bites her thumb.

I know of this cabin, I say, in Mystic.

Well alright, she says, give me your phone. I'm gunna put my number in there. She keys it in. Now you text me the address and I'll come meet you tomorrow.

As I walk out, I see Pinault. He is trying to look into my Dodge and my heart goes cold. And there was me thinking I was ready to face him!

I get into my car, put my fist to my cheek and duck my head to the side and see in my rearview Helena brushing up straw and smiling as Jordan walks toward her, both of them looking at my car.

*

The next day it snows.

Be like snow: beautiful and cold.

I heard Alexa Last Horse say that once.

It's funny how these things stick in your head. Every time I picture Alexa, I hear her say that phrase, just as I align Candace's flippant remark about her assault: So what, shit happens, too late to do something now. And I hear myself say something can be done, but this reads false.

It's never too late. Is it? I think, do I do it for her or do I do it for me? Can we share a win?

Perched in a pass in Mystic is the cabin. The place looks like a ghost town, like there has been a natural bombing and all that is left is a roof held up by splinters. Any pines that have not been killed by pine needle or heavy snowfall, sit thick and strong.

I sit inside my grandmother's cabin and look around me, remembering, clutching my fists into my thighs, my stomach expanding with cotton, until I hear her car.

She rushes inside.

You're early, I say.

I can't help it. Nothing worse than being late, Helena says. She is wearing a long glossy wig.

I can't believe you found me out here, I say.

I did, with my cell phone. And, I know the area. Helena looks around. I've been here. Lately.

Really? Out here?

Yeah. But, go on. You want to tell me some things.

Maybe I wanted you to see me here, I say. Subliminally. Subconsciously! Here is where it started.

I look around.

So, tell me, she says.

I twist my ring. I was sitting here, I say. I was talking to Jordan Pinault when he first raped me. Beverly Burgess was sitting where you are now, watching, beating off.

Helena does not look surprised, just sympathetic.

My grandmother had just given me this ring for my thirteenth birthday. I show her my hand. It was my mother's ring. My mother was wearing it when she lived herself out. Her father had melted it into shape from a state crest spoon for her when she turned thirteen, and he plated it with silver.

It's real pretty.

I felt Jordan's hands around my neck, he did that. He does it to you, doesn't he?

Sometimes, lately. Yes. Helena shivers.

I thought I was gunna die, I say. Helena, I remembered a girl in a movie I watched before, how she left a hair pin under a cushion and when she was killed that's how they found her. So I thought, when they take my body and hide me in the canyon, or some crawl space in some basement, then my grandmother, or the police, will come to this cabin, and they'll find this ring, and my grandmother'd know that we hadn't been to the cabin together since the summer before, and she'd remember giving me my mother's ring on my birthday that September.

I see.

She'd know something was up. She'd ask my cousin Stone about the cabin keys that he had and I didn't, the police would work out that I'd been murdered here, on this very couch. There'd be justice.

Oh Elijah …

I retrieved the ring, a month later, when I came back here with them, and I did it every time.

I take my ring off and hold it to the light.

It has been exhibit A in the court case of my crazy mind, because I *am* crazy. Ever notice that? When a man wrongs a woman, or a girl, she's the crazy one. I hear a boy call a girl crazy and I know what's up.

Damn, says Helena.

I pull a necklace out of my shirt, it is gold with a boulder opal pendant in sheens of blues and pinks, with a bright pink ruby offset in the metalwork.

He brought me this back from a trip to Hawaii once, I say.

Helena looks at it. It's worth a pretty penny, she tells me and she should know.

I push it back down my collar. I've never worn it, I'm only wearing to show you because I noticed your ring.

Helena looks at her finger, at the boulder opal and diamond engagement ring.

He likes showy, I say.

So, why now? Helena asks, she pushes her left hand deep inside her coat pocket.

I feared him for more than a decade, for nearly two, then people were talking about MJ McCord, like, a lot, he was in the papers. You and him were, and the animal sanctuary.

Oh, yes.

MJ's death happened in his house, so he was always the victim.

Was he?

I couldn't get rid of his face, then I had this dream right after Christmas, in which I saw him and laughed in his face. I was happy and peaceful. I thought if I saw him again I'd laugh. But I saw him yesterday, and I didn't laugh. Because what he did is not fuckin' funny. You know, I thought I knew something about him, that he was incapable of love because he'd been hurt. That he only knew how to hurt me because he'd been hurt the same way. Like Ephraim does to people. Stone, I mean.

I can't understand that man. Nor what Thisbe is doing with him now after what she accused him of! Helena says.

I look at Helena kind of shocked. I think, she might not be an ally after all, but I need to say what I came to say.

They are hurt, pained, bitter men, I say. So suddenly we all understand each other. Does that matter? Does it make a difference? My cousin would meet Pinault and Burgess here, they must have given him money for me. There was another girl too, she killed herself in '98. No one remembers her. They must have kept us apart. There is never only one, it just starts out like that. I've had that guilt all my life.

Survivor's guilt.

I suppose.

I'm sorry, says Helena. You are so very brave.

I haven't the voltage to be brave. And you shouldn't be sorry.

But you look so angry, Elijah.

I'm not angry with you.

She shrugs. What next? You go to the PD? You want me to come?

I sigh. That had been the plan. Justice. Karma.

What if he gets let back out, posts bail? Helena asks.

Then you come stay with me.

Yes, but there's my mother to think of …

I can go alone, Helena. That's fine. I just need for you to know, so when you are home alone with him and he has been released, or wrangled his way out, so you know that I am not in danger anymore, but that you probably are. I mean, has he ever hurt you?

No.

People like that can't help themselves.

She looks at me. She doesn't seem like the type but I realize now that she might be a woman who likes dangerous men. Some women, even smart, kind-looking, wig-wearing ones, can be attracted to that. She thinks she'll save him. She's a fantasist. You just can't tell by looking.

And how long are you together? I ask.

Just over a year, she says.

She still seems forthcoming but I've seen it before, with girls I went to school with, with teachers I've worked with, making excuses for deadbeat men and what they will put up with before they will allow themselves to be lonely. How one day they want you to hate their man and the next day they want you to excuse them.

So, Beverly Burgess brought you here in the past? she says.

Stone arranged the location. If it wasn't the house in Colonial Pine Hills, it was here: my grandmother's secret hideaway. My grandfather died ten years ago, and he never ever knew she had this place. I was sworn to silence.

No, says Helena. Olivia Burgess – Beverly's wife – visited my home a couple of months ago. He hasn't been well …

245

I know that.

Well, it's not looking good for him. His time's coming.

Good.

Thought you might say that. Olivia, his wife, was getting his affairs in order and she found the deeds.

Yes?

Of here. That's why I was in the area. Jordan brought me out here for a drive and … showed me …

I stare at her to finish the thought.

Bev's love nest, was what Jordan called it, says Helena smiling unhappily. He used it for that purpose with that medium from the paper. Madame …

Barbra-Jean?

A place in Mystic for the mystic. I suppose that was cute.

I go to the window and look out.

Oh shit! Is she your grandmother? Helena asks me.

I've been stupid, I say, my grandmother could never have ever afforded an extra place. I never questioned anything. I'm bringing you here to tell you and all the while, I'm the one who doesn't know.

A Jeep pulls up outside.

Shit! Jordan's here, says Helena, rising to look out.

Did you tell him? I say.

No! I promise.

I grab my purse and take out my gun.

Don't! says Helena. Shush!

She grabs my arm and pulls me, so we creep through the back door, and along the dusty mat of snow, into the falling-again snow. He is at the front of the cabin, kicking open the door. We jump into Helena's car since she is clutching her keys. He runs back out of the cabin and at the Cadillac. Helena and I press the lock button at the same time, so the car locks and unlocks again.

I press it once more while he grapples for the door handle.

Stop, Helena shouts at me. She unlocks and locks it again.

I am still holding my gun in my trembling hand. I am thirteen years old again. The violence washes out of me and I am completely unarmed. Not even a giggle in me for him.

He runs back to his car, gets in and chases us through the hills through the snow.

Go right, I say, we can try to lose him here.

He follows us, firing shots from his window.

Helena races out past the reservoir, past Verboten Clubhouse, where there are about thirty bikes outside it. She doesn't notice the cop car but it's not like we can stop here anyway. Not with Ephraim and his ilk about, listening in, denying everything.

She can drive fast, even in the snow. I turn to watch Pinault and I try to force a laugh.

Please don't shoot back, she says.

I didn't tell you, I say, Jordan killed Mary Jane McCord. Remember Mary Jane?

Yes, we were neighbors. Helena is clenching her teeth.

It was Ricky Nwafo who was having an affair with her. That's why he keeps quiet, man of God and all. And MJ ... she got shot trying to protect me.

I hear you. Now be quiet. I need to concentrate before we get shot too.

That's why I wanted to get to you, because it could be you next.

Elijah, Helena says, I really need you to be quiet, I can hardly see where I'm headed.

I will be quiet, but earlier, you asked me why now.

She glances at me as she turns into a residential area, a boulevard. A tree falls in front of us. Helena swerves to avoid hitting it. I think I see Wanda's face in the bark.

The Scorpion

2015

Since his woman has her family visiting for
Thanksgiving, he leaves them to it and rides to Custer.
On his way, a few mountain miles south of Keystone,
Stone stops at Wolf Camp for a dollar-fifty beer and a
breakfast to eat alone while he listens to Johnny Cash
chew his way through a song on the radio.

Stone has no idea how things will go when he gets to
Custer. Sometimes, when he calls, he hopes Elijah is
there so they can finally address the thing that is always
between them. When he gets there, she stays in a room
upstairs. No matter, it's for his grandmother he is here.
She is sitting by the fire, there is gravy bubbling over on
the stove. He lifts it off the heat and calls out to her.

Ephraim? she says. I'll be darned! What are you
doing here?

Happy Thanksgiving to you, too, he says.

Elijah had to go fetch something, says Barb, dithering back and forth, then suddenly businesslike, she lifts the turkey from the cooker, her arms shaking.

Give me that, says Stone, resting it on the counter, finding two plates on the oven rack below.

Barbra-Jean goes to the bottom of the stairs and calls up to Elijah while Stone lifts the hot plates and drops one on the floor. He holds his hand under cold water from the faucet.

Oh Ephraim, now my good Thanksgiving set is ruined, his grandmother says as she retrieves the dustpan and brush and hands it to him to catch the fragments that are lying on the linoleum.

I'll buy you a new set, he says, thinking of the boxes of china in Thisbe's dining room sideboard, among other still-unopened wedding gifts from super-moneyed schmucks. It's all still like-new, while the marriage itself was nixed long ago. Thisbe surely wouldn't notice, at least not immediately, if a dinner set was to grow legs and walk.

Barbra-Jean calls Elijah once more, then she says: Why don't we start. They dish up and sit down to it.

Oh, I don't know, says his grandmother, maybe the gap was too big. Y'all never been close, have you?

Nope, he says.

It is what Elijah would and did herself say: It was Barb's seventieth birthday, a long time ago now, and one of the only times Elijah forced herself to be in her cousin's company. A friend of their grandmother – a woman named Laberta, who was once a nurse in Custer State Hospital, and no doubt worked part-time as Madame Barb's psychic informer – had said: Bring your cousin over here, Ephraim, and tried to talk to them both collectively.

But they avoided talking, just as they side-stepped looking at each other. At the party Laberta asked: Y'all close, as cousins? and Elijah said, without missing a beat: Nope. And excused herself.

Eventually, she comes into the dining room and lifts her plate.

It'll be cold, her grandmother tells her.

Cold as hell, Elijah mumbles and brings the food upstairs.

What in the world is going on? says Barb. You two really don't care about getting on with each other. And I don't get it. It's like I am gunna live forever.

Meaning? asks Stone.

Meaning, are you both gunna ever pass a civil word, or will it take my death?

He raises his shoulders in question, so she asks him what he is thankful for, and he laughs at the question. It is none of her business, he thinks.

It has been a lucky year for Stone, the luckiest he's had. He has a beautiful, strong woman by his side, and is living off the fat of her alimony. He is finally getting to screw with Jordan Pinault in the best possible way. Stone has fucked him out of his own life and how. Now he is living it in Colonial Pine Hills. Seven beds, five baths. A pool house. Guest cabin. Garage, workshop. Acres for the horses Stone pictures himself having like they once had here in Custer. And, he is finally warming to Thisbe's older kids like he instantly warmed to the youngest. Soon he'll have them calling him Papa and really twist the knife in Number Eight's back. He is thankful.

Stone's closest brothers from the Marcach are either dead or jailed, but he is free, and plans to hang up his leathers soon for a normal life. Very, very.

I'm thankful that I don't have to look at Elijah's cold as hell, lemon-sucking face while I eat, he says.

His grandmother scoffs.

*

Thisbe and Zoey are in the kitchen eating cold cuts. Their father and brother are sleep in front of the TV in the lounge.

How was your Thanksgiving? Stone asks Thisbe.

Busy, she replies. She looks happy, she has her kids and the family she'd lost contact with for years, and in this house, and with this wealth. Stone feels an envy-pang pound his chest.

Guess who called around, with his boo-thang? says Zoey.

Who? Stone asks. He likes Zoey more than the male Hartfields, who he knows can see straight through him.

He took me by surprise, Thisbe says.

Not Jordan? says Stone, he won't call him Pinault around her. Her kids are Pinaults.

He only called in for an hour. Thisbe holds up a finger to emphasize the small singularity of the visit.

With his boo-thang, says Zoey. With her *wig*.

It's Thanksgiving, Sis, says Thisbe.

What do you think about that, Stone?

I can't say I like it.

And I don't either, says Thisbe. They caught me unprepared.

Do you regret it now? asks Zoey.

What?

Letting him in?

I don't know, says Thisbe popping turkey into her mouth.

Does he know about us? asks Stone.

He does now, says Thisbe. Zo told him, and she took great pleasure in doing so.

What did Jordan say about that?

He tried to pretend he could care less. Wanted to see his girls. Says he's getting married.

You let him see the girls? Stone asks. Don't do that again.

I agree with Stone, says Zoey.

So, when we have our kid, it's okay if I don't let them see you? asks Thisbe.

What kid is this? asks Zoey, looking at Thisbe's belly.

There is no kid ... yet, she says.

Thisbe and Stone stand looking at each other angrily until Zoey asks if they'd like her to leave the room.

If you would, says Stone.

Thisbe wants her to stay, but Zoey takes her plate of cold cuts and says: It's okay, y'all need your space.

Pinault's fucked in the head, says Stone, quietly.

Well, yes. Granted. But aren't we all moving on? asks Thisbe. It wasn't like I planned for him to visit and I would like the kids to have a relationship with their father. Maybe ... I don't have to be part of it, and you can keep all the way out.

He grunts. Elijah wouldn't sit with me, he says. She took her plate upstairs like a damn dumb kid.

What's her beef?

Funny thing, Stone says, it's Jordan.

Why?

You should ask him about it next time he drops by. Ask him what he's hiding.

What *is* he hiding?

That he likes little girls.

Get the fuck out of here. You need to explain now.

Little girls, like Ever's age.

No. She laughs nervously.

I'm telling you, he used to have these parties back in the mid-nineties, Elijah was thirteen, something like that, a kid, okay?

You better keep going now you've started, says Thisbe.

And he used to have her come to him, him and his senate friend, Burgess.

What are you saying? They used to fuck her?

He exhales and leans on the counter.

Jordan's a lot of things, he was a motherfucker to me, but … that can't be true.

Ask Elijah. Stone leans back and folds his arms.

Did she tell you this?

She didn't have to.

Then …

I was there, Bee.

What does that even mean?

They used to give me backhanders, tell me to leave her with them, said they had model agency friends coming.

Alright …

Never happened.

You were goddamn pimping her out.

No!

You didn't tell them to stop!

I did. When … He points to the ceiling. When MJ killed herself, I stopped it all. That's if he didn't do it … but he did. And she wasn't the only one, so I hear.

Elijah has to tell the police, says Thisbe. Tell her she has to tell the police.

The police, Bee? That's not our style.

Not usually, but, jeez. If you're telling the truth …

Whaddaya mean if?

You're telling the truth?

I've been called a rapist, he says, remember? I'm not gunna be that one who does that to some guy. Not even my worst enemy.

Thisbe exhales. Poor Elijah, she says.

She's still fucked up, you can tell. She wants to … tear my face off.

She should want to!

Meantime, he is here … with your pre-teen kid. He's not her father. It's just time, is all.

Fuck! She grips her waist. Fuck!

But the police? No. There are other avenues, says Stone. Just say the word and I'll keep him away from your girls, forever.

Regardless, she says, we can't be quiet any more. Silence is exactly what that bastard does not need. And you promised me, Stone, a few more months and you are done with your crew. Don't go doing anything stupid. Not now. He's not ruining what we have here, too.

*

He knows she changes her mind about people, that she has a baby-fever now, but she could change her mind about him, have his baby, change her mind and kick him out. He knows he can leave the gang now and then return. They'll dig him out at first, but they'll never turn their backs.

He is having a normal relationship, and things like this, love and shit, do not happen to Stone Shea. He grabs her close to him and kisses her. She takes her winter sweater off over her head and he removes his jeans and lays on the bed. She gets up and sits astride him.

255

So, when we make this baby, she says, you'll let me meet your family?

Not this topic again, he says.

Just like Jordan, she says.

Why do you have to talk and ruin a moment?

You are, she says, just like him.

How? Tell me.

Every time, hot and cold.

I'm not hot and cold, he says, you're hot and cold. He unbuttons her jeans, reaches up and bites her upper arm.

But I want an introduction to the famous Madame Barb, she says. She was here before, she actually exorcized this bedroom.

Buzz-kill, he says looking around the room Pinault shot MJ in, the room he beat up Thisbe in, the room he called the cops from and accused Stone of rape.

Thisbe runs her finger up his thigh and his erection pulses.

When will I meet your grandmother? she asks.

You will meet, he says.

When?

New year.

New Year's Eve?

No, he says, trying to pull at her bra straps. She has plans with her precious granddaughter, I believe.

Invite them here, Thisbe says, holding her breasts inside her bra.

I will, if you'll only give me a chance. He reaches around her back.

God, always so secretive with you, she says, grabbing his fingers. Always take, take, take.

Bullshit. He puts his hands on her thighs.

Is it, Ephraim? She wraps her hands around his throat.

Don't call me that, he says, pulling at her wrists. You sound like Barb now.

Thisbe laughs, pulls his hair at the roots. Good, maybe she'll like me.

Who cares if she likes you? She's a crazy bitch.

Does Barb know about me?

Sure.

Have you told her? She tugs his hair harder.

Of course. He releases her thumbs.

Then what ... she's racist?

You know ... probably. A little bit.

Thisbe scoffs and climbs off him, smacking Stone on the chest.

We just aren't real close. I raised myself, he says, sitting up, pulling her on to his knee and gently gnawing her neck.

You probably think you did, she says, pushing his forehead away. Like I thought I did. But I assure you, you didn't.

He pushes her up to standing and gets off the bed, pulling his jeans back on. There is no point getting into it. Women never lose an argument, they remember every little thing you say.

*

On January 2nd, it storms generously and swift. The morning before the meeting at the clubhouse, Thisbe wraps her arms around him. You haven't asked my new year's resolution, she says.

Spill.

Jordan is gunna get his day in court. I'm gunna see Elijah, talk to her, make peace, bribe her to speak up, if that's what it takes.

Stone looks at her, her eyes are sparkling.

257

You could be putting me in the firing line, he says. You want to put me back inside? I think that's what you want, to see me behind bars.

No. She holds him. I'll get to Elijah, since the police couldn't care less, I'll tell her to leave your name out of it. I'll even do it, if you won't. People tell me things and I can be very persuasive.

Don't I know it.

But I can't have my kids get older, decide that they want him in their life and not know that he is a monster and a possible murderer.

A definite murderer. There are rumors, girls younger than MJ McCord. God knows how many kids he has done this to.

God knows he won't do it to mine!

We'll talk about this when I get home from the meeting, Stone says.

Thisbe kisses him sorrowfully. If you love me, you'll do it, she says.

I could say the same to you. Leave it.

He lifts his leather vest from the back of the closet and puts it on. He will miss this. Maybe he doesn't have to. He walks down the stairs, goes to leave, gathers his wallet and feels in his pockets for his cell. Thisbe comes behind him, grabs his hand. They release their fingers with uncertainty. He walks outside and gets on to his bike.

He'd not been able to get through to Barbra-Jean the day before, so he heads out with the stony eyes of the founding fathers at Mount Rushmore on him at every turn, white flecks of mountain goats on their noses like blemishes, and around wooden pigtail bridges as he rides the curved roads home to Custer.

She is there, wearing her old mink coat and sitting on the porch with a duvet wrapped around her.

She has her scribble-pad and pencil, is writing the Friday horoscopes. They go online and in the paper. They don't pay her more than a nominal fee. What does anyone expect for that? he thinks. It is only a hobby. Something to do. And don't chicks dig that kind of shit? he thinks, wanting to think they are special? that their disappointing past wasn't in vain? that something wonderful is right around the corner, waiting?

Happy '16, he says. What are you doing outside, it's about to blizzard?

Measuredly Barb sets her pen and pad down. She used to be annoyed with him if he'd been on the road and avoided calling her at New Year. She didn't mind him forgetting her birthday, she would have to remind him anyway. She does not expect a Christmas present, nothing at Thanksgiving but his company. But New Year, it's important to her in a way he doesn't get.

Who in their right mind wants to celebrate a new year of the same old same old? he thinks.

Barb goes inside, leaving the duvet outside. Stone asks her if she wants it left there, if she wants it brought inside. Nothing comes in response.

How was your new year? Stone asks.

He notices that all of Elijah's pictures on the table are gone.

Elijah is dead to me, his grandmother replies. That's the last time I'll ever say her name and I never again want to hear it from you either.

Why is that?

I'm not discussing it. That girl is wired wrong. See, I knew it from she was young.

Stone laughs.

What a waste of skin, he says. And time.

Barbra-Jean looks at him in surprise before he turns and looks for his phone.

He has a message from one of his gang brothers, they are bringing the meeting forward a few hours to avoid the police. Stone hops on his bike and rides fast through the black hills and out to Verboten clubhouse in the whisking snow.

RAPID CITY WOMEN ONLY REPLY

2015 – 2016

I don't think I need to be any clearer than what the title says. If you are not from Rapid City or South Dakota then don't waste my time. I am being serious here and putting time and effort into trying to meet someone who is easy going, fun to be around and has a great sense of humor. I'm a nice guy, I have great morals, enjoy being active and enjoying life. I expect someone who can be just as talkative as I can be, so if you email me with Hey, how you are you, chances are you're going to get ignored. Sure, I'm picky and I have every right to be, I expect someone to have plenty to talk about, nothing worse than trying to talk to someone who has nothing on their mind. At least tell me more about yourself, your age, where you are from, your interests, etc. I love getting to know people and the whole point is having a nice meaningful conversation with someone.

If you have a few words how can you get to know anyone unless their motives are sex.

I am separated (in the process of divorce soon), and I would love to treat someone right. I have always had a great outlook on life, been kind and polite and I can't be anyone but myself. I really prefer to get to know someone, friends is always the best way to start things out, and see how things go after that. I am in no rush, I know there are a lot of guys on here who just want one thing, but I just want someone to talk to, hang out with and just enjoy everything with.

I am a very romantic guy, so if you send me a nude picture of yourself or you start to talk about sex then you are going to just get ignored. That, to me, shows insecurity big time and I want someone who is worth waiting for, someone I can get to know very well.

I could go on and on and tell you more about myself, but the whole point is to just email me and let me know you are interested. I would be happy to hear from you, so if you are real and you are from South Dakota then I look forward to hearing from you.

Spammers, people that are not from SOUTH DAKOTA, and let me say it again IF YOU ARE NOT FROM RAPID CITY then don't even email me, you're going to get ignored. :) I know there are women out there who are from Rapid City, who are easygoing and fun to chat with, so don't be shy, say hi! :) I mean this most sincerely, do not mess me around. I mean it.

Sheriff Heath Noteboom looked at his post one last time before he published it on the personal ads on his local Craigslist, then he scrolled through the Missed Connections page once more, looking again at the post he'd added back in April for the girl in the Cadillac he'd seen at the gas station. Beautiful, she was. She had still not replied.

By now it was highly unlikely that she ever would, especially now he knew who she was, and who she was betrothed to. Regardless, Heath clung to the hope that she would see his message soon, realize how he felt about her and in turn discover that she too loved him, in passing, from afar, across the forecourt.

Heath had been with the police force now for twenty-two years and was considerably fatigued. The bikers were steaming through town again and he had the tribal police to deal with too. Heath had given his life to justice, and now he deserved to have someone come look after him a while, he decided, as he sat back and took measure of the room, loose with long drapes and baggy carpets, the snow gathering on his window ledge.

October, and there was snow already. The only thing you could not depend on in Rapid was the weather. Hate the season, wait fifteen minutes for the next one – that was always the thing Heath said. He missed having a woman to say it to. He'd always liked female company, but for undetermined reasons, he was never a smash with them.

He'd spent hours looking at Craigslist now. He found it addictive since he started using the site to get wind of house parties. Through the site, he could intercept any problems before they started, and he liked that very much. He liked to be one step ahead of the game.

*

The day after Thanksgiving, in the bashful November light, Thisbe Hartfield came into the Pennington County Sheriff's Office and demanded to speak to Heath Noteboom, nobody else but Noteboom.

Just as well he was there.

Heath told her to step inside his office. He was drinking tea when he asked her to tell him what she wanted to say.

Jordan, my ex-husband, she said, he murdered Mary Jane McCord.

How Heath had laughed. Oh really, he said.

Yes, she uttered and he laughed some more.

Thisbe furrowed her brow. How is that funny? she asked.

Where were you back in '95? Texas, isn't that right? High school?

So?

Guess where I was? Heath said.

Here? she guessed.

Yep, sure was. I was in Colonial Pine Hills that night, driving by the crick when a call came my way. Not that this is your business, missy, don't even know why I'm telling you. Who was the first responder there that night?

You? she asked, growing an attitude that he would have to cut at the knees.

Yep, he replied, so please, don't come in here, twenty years later telling me that you have done my job for me. Thank you and good day.

You know it's public knowledge, right? she said.

Oh, is it now? He pulled a face and sipped his tea.

Aren't you gunna do something about it?

Isn't this the man you married?

Yes, she said, so I know better than anyone what he's like.

Really?

There have been posters over town about Mary Jane for months. You say you're looking for information.

Woah, hold up, said Heath. I'm not looking for anything of the kind.

Who then? Her family?

Now I see that your reading comprehension ain't that good, I'll not worry about your new information. He laughed.

I can see you don't have a daughter.

Excuse me?

If you did, you might care.

Excuse me, missy, I was the one who had to tell Mary Jane McCord's poor mother Marjorie that she had shot herself in the head, not you. So when you're ready with an apology, I'll be here waiting. Good day!

I know the truth, she said.

And who told you the truth?

Ephraim Shea.

Ha! Stone Shea. Isn't he the man you accused of getting rough with you? Why would he tell you anything?

We're together now, she said proudly.

Damn, he thought, this bitch is damn near unbreakable. Hold up! Heath said.

Ephraim has told me that Jordan murdered Mary Jane McCord, and had sex with a whole crew of minors. Probably murdered one or two of them, too.

Thisbe, you have wasted a lot of police time in the past and you sure as heck ain't gunna waste more.

I'm serious. And I won't go until I'm listened to.

Shea has a vendetta against Pinault, said Heath. Shea has a vendetta against most people. Is he blackmailing you now? You can say and I won't be mad, but the sooner you tell me the better.

Heath hated that man, rolling around on that Harley as if he owned the town.

There had been a small vacation from them until factions of the gang, who were not imprisoned, started to flock together again. Heath would have happily locked Stone up too, with the rest of them meat heads back in May, only he had an old honor code towards Senator Burgess. He had promised to look after Ephraim Shea, who had done the senator a good deed. Heath never asked what the deed was, and although the senator was in no condition to question anything now, Heath still could not renege on his promise.

He'd received a golden handshake from Burgess at the same time and nobody had ever given him a thing he did not have to work for. And no, Heath did not see it as bribery, there were no conducive requests attached. The cash he was given and the request that was eventually made, were not exactly at the same time. The senator purely saw that Heath was young and still living at home, and he said: Listen, Noteboom, you can't be a new sheriff – for he had gone through the police ranks at top speed – and still living with your mother, you just can't, so here is a down-payment for a home, you deserve it, you keep this city free from vermin and that is all anyone ever expects from you.

Beverly Burgess had been fatherly to Heath, to be clear. And Heath had not been in uniform when the handshake occurred. It was not a business transaction. Beverly had come to him a little later, a week or so, the down payment paid out already, the house already Heath's, when Bev said: That guy, Stone Shea, he's a good guy.

And Heath, rubbing at his shiny new badge, said: He looks like he's starting up some kind of gang – expecting that Beverly would say: Then you keep them off our streets, and Heath, eager to please, would have said: Well, yes, sir! but he had not said that.

Instead Beverly said: A gang? No, Sheriff. They're just young men that enjoy motorcycles, and then he added, Listen, Sheriff Noteboom – because he respected Heath's title an enormous amount – Stone did a favor for which I will be forever indebted, it's a personal thing, nothing that would interest you, but what I can say is that, he's good people. Beverly put his slim tapered hand on Heath's arm and said: He's one of us, Sheriff, one of us.

Heath had taken this on board, exactly how he was one of them he did not know, but Heath would reprimand him up to the point of arrest and then let Stone off with a caution. And when he messed up around Pine Ridge, the Sioux folk avenged for his crimes themselves, as did the rival gang of bikers. So he was usually not much trouble.

But there was another thing, one thing, that's all: Jordan Pinault calling the PD that night in 2010, claiming that his wife had been raped by Stone Shea and what could Heath do but arrest him? His hands were tied. Heath went to Beverly's bedside after the arrest and asked him for forgiveness, he even considered losing evidence, and there was a lot of it, semen, saliva, bruises and cuts, and then Heath saw the fear in Thisbe's eyes, and her kids crying at her side, confused, clinging to her, and he saw how angry Pinault was about the whole situation, and Heath thought, Okay, she is someone's mother, and my mother … well, she is someone's mother too, making Thisbe human, kind of. And he looked again at Pinault, whom he'd always admired a great deal, so if he'd liked Burgess like a father, he liked Pinault as a cool younger brother he wished he'd have had, and Heath thought, right this moment, *this* guy is the one I need to please. Plus, Beverly always liked him.

Heath looked at Thisbe Hartfield, standing in his office now, the familiar look of pain in her eyes when she said: There is no vendetta. Ephraim never raped me. My husband? Now there is another story. And a couple of boys back in Lubbock … but let's forget that for a second. With Ephraim it was consensual. Sheriff, you know, sometimes you are just so lonely, so starved of affection, and Ephraim gave me that.

That's TMI, he said, too much information.

But Heath did know that loneliness. Those prolonged periods of separation that corroded the soul. Another potential association would fizzle and die. His own marriage lasted only six weeks. There was nothing he knew more than loneliness.

Sure, Jordan had a right to be angry, she said, but did he have a right to rip my dress off me? To hit me, to kick me, to phone the police and lie, to say to me: Tell them you were attacked. And did I let it go too long? Yes, I did, but I was scared. I needed to time it right to get rid of Jordan. I needed to have protection and my own money. But now, Ephraim has forgiven me. Doesn't that stand for something? That I told the truth?

I'm sure you do not want to go down this route, things could get very slippery, Heath said.

Slippery is the game Jordan has played his whole life, said Thisbe. Let me tell you, he always said he was up before anyone, perfecting his throw in a field full of morning dew.

Mrs. Pinault …

Uh-uh, she said.

Thisbe, Heath said, I'm working on something right now. I'll call out with you in a couple of days, okay.

Fine, she said, looking unsure whether to leave or stay, but she left.

Heath rolled his eyes. Jeez, always a telenovela with some folk, he said as he reopened the tab on his laptop for Craigslist. There was still no reply to his Missed Connection post, but in the long, dead days after Thanksgiving – and not visiting Thisbe and not being visited by her again – he finally received what he estimated was a sincere reply to his personal ad among an arsenal of ridiculous ones.

Hey, read the sincere one, *you sound real nice and I think we would make a great pair. Not only do I like to talk but I'm a real good listener. I'm lonely – truthfully. I want to look after someone and you sound like someone who needs looking after, I can tell. You deserve that, and I deserve that. Let's meet up for a lunch.*

He agreed to, even though she had blatantly disregarded most of his rules of engagement. She chose Klinkelton in Main Street Square. She would be the woman with the flower in her lapel and Heath said he would be the man in the cowboy hat.

*

And he went for lunch, all in uniform except for a cowboy hat. He sat in his booth and ran his sweaty palms along the thighs of his slacks, blew slowly out when in walked a woman with short silver hair. She sat in another booth. She had the flowering bruise of a silk pasque in her lapel and the day's copy of the Rapid City Journal in her hand. When she saw him, he tipped his hat. And she got up and walked over to him.

Well I'll be damned, Sheriff, she said, regaining her usual confidence.

Marjorie! he said, gesturing for her to take a load off on the red leather seat adjacent his.

269

He could have said that he was simply a man wearing a cowboy hat having lunch, but he could not once he saw her. This was finally it.

He thought back all those years ago and how he had broken the news of MJ's death to her and how she had crumpled into his arms. He'd thought about her from time to time since, she had liked younger men and he had been put out that she had not liked him. But now he still looked kind of young, it was the prominent teeth and how his ears stuck out, they gave him a boyishness that he usually did not like about himself. But now Heath pitied those men he had envied when he was younger. It must have been the worst thing to peak so early, then spend the rest of your life trying to grasp back something of your past. Not him, this was as good as he got, a dependable mediocrity.

Heath asked her what she would like and she said: Quinoa and kale, and a coffee. He ordered that and a burger for himself, when the waitress approached the table.

Then they sat quietly, then suddenly he found the weight of his Craigslist post overwhelming; all that talk about talking! And all this silence! He knew they both had heads full of things, Mary Jane most probably.

Heath hadn't seen Marjorie in years, not since it happened. How could she see him and not see that night as clearly as he was?

It's been twenty years, can you believe? he asked.

I can believe, Marjorie said smiling at him. She had always been uptight and hyper-wordy but dripping with sexual spirit. Now she was at ease, that was the only thing he could think, that she looked well, and content.

You know, Ms. McCord, you look good, he said.

Bless your heart, Heath. I can't believe you haven't got a woman.

Not since my marriage ended. If you count that. I wouldn't.

What's the deal with that?

It was short.

No, she said. I mean, lovely man like you and no woman.

I don't rightly know.

You're right, Marjorie said, in what you wrote. Heath, you do deserve a nice woman, and a local one would be ideal. Who wants to have to travel these days? You're probably behind the wheel often enough.

His face heated when he remembered his post, and her being older felt like authority, and he had always bristled at authority, which was what drew him to the police department and then the sheriff's office, to be it rather than fear it.

Something about her made him feel demure, right there, two civilians both laying it on the line that they just wanted to have companionship.

I've been single for a long time, Marjorie said, I didn't think I wanted someone, and then, well … you are not the first person I've met through the personals.

No?

No, there have been a few, none I could see myself with. They were either too young or they were old. Getting to the point, Heath, I want a match. I want an equal. I work hard. All those things you said about yourself, that you don't want someone just using you for sex, how many men can say that? Beside the bravado bullshit – and I could see past that into a good heart – behind all that I thought you sounded more like a woman.

I don't know how I feel about that, he said, embarrassed again.

No, no, I liked that, said Marjorie. It's not an insult, unless you have something against women.

Well, I certainly don't fear women, if that's what you're meaning.

Fear them? No. Heath, I mean that you are honest and you don't want to be used, and, getting to the point: I've spent a lifetime getting used by people, being some man's sidepiece. I'm talking of when I was younger, in particular.

He looked at his napkin.

None of this is news to you, I'm sure, she said.

You were using what you had and you had your looks.

I don't anymore?

That's okay, they don't last forever.

Are you serious? she said loudly.

Oh, it was a question. I thought you meant that you don't have your looks.

No, listen Heath, I am a beautiful woman, I always have been and I always will be.

Sure! I didn't like to say.

Attraction has to come first, it just does.

You're right.

But …

Marjorie sat back to receive her quinoa, she looked at it. She put salt on it. Heath looked at his burger, sniffed it and set his hat down by his side. He discharged the waitress when she asked if she could bring them anything else.

But I want something extra now, said Marjorie. I don't try to maintain my looks but I look after myself.

Shows.

Heath, stop it and listen, would you.

Yes. Sorry, Marjorie.

Heath, let's cut the bull. I know you say you don't want sex and I don't want *just* sex, so can we cut to it? We know why we are both here, now let's be adult about this. I like you, she said.

And I like you.

You are kind of special.

Thank you, he said.

I mean it, Hun.

And I mean my thanks. Do you mind if I get tucked in?

Please, she said. She watched him eat. You do have nice manners, and you do deserve a real woman.

Thanks again.

And I deserve a nice man. I do.

I know you do.

So, tell me straight. Do you want to see me again? Starting of as friends and seeing where it'll go? She lifted her fork and played with her kale.

Marjorie, let me narrow with you first. There is someone else.

Already? She smiled.

I need to take her temperature first. That's me being straight.

Fine.

You're not offended?

Hun, you couldn't offend me if you tried.

Thanks for taking that so well.

Gosh, aren't you a well of gratitude?

So, if I can find this woman and see how she feels, and if she doesn't feel the same …

Heathcliffe! You haven't even spoken to this woman?

No, I did. Briefly.

Oh, come on!

273

Give me a day or two. I'll find out and I'll be in touch.

How are you gunna find out?

I know her car.

You have her plates?

Yep.

How long have you had them?

A few months.

And you haven't run them yet?

It's not ethical.

Screw ethical, Marjorie said. You are posting personal ads, and was that you too, the ad in the missed connection? I recognize the writing style. The same weird use of capitalization.

Heath blushed. She's engaged.

Oh, Heath, she said.

He looked at the time on his watch. Put his hat back on. Sheriff Noteboom, he said, I'm back on the clock.

Heath, she said. You're gunna live your life like this, be my guest.

How do you mean?

Afraid.

I'm not afraid of anything, he said.

Let's Stay Together by Al Green came on the radio. Marjorie smiled. I love this song, she said, isn't it the best song?

I like it, Heath admitted.

Would you dance with me?

Here?

Where else?

No. No, Marjorie. It's not … I'm not someone who dances, you know?

I hoped so but thought probably not.

He looked at her face, he remembered how the sweat had run down his spine standing at her door that August night. The instant he said: Mary Jane has shot herself in the head, he'd looked away so as not to see her face. Then Marjorie had fallen against him in a way that seemed contrived, and yet it could not have been. He'd held her in his arms, it was the first time, besides his prom when he had held a woman in his arms. She had pressed against him and cried in his ear. She had a sweet small bald spot at the top of her head he wondered if she knew about.

He had revisited that moment for months until he finally lost his virginity at the Christmas party to sweet little Penny Lawhun who had since worked her way up but back then she worked the phones. With Penny, he thought of Marjorie's body. Any other young man would have preferred poor dead MJ: she was the kind of girl men went wild for, but Marjorie had become a fascination for Heath. He thought about her more than he thought about her daughter. Though he tossed MJ's death over in his mind for years. These crimes of passion put him off developing relationships with women.

When he was young, women of his own age bored him with their chat and their insecurities, then they married and bored someone else, or changed their mind after less than two months, and he got to hide behind his uniform and stay at his mother's house.

He often wished he'd been a little bit wilder, that he'd been one of the boys Marjorie deflowered; or that he'd called in on her another time, to tell her that he was sorry for her loss; or that he would happen upon her when she was out sometime and he was out and off duty, and she would try to seduce him.

She had held him so tightly that night. And afterward, he hadn't the cajones. And then she vanished from the Rapid City bar scene.

Now, although he wanted nothing more than a reason to hold her in his arms again, Heath could not get up and dance with her. It was ridiculous that anyone would dance in a diner in the middle of the day. But he wanted to be that man, badly. So very badly.

I know who the girl is, he said, the one in the car. I don't need to run plates.

Then go after her, said Marjorie.

No, he said. She's getting married. What would she want with me? He glazed over.

What is it? she asked him.

You look beautiful, he said.

You know, no man has ever said that to me, I mean outside of bed.

And I've never told any woman that they are … he struggled to say it again.

This is like some sort of eclipse then, or a comet, said Marjorie. Maybe it will never happen again in our lifetimes. Now that's tragic!

He looked at her face, the sweet smudging of her features. She was no less intimidating, she was maybe more so. What happened to it being about friendship? He wanted to be in her bed, telling her how beautiful she was, without any humiliation.

What are you gunna do about the other woman, prize her away from her fiancé?

He lifted his burger and took another bite.

He'd known it was Helena Russo for weeks now, he'd seen Pinault drive away from the care home where Burgess resided in that car, and who in their right mind would choose Heath Noteboom over Jordan Pinault?

*

That August night twenty years before, Jordan was being tended to by a paramedic when Heath found the letter in MJ's purse: Dear J, it started, etc. And below that was an apology for hurting a person and explanation – he won't ever forget it – that she would 'leave now'. Heath instantly said it was obviously a suicide, with Jordan sitting there scalded, saying they'd been having an affair and she had gone crazy. Demanding he marry her. That letter wrapped everything up.

Now Heath thought about MJ's husband John that night saying: She is married. Why would she be angry with someone else for not wanting to marry her?

John Kloster said he knew someone else was involved with his wife. A small friendship, he had called it. The letter could have been to him. He was also a J. And sure, that made sense too. That she was leaving him. That she was sorry for *that*.

It also gave clout to what Thisbe said that day after Thanksgiving about Pinault and how MJ's death was no suicide. There was no Beverly to keep happy anymore. Not in the way there had been. Heath could do it, there was nothing stopping him, Pinault could be prosecuted, Helena would be free. Marjorie would be thankful.

Sweet Marjorie! There was a sexual adolescence he was living in his mind with this woman in her mid-sixties. Now Heath thought of her.

If he was to tell her that now – lightbulb moment! – it suddenly made sense that her daughter had written that letter for her husband and that she had been having an affair, not with Jordan Pinault but with Eric Nwafo.

But nothing was suddenly.

Heath copped on to their relationship immediately after the death; Eric Nwafo promptly gave up football and got into the church; he had real tears in his eyes at the memorial service like only her husband had. And after it, Eric wanted to be alone. He was devastated.

And MJ had liked him, too. From what Heath has heard since, it was a mutual sort of haunting. Then Eric lost his brio and, some might say, married beneath him.

Heath realized everything, but then, he thought, maybe he should not pick at old wounds, open those files of the five or more barely-teen girls from the furthest corners of Pennington County – all Caucasian, all blonde, all with hopes of becoming models – who suicided in '95, and the following year, in some sort of contagion.

All those cases where Pinault's name was brought up in question. Or Burgess's.

Waking up the dead never helped anyone, not when all was gone and already dealt with. The families of those girls had already closed that door and it did no good to open it now and storm through a whole building of pain.

Maybe how he could pay back Marjorie for all she had lost, was by being her lover and companion, by looking after her and allowing her to look after him and allowing them both to have something good finally.

But he could not stop thinking about details: like the champagne flute that was smashed in Pinault's hallway and how he'd ignored it like he had ignored the patch of oil on the bedroom floor, under the towel.

Heath had let that slide because it didn't make sense.

Then he let it slide back into his head once in a while for years. He had, ten years after, been toweling himself after a shower when he thought, someone brought that fryer into Pinault's bedroom too, not just the bathroom.

And he had a thought as he pictured Pinault in the bath, remembering that he was not particularly burned despite having a whole fryer of hot fat thrown at him, as he'd claimed. Heath saw a vision of Jordan Pinault shooting MJ and placing the gun in MJ's hand and going downstairs, then getting the oil, bringing it upstairs, and scalding himself, adequately, just enough. The letter in her purse was probably nothing to do with MJ's death, the tone wasn't right. So there was that, the towel, the glass, the oil that sat on the top of the bathwater.

Few people would have blinked. Heath didn't. The Justice of the Peace didn't order an autopsy. It was done. And until it became something, it was nothing.

*

It was the second day in January when Heath made breakfast in bed for Marjorie and then got ready for work. He set the newspaper on the bed and Marjorie opened it straight at the horoscopes.

It's my thing, she said. I live by this.

That's just some old crank writing them, said Heath buttoning his beige shirt and putting on his tie and badge.

No, said Marjorie, Barb believes that your star sign says something about your character.

So, what would she say about me?

You're a Virgo, she said. You're shy. Worry a lot. All work and no play.

Maybe there is something to that, he said. Go on, read mine out.

Marjorie read it inside herself first, then she closed the paper. Barb's column kept me going, after MJ's death, she said.

Was she going to bring her daughter up in every conversation? Heath didn't know if he could stomach it. It was bad enough that he was thinking about her persistently, guiltily. What star sign are you? he asked, deflecting.

Aquarius, said Marjorie.

What does it say for you?

I can't tell you that. She stretched out. That I might meet my prince charming.

Really? Heath said and Marjorie looked at him whitely. He was almost out of the door when she muttered – They're talking snow – and opened the paper again.

Hate the season, wait fifteen minutes for the next one, said Heath with insurmountable satisfaction.

But it wasn't just snow, it was a full-blown storm. He was out in it now. He could have gone to the office, he should have, but curiosity got the better of Sheriff Noteboom. He had this feeling he rarely had, like he was intuiting something, so he drove in the snow to the clubhouse when he received a message on the way.

The Chevaliers are in town, said his deputy.

Yes, that's why we're gunna have a heavy police presence here later, for their biker meeting.

Seems like the meeting is done, the deputy replied, the Chevaliers were seen at Verboten clubhouse a couple of hours ago.

So why are you only telling me now? he asked irritably.

I did try to contact you.

Noteboom looked at his cell phone and saw the missed calls. Marjorie had an awful habit of silencing his phone. You deserve time to relax, she'd say.

When he pulled up at Verboten there were no signs of any fighting. There were no Chevaliers but twenty members of the Marcach gang, most of the ones who had been released from jail just before Christmas. Heath suddenly felt like he should not have come out there alone. Stone Shea was giving him the eye.

No homes to go to, Heath muttered.

The snow was coming down hard in Hisega. He got out of the car and stood there watching them, but besides Stone they didn't take any notice.

I thought we had a deal, Heath said.

What? asked Stone, he walked nearer and Heath inhaled and tried to count to five, tried to read the situation. He'd never found it an easy thing to do.

You coming back later for the meeting? Heath asked Stone. He was about to radio in to his colleague not to bother coming out this way when Helena Russo's Cadillac sped past him, Helena was racing through the hills, he could tell it was her despite how often she changed her hair, and there was a blonde-haired woman in her passenger seat.

Had to be flexible, said Stone.

Heath took his radio out, there was no doubt that Helena was speeding, this was his chance. Next Jordan Pinault was right behind, speeding too, chasing Helena.

Sheriff Noteboom jumped back into the sheriff's car and turned, trying to tail them. The snow and wind swirled heavy. He put on his wipers at full force. He could feel his car being pushed to one side, buffeted by the wind. Heath was almost blinkered by the snow, struggling to keep going straight and forward.

He heard shots. Gunshots. He drove, hunched over his wheel. He sped in the direction of the city. Ahead he could see Pinault and Russo directly in front of him.

He put on the siren to get them to stop but they did not heed his warning. Helena traveled into a residential boulevard, while Pinault's wheels skidded on the ice.

A tree in front was shaking, it wobbled in the distance, and soon Heath was almost at it, his foot hovering over his brake when the tree came down, right in the middle of the road. Heath swerved to avoid it. He got out of his car, blinking away the snow that sat on his lashes. He killed his siren. It echoed in the swirling wind.

He could make out Pinault's car there too, but Helena had got away. Heath would be lying to say he wasn't relieved she was safe.

Adrenalin was coursing through him, he felt like a hero. The tree, he now noticed as he gained on foot, was not fully down but hung on the powerlines for a moment before it pulled them completely down. Electricity was jumping up from the ground as Pinault's passenger door opened. Heath was expecting to see someone else, but he recognized that meaty leg.

Hang tight, Pinault. I'll get help to ya, Heath shouted at Jordan, thinking he must not have seen the wire hanging in a puddle next to car. But Pinault either could not hear him or he decided to ignore Heath's good advice and he stepped out, jerked and jumped, a glaze of electricity traversing across his form. Then he fell, like a lightning bolt, with the now seen from behind. Pinault rolled flat as the asphalt. Something in it awed and terrified Heath. Pinault hadn't moved that smoothly in a decade or more.

Heath bet Pinault was dead. Ceasing to exist, now that was another matter.

He took out his radio and called for backup.

Jordan Pinault's down, he said. We're gunna have to get an electrician out, know of any?

We'll have to get the electricity disconnected before anybody can get near him.

A motorcycle behind Heath slowed to parade speed. Stone Shea was on it, he stopped, took off his helmet and got off his bike.

He looked at Pinault, shrugged and laughed.

Well, well, he said. Saved me a job.

There was a blaze of motorbike engines roaring in the distance. They slowed to pass the scene, then they bypassed the tree, cutting through front yards, and then the bikers were gone.

What are you talking about, *saved you a job*? Heath asked Stone.

Stone remained looking at Pinault.

All that business, he said. All those young girls who killed themselves because of him and Burgess. And MJ McCord …

You don't know what you're talking about, said Heath.

He always feared men like Stone for a multitude of different reasons. Most men did not look to Heath with admiration, though they might have pretended to. Not Stone. His contempt was palpable.

Stone lifted his eyes from Pinault to the sheriff.

Still Burgess's little bitch, are you? he said.

Watch your lip, said Heath, caressing his gun with his thumb and feeling safer, instantly.

Stone turned to face him. I was guilty, he said, in my own way … with Elijah. My little cousin … I allowed myself to be bought by evil, a lot of us did. You included.

What were you doing at Verboten this early? asked Heath. We have a deal, since the massacre in May, that the department will always be present at your clubhouse meetings.

Listen, Heathcliffe.

Sheriff, to you.

Number Eight is over there, look at him. He's going nowhere. And your friend, Bev, is on his way out and maybe that's enough, right? But I can't help but think about all those other families with no answers, or the wrong answers. Photos in the Journal. White girls. Blond. Twelve. Thirteen years old. And, then there's Mary Jane. It was always obvious to me that that was no suicide.

Get on your bike, Shea, said Heath, and roll on out of here. Just roll on out with your cronies and your conspiracy theories.

I'll roll out when I'm done. When your associates get here and I let them know what's on my mind.

Yeah, right.

I'll go down for my part, no sweat. I'll do it the right way. I'm done but I'm not done, bitch.

The cold in the air felt hot and smelled like cloves, reminding Heath of a toothache. His tooth ached when he freed his gun. Heath's tooth hurt when he shot Ephraim Shea, road name Stone, aka, Agri-Supplies Boy in the chest.

When Ephraim Shea hit the snow and moved a bit, a nerve in the sheriff's jaw twinged. He's probably wearing a vest, thought Heath, and he panicked, walked over and shot him at closer range in the head, at the same time pressing his knuckles against his own cheek.

The mess that was Stone's head was shocking but contained. Heath felt calm, safe.

But beyond the snowflakes, were faces at the windows of the houses, a young man came out on to his veranda and lit up a smoke. Sirens were whipping in the distance. There were witnesses. Too many. There was no way to cover this.

Heath would never proceed beyond it. He'd had his one strike when he opened fire on the unarmed Lakota boy back in 2002. Heath's career was done and he was afraid. But he was always afraid. He let the streets of Rapid City crawl with junkies and he stayed away. He hid in his office, and if he had to confront any male at all, even youths, he hid behind his weapon. His fear had gotten worse the older he'd got. He was tired of being afraid.

Heath could cease too. Heath could die right now, at more or less the same time as Pinault, on the same boulevard, on the same day. They'd at least remember his name, thought Sheriff Heathcliffe Fitzgerald Noteboom. His last thought, he'd hoped, wrongly, as he put the gun in his mouth and aimed upward, blowing off his face, but leaving his brain fully intact and alive with thoughts that screamed through him like the early morning locomotive, smelling metal and blood through the hole in the middle of his face, while his nose lay waiting on a blanket of snow.

Life goes on, the sun comes up

1972

Aquarius, weekends are meant for relaxing, but these next two days will test you. On Friday, the competitive Scorpio moon is linked up with lucky Venus in your money sector. Don't underestimate the impressions you make on people. Devote more attention to the way you dress and how you communicate. Aim high and don't settle for anything less than that! Take a breather on Saturday, when the Sun in your sign aligns with the moon in your eleventh house of group activities. Your humanitarian spirit may be craving something meaningful. Help those who need your help, that will not only fill your heart but could introduce you to a new kindred spirit.

Marjorie Crapper reads her horoscope, then sets down the paper and goes into her apartment bedroom.

Mary Jane totters about in her mother's shoes and the soft rain outside that has fallen like ash for days, grows fuller, stronger. Marjorie sweeps her daughter up in her arms singing *Brand New Key*, then sets her down on the bed as she dresses the child in a purple soft-knit mini-dress. Marjorie dons her own matching one, and on top of it, fine raincoats for a rather bitter evening.

She puts Mary Jane into her stroller and walks downtown to the new Taco Stax where Arthur is standing with his back to them. When he turns, he instantly guides Marjorie away.

Let's go to the diner, he says, his smile skims over the baby.

Butterflies go at it in Marjorie's stomach, she has not seen him in over a year. She has had to make do with the thought of him, minus his scent and touch. She is ready for the child to meet her father now he is talking about Taco Stax as a completed task, and all he has achieved, telling her, as they get seated in the diner, that the place is coming together beautifully, as planned.

He takes a break from talking about shop fittings and flights and releases his shoulders, gives her a broad smile as if to say: Okay, I've been talking about me, but what about you? Tell me.

This is Mary Jane, Marjorie says, clutching Art's hands in hers.

Sweet, he says. You minding her for someone?

Take off your jacket, Arthur dear, says Marjorie, letting go of his hands.

If I take it off and hang it up, then, if the sun comes out, I'll walk outta here and leave it behind.

That's not likely to stop. Marjorie looks out of the window. The baby climbs into her lap and reaches for the sugar bowl.

287

I'll keep it here, even so, says Arthur, pulling his coat around him. What kind of weather is this you got here in June? he asks.

Marjorie watches him as he looks at the puddles on the ground outside. Maybe there is something in his pocket he wants to give her, she thinks hopefully, money, a ring. He pats his jacket around the breast, then tucks his hand inside and frees a packet of smokes, takes one out and offers one to Marjorie. She accepts it.

Arthur lights her cigarette, looks at her then at Mary Jane.

She's yours? Art says.

She is, says Marjorie, she inhales, exhales. Look, Hun, I didn't want to tell you over the phone. You'd gone quiet and I am fiercely independent. I never ask nobody for help. She inhales her cigarette again.

She's mine, isn't she? he asks. Yours and mine? He lights his own cigarette.

Yes, Arthur, she says gently.

I'm sorry, he says. I'm just shocked.

Shock is good, she says, puts you in touch with your heart, helps you recalibrate. Marjorie smiles cautiously. It was never going to turn out the way she'd pictured it.

You must have already had her last time I saw you, he says.

Yes, I did. Marjorie gives the baby her pocketbook to play with.

The last time Art Garber was in Rapid, Marjorie had got her mother to mind the child in case she scared him away, because Marjorie really likes Arthur and didn't want to put pressure on him. When they first met, Art said he had plans, a four-year plan, and wasn't that four years ago, now?

Isn't she beautiful? Marjorie smiles at Arthur. Like a perfect baby doll.

She's sweet, he says. Real pretty like her momma.

Wanna hold her? She holds Mary Jane up under each arm.

Erm. He recoils but holds out his hands.

You strange around kids? Marjorie laughs. You get, don't you, how I didn't want to tell you in a letter ... over the phone? Last time you came to town I wanted it to be me and you, and you were saying, you know, give me one more year, I'm slowing down. You were gassing about that four-year plan of yours.

I did say that, didn't I? He chucks the baby under the chin, makes a face at her and she smiles at him. He is good with kids.

It's been four years, Artie, Marjorie says, her tone sharpening.

Has it? He takes a drag of his cigarette and blows the smoke away from the baby. I'll call over the server. Should I? I should. I'm not hungry ... or thirsty, but you both should have something. Let me buy you both supper.

He hands Mary Jane back to her mother and waves the server over. Marjorie orders two coffees and a glass of milk.

Hey, you've been real quiet, Artie, she says.

Marjie, it's like this ... He looks up, his beautiful face, it has a look of something that is about to break, like he has seen a glass in the process of falling from the counter behind Marjorie's head, and he is waiting for the crash. She turns to look and turns back again, catching him trying to cover the gold band on his finger. He goes to say something when she tells him to stop. He has gotten married in the meantime, she knows it now. Some whirlwind affair. Lustful, thoughtless. Selfish and wrong. It is the reason she hasn't seen him.

Marjorie stubs out her cigarette. She bursts into tears.

He tries to put his hand under the table but thinks the better of it. I'm sorry, Marjie. I'm so sorry.

When did you do that? she says.

Well, no. I've been married. He puts his cigarette in the ashtray beside hers, to slowly burn away. I have a family, he whispers. Two babies. Twins: boy and a girl. He nods at MJ. They look so like your ... our ... this little one.

Marjorie lifts Mary Jane abruptly and takes her out of the diner into the street into the rapturous rain.

Art leaves a few dollars on their table, picks up his cigarette and follows after her, pushing the empty stroller. Let me give you a lift to your apartment, he says around his cigarette. I've a rental car. A Buick Skylark, gleaming new. It's got the 2-barrel Rochester carburetor, says Art.

I don't know what that means and I don't care to know, says Marjorie.

She gets into the passenger seat, Mary Jane on her lap. Art puts the stroller in the trunk like a professional stroller-collapser. He is soaked through as he gets into the car.

So, he says.

So?

The rain is coming heavy and dull, the wipers cannot remove it fully. Don't cry, Marjorie tells herself.

You walked down here in the rain? Art asks her. I should have come collected you, kiddo. Should have done a lot of things ...

And now she cries, and Mary Jane cries too.

Hey, I'm sorry, Marjie. Please, don't.

He puts his hand on her shoulder.

He is pathetic, she thinks. Pathetic, stupid, and she will never let herself feel this humiliation again, never.

Keep the car, he says when they get to her apartment.

But ... she goes to say.

I'll pay it off, he interrupts. Buy it outright, send you the papers.

She pulls at his arm, then she stops. This is what he wants, she knows that, for her to bring him back into her bed, for her to be fun, carefree Marjie again, but she is not that person anymore. She is running the show of her life with little help from her dregs of a family. Counting on him, she'd hoped. He'll go back to his twins and be the perfect father. His wife will take him to her bed, loving him, sleeping beside him, feeling safe and secure with him. Marjorie won't have him now, not even if he begs.

Maybe I can come in for a chat? he asks.

No, Arthur.

I'll set up an account, I'll make sure the child is okay. I'll back-pay even. How old is she?

Two, Marjorie says, she sets Mary Jane on the floor and pours herself a Jameson while Art hangs back for a moment.

I'll walk back, he says, don't worry about me. Keep the car.

You said already, she replies.

He sets the key on the hall table and closes the door. She goes to the window to see him outside in the rain.

*

That night and the next day, it thunders and thunders, it rains and rains heavy for eight solid hours.

But in a matter of minutes, and while people are sleeping, if they can find some peace for it, a mountain moves upon them and a suffocating tide of water swallows everything ahead of it for miles, starting at the creek and washing out the city. It does not stop until parts of Rapid is underwater, not until there are a couple of hundred people gone. Looking back, it will be as if they died at once.

Times like these, you are cut off from the world with only an old, outdated newspaper for comfort, and the world completely changes.

In the morning, Chad McCord, a young farmer who rents a plot from Marjorie's parents, knocks at her apartment door. Usually, anytime she sees him, he is wearing striped overalls, driving a John Deere, with Dale Russo standing on the drawbar, spikes of sunlight behind him.

Oh, thank God, Marjorie says.

Just checking in to see you're okay, you and the little sweetheart, Chad says.

Once Chad had climbed down from his John Deere and lifted little Mary Jane, who was out playing in the field. He'd gathered her up, the girl was as unsuspecting as water before it finds itself in a bucket. They had both laughed when he brought her to the Crappers' front door. Lost a sweetheart? he said, thoughtfully, smoothing down his tidy side part.

Marjorie had taken the child from him, hadn't even realized she'd gotten out. He'd laughed some more as he tickled Mary Jane. Mary Jane cried for Chad after he left and went back to work. He'd always seemed very the-meek-shall-inherit-the-world to Marjorie: a real boy-scout. Not today. He is suddenly older and worried-looking, not unhandsome.

Your parents are okay, just thought you should know, he says.

God, aren't you good, she replies.

He smiles then looks away to enjoy the smile. Chad looks to Marjorie like some sort of stupid angel. Or a messenger, at least. One who brings with him a naïve kind of faith, if there isn't any other kind.

Marjorie has cried all night, she touches her puffy face with her fingertips, embarrassed. He has always liked her, she can tell that.

So, what is the damage? she asks, sounding like an old boyfriend she had before Arthur no-good Garber. It was always the thing he said when he'd taken her out for a meal and was looking at the check. What's the damage? Reaching for his wallet.

She should have known with Art, there had been no meals out, just nights in. Few and far between, too. She'd turned perfectly acceptable men down while holding out for Art. Holding out to tell him, when the time was right, about Mary Jane. Meanwhile, she'd been making her own four-year plan that involved her and the baby making the move to Memphis, and Art becoming a semi-permanent fixture, in between all those long hours working and traveling. She didn't want a lot from him. She should have known.

Keystone is completely wiped away, they're saying, says Chad, bringing her back to earth. You hear that thunder last night?

Couldn't miss it, she says.

The soil has been saturated for days. On the ranch, that is.

Everyone else okay?

I shouldn't think so.

Marjorie groans and puts her hands behind her head.

293

I thought, she says, the roof was about to rip off the apartment or the windows were fixing to come in, she says.

Sure, he agrees. It was scary. Homes, businesses, they're no more.

All she can think of is Arthur and Taco Stax. It is still fresh, the break in her heart, it has the potential to go all the way. Wouldn't that make sense? She is already mourning him.

You're lucky you're out a-little-ways, Chad says. I'm gunna go help some. Seeing you're good, wanna come?

I would, but I have the baby.

Let's all drive around and see.

Outside cars are piled up like dominoes. People are standing in the street calm yet nonplussed. She sees Art eventually, he is standing outside the decimated Taco Stax. She is so relieved a tear falls from her eye.

It's not till you see it it hits you, huh? says Chad.

Her face feels so heavy it feels like it might fall off. Marjorie blows her bangs out of her eyes and hates everything in the world as strongly as she once loved it. Marjorie is thinking of all the things it said in her horoscope. Madame Barb had it right again, in her own way.

For the next couple of years, until what happens to Chad McCord happens, Marjorie believes in Barb, and the thought of anyone – even Barbra-Jean Shea – knowing anyone else's destiny, makes Marjorie feel very safely small. But now, she has an overwhelming notion to wrap her arms around Chad's as he changes up the gears. She inhales his waxy coat.

He is surprised when she does it, although he keeps his eyes forward. But he does not recoil, not even slightly, not back inside his sleeve.

He reaches out and puts his hand in hers. His hand is rough and ready as wood, hardened by years of ranching, hangnailed but honest. There is a glow all around him.

Chad McCord, she says, through a yawn. Would you look at that. You're a soft, hopeful sonofabitch. Rub some of that on me.

He lets out a little laugh as he drives through the detritus of the flood, under a gray sky that is moving on, slowly, to somewhere else. Every time they come to a roadblock of debris or destruction, they turn and try another route. They try again, again and again.

They move against the grain, through the damp city and out north to the flat forever land of sliding prairies and everything familiar, Chad driving slowly and steadily, so he won't have to let go of Marjorie's hand. And tenderly he rubs his thumb along hers, while Marjorie's daughter sleeps on her lap, blissful and unbuckled. Marjorie kisses the crown of her shiny blonde head.

ACKNOWLEDGEMENTS

I owe a debt of gratitude to the Arts Council of Northern Ireland and the ACES scheme, through which I was able to go to the beautiful setting of Rapid City, South Dakota, to research for *Souls Wax Fair*. I haven't been able to get the place out of my head since.

Special thanks to Ards Arts Centre, Tyrone Guthrie Centre, River Mill Retreat, Damian Smyth for all his support over the years, my writing community, especially Claire Savage, Gaynor Kane, Anne McMaster and Karen Mooney, and to the cracking NI crime scene, particularly my partners in crime, Sharon Dempsey and James Murphy. My heartfelt thanks to all.

Finally, thank you, as always, to my family, Ryan, Maddie, Jude, Jonah and Martha. I appreciate all the love and support you have shown to me, and all the patience you have for my double life.

BOOK GROUP QUESTIONS

There is a lot to think about in *Souls Wax Fair*, making it a perfect book for book clubs and groups.

What questions would you ask the author?

Here are some ideas to get you started:

Which scene has stuck with you the most?
What did you think of the writing? Are there any standout sentences?
Did you re-read any passages? If so, which ones?
How did your opinion of the book change as you read it?
If you could ask the author anything, what would it be?
Did this book remind you of any other books?
Who do you most want to read this book?
Are there lingering questions from the book you're still thinking about?
Did the book strike you as original?

To get in touch with the author with your questions or an invitation to visit your group, email fridaypressbooks@gmail.com.

THE BONES OF IT

Thrown out of university, green-tea-drinking, meditation-loving Scott McAuley has no place to go but home: County Down, Northern Ireland. The only problem is, his father is there now too.

Duke wasn't around when Scott was growing up. He was in prison for stabbing two Catholic kids in an alley. But thanks to the Good Friday Agreement, big Duke is out now, reformed, a counselor.

Squeezed together into a small house, with too little work and too much time to think about what happened to Scott's dead mother, the tension grows between these two men, who seem to have so little in common.

Penning diary entries from prison, Scott recalls what happened that year. He writes about Jasmine, his girlfriend at university. He writes about Klaudia, back home in County Down, who he and Duke both admired. He weaves a tale of lies, rage and paranoia.

Out now in paperback and ebook

DI HARRIET SLOANE SERIES #1

THE SLEEPING SEASON

Someone going missing is not an event in their life but an indicator of a problem.

Detective Inspector Harriet Sloane is plagued by nightmares while someone from her past watches from a distance. In East Belfast, local four-year-old River, vanishes from his room.

Sloane must put her own demons to bed and find the boy. Before it's too late.

Out now in paperback and ebook

DI HARRIET SLOANE SERIES #2

PROBLEMS WITH GIRLS

Where are the young women here? Can you even see them?

After taking some leave, DI Harriet Sloane comes back to work at Strandtown PSNI station, East Belfast, to be faced with a murder case. A young political activist has been stabbed to death in the office of a progressive political party where she works as an intern. The killer seems to have a problem with girls, and is about to strike again.

Set in 2018, a month after the Belfast Rape Trial and the #ibelieveher rallies that took place throughout Ireland, this novel asks questions about cyberbullying, mental health and consent.

Out now in paperback and ebook

DI HARRIET SLOANE SERIES #3

THE TOWN RED

If it had been me, she would not have stopped until there was justice.

Just as DI Harriet Sloane turns forty, an old case reopens from before she was born. In the late 1970s, Karen Ward was a teenager when she was murdered just yards away from her Belfast home.

At the time, people thought they saw Karen with a man, but time has moved on and now witnesses are thin on the ground. With the help of the victim's sister, Sloane must travel back in time, while her own family evolves and someone from her past resurfaces.

Codes, and rules, need to be broken if justice will ever be served.

Out now in paperback and ebook .

EVERYBODY'S HAPPY

SHORT STORIES

Creighton's second short story collection introduces us to a gallery owner who worries her husband will leave her for a doppelgänger; an artist whose creativity is blocked by intense fear on a retreat; a would-be writer who opens a PO Box to gather other people's letters to God; two mothers with guilty secrets; a young student contemplating suing a lecturer for boring her into deep slumber; a geologist traveling the earth to find herself; and a woman who flies home to bury her dead uncle, only to end up in a compromising situation.

Out now in paperback and ebook

Printed in Great Britain
by Amazon

79375107R00180